Ne

# THE AFRICA BAR

*Also by Nick Maes*

Not Dark Yet

# THE AFRICA BAR

Nick Maes

review

First published in 2003
by REVIEW

An imprint of Headline Book Publishing

10 9 8 7 6 5 4 3 2 1

Cataloguing in Publication Data is available from the
British Library

ISBN 0 7553 0013 0

Typeset in Garamond Light by Palimpsest Book Production Limited,
Polmont, Stirlingshire

Printed and bound in Great Britain by
Clays Ltd, St Ives plc

Headline Book Publishing
A division of Hodder Headline
338 Euston Road
London NW1 3BH

www.reviewbooks.co.uk
www.hodderheadline.com

For Jonah, a very good friend

With thanks to: Emerson Skeens, Tom Green, Liz McKee, Elly Mlang'a, Frank Talitwala, Hasan H. Wambi, Thomas Scherer, Reto Ernst, Rashid Juma, Simba, Wolfgang Dorado, Professor Abdul Shariff, Rebecca Osborne, Hazel Orme, Fundu Lagoon, Charlie and Philip Mason, Damon Richards, Geraldine Cooke, Janice Brent, Daniele Dodd, Salon des Arts and Mary Pachnos

'An illusive place where nothing is as it seems.'
Dr David Livingstone, Zanzibar

# CHAPTER 1: GETTING THERE

## Dar Es Salaam

She was mugged last night – done in by a whumph of warmth. It had come as a grubby shock after the refrigerated confines of flight BA 065. Where was her watch? It didn't matter: she was awake now. Not only was it unusually early but she was also refreshingly unhung-over. The heat was pounding and Camden Town was an aeon rather than ten hours away. She could kill David for his bloody stupid recommendation, and slap herself for listening to him. The Karibu Hotel. What was wrong with the Dar es Salaam Holiday Inn? At least she'd have had air-con and a mini-bar to empty. Light poured into the room from behind an ill-fitting blind.

The phone rang. 'There is guest in Reception for you.'

'There is? What guest, Muhammad?'

Voices at the other end of the line spoke in Swahili.

'He say he come to you for safari.'

She was puzzled; why on earth would a stranger be offering her a game trip? 'I'll be down in a minute. Thank you.'

Francesca's eyes felt sticky; she wasn't with it. The constant heat made her vague; she couldn't quite be bothered to make sense of it all. She hadn't unpacked on arrival, except for her makeup bag, a clean pair of knickers and a bottle of duty-free whisky. She wore the fresh pants now, her lips were red but the bottle had been packed away again. These basics were her idea of urban survival: she'd kidded herself that nothing else was needed. Nothing except a fan, that was – a luxury the hotel didn't stretch to. Her suitcase was by the door – a tough red plastic job on wheels – and she went to trundle it through the dim hallway. She was feeling claggy, stuck with sweat, trapped in a fur of warmth.

The case clunked on the bare concrete stairs, forewarning Muhammad of her descent. He came up to meet her on the landing, apparently unaffected by the humidity. 'Mama, let me take for you.'

She surrendered it – delighted she had no need other than to walk in the heat – and followed him to the front desk.

'Here is him.'

A tall, startlingly handsome man was standing by the street door. He was aloof with good looks, but his posture suggested he had not mastered the length of his body. It was a beguiling combination of characteristics.

'Mama Francesca, I am Abdul.'

'Hi there.'

'I come to airport last night, but you gone already.'

He didn't make any sense; she hadn't expected anyone to meet her, least of all this tall black stranger. She shook her head slightly, a nervous twist of a movement that signalled her confusion.

'I come to tell you of safari business.'

Francesca was still no wiser. The sweltering atmosphere pushed down upon her, attempting to empty her head of reason. 'I think you've got the wrong person. I've not ordered a safari.'

'I tell you of mine. Special safari, very good rates.'

'I'm afraid it's not for me, I'm sorry.'

She turned to the other man. 'Could I settle up, please?'

Muhammad went behind the desk to look at his paper-work. Shuffling papers and cross-referencing was a good idea: he'd seen it done in any number of TV movies. Reception staff in flashy American hotels always had something to look at, or internal calls to make from state-of-the-art switchboards before they tallied the bill. But it wasn't like that at his place: there were no computer screens or buttons to press, or room-service charges to add. It was a bed-only joint. He still took ten minutes to arrive at a total.

'Twenty-seven thousand shillings.'

Abdul stood to one side, quiet, passive, clenching and unclenching his fists. He'd waited like this many times before – it was part of the procedure: the white woman wasn't to be disturbed when she was concentrating. He knew to remain silent, to become momentarily invisible, to suck at his lower lip, to view the proceedings through half-closed eyes.

Francesca searched for her money, trying to ignore Abdul's presence and concentrate on settling the bill; his bearing disturbed her, she found it difficult. Both men watched intently as she counted out the foreign notes from a bundle she'd acquired at Dar es Salaam airport. It was a wad more suited to a gangster than a dark-haired girl from Camden Town who was happier with plastic.

'Could you call me a cab, Muhammad?'

The receptionist grinned, and nodded towards Abdul.

'No, you don't understand, I don't want a safari.'

Muhammad continued to smile.

What was it with him? Everything was answered with a silent, gentle laugh. His friendliness disarmed and annoyed her. Was he actually listening? Perhaps he didn't understand.

She spoke again, stressing each syllable as if she were addressing a moron. 'I want taxi to take to port. I want boat to Zanzibar.' Hadn't she promised herself she'd not do that? Her first morning in Africa and already she was speaking *at* people. Where was her phrase book? '*Nina kwenda* . . . Sod it, how did you say the word for "port"? . . . *Zanzibar.*'

'Yes, Abdul is taxi, Mama, he can take you.'

Muhammad was as puzzled as the woman in front of him; why couldn't the *mazungo* understand that Abdul was a taxi-driver *and* a safari rep? It wasn't difficult, but then he'd found white folks on holiday were always hard to understand. He smiled at her again as he put the cash into a till, then tidied away the remains of his breakfast.

Abdul made for the door, dragging the red case behind him. He looked back. 'Is only two thousand to boat, Mama.'

She wouldn't argue. 'Fine. Let's go, then.'

The Mama thing irked her.

'Abdul, why do you call me "Mama"?'

'Because that you. You Mama. Everyone Mama who can have baby.'

Abdul toyed with the ignition key, eventually tricking the car into life and forcing it into gear. Francesca adhered to the plastic back seat and they bumped through some of the odd mixture that makes up Dar es Salaam. Low, dusty buildings with something Deco about their architecture were vaguely reminiscent of a movie from another era. The precinct was Bogartish. The uncommon remnants of Victorian additions to the city stood on another street, the senior citizens of a changing neighbourhood bent double with balconies. The British High Commission displayed all the charm of a low-rent shopping centre in a poorer South London borough. In London Francesca had pictured Dar as a primitive Marrakech, souked-up and windy, jammed with silk bales, camels and snake charmers, decorated with red-earth streets, ornamented by turbaned nomads.

But reflective glass had been wrapped round efficient offices and high-rise banks. The sleek structures exploded her fantasy. She thought buildings belonging in Croydon shouldn't be in East Africa.

'We here.'

Abdul drew easily into the crowd, scattering taxi-drivers, punters and hawkers flogging small packets of cashews. A child yelled at them. Cops, boys selling sunglasses embedded in polystyrene blocks, paperback vendors, a bewildered tourist clutching a child and students hugging backpacks blended into the confusion. It seemed that everyone wanted a passage on the Zanzibar boat.

The mass of faces unnerved Francesca. 'Where can I get a ticket, Abdul?'

'Give me money, I get for you.'

She was glad of his assistance: perspiration had started to dampen her independent spirit. It was too much: she wasn't ready for the scramble and her energy evaporated in the sunshine.

Back in London she had been . . . ready? Hell, she couldn't wait. 'I know exactly what I'm doing, Mother. I'm going, and that's the end of it.'

'But it's a Muslim country, Francesca. You won't be safe. You know how they treat women in those places.'

She had expected no different from her parent.

'They're no better than heathens. I can't stand the idea of you getting mixed up in all that, especially now. I imagine Bin Laden has terrorist cells out there. You really have no idea, do you, you silly girl?'

It had been the same with her best friend. 'Davey, hi. I'm going to Zanzibar . . . Of course I'll be fine, I'm going for a break, it's not a convalescence. Where's your spirit of adventure?'

She was leaving, there was no reason to stay. That was the point, wasn't it?

Dar es Salaam wasn't as easy or as obvious as she had anticipated. Abdul looked effortless, nothing strained in him. He stepped over the boisterous crowd in a couple of gangly, elegant paces. His catwalk made her feel clumsy. She stared at the back of his head – thinking her shades made her disappear – but he turned and saw her looking. She felt foolish and diverted her attention awkwardly to the duty-free bag sitting on her pink silk knees. Relief also figured: she was pleased he'd not done a runner with her money even though she was still sitting in his car.

After ten melting minutes Abdul got back in the driver's seat and turned to his passenger. 'Here your ticket. But boat don't go for one hour.'

'I thought it left at ten.'

'It does, but today, no.'

Francesca looked at the crowd, which was pushing in all directions. She didn't want to leave the safety of the car or admit defeat. 'Is there somewhere I can wait, Abdul?'

'We have café here. You want to stay in café at port?'

Anywhere would be better than being left to stand in the heat and crush; and the café would be an illustration of how *natural* she was. Francesca daydreamed about being mistaken for an ex-pat who'd lived in the area for years. She was about to spend three months on the island, a period of time that made her more *aware* than mere holidaymakers. It was a ridiculous conceit: she imagined she was above tourism. Abdul grinned at her; he was oblivious to her foolish insight.

At the far end of the long, slim café there was a counter, a relic from the 1950s. Upholstered in vinyl and velour, the cocktail bar was ill prepared for its new career. Francesca edged past it and found a seat by a huge woman who patted the empty space beside her. She wore a green uniform a size too small, the fabric pulled over her enormous bust. Her outfit, although filthy, was carefully patched and immaculately darned.

Abdul stood beside the door. Only his head poked inside the sticky room. 'OK? I go now. *Kwaheri.*'

Francesca panicked. A fat sensation of exposure settled on her, but she had no intention of revealing it to her neighbours. Did he have to leave that minute? She couldn't let him go now. Was there a way of keeping him a little longer? 'Could I treat you to a drink, Abdul?' She needed him to stay; he would camouflage and protect her with his presence. He was the perfect mask. 'Go on, Abdul, join me as my guest until the boat goes. Is soda OK?'

Francesca exuded an artificial self-assurance, acting as if she were doing *him* the favour. A simper stuck to her face, lopsided, lips thin together; she tried to project confidence and unconsciously blinked to the pips of the Greenwich time signal coming from a radio propped on the bar. The Ray-Bans were still glued to her face so Abdul missed the bizarre ocular display. Time slowed with the echo of 'Lillibullero'. The tune sounded incongruously garden-green in the hot, cramped yellow room. Abdul sat opposite and ordered the drinks.

A child, wearing a bright red fez and dirty grey rags, delivered Sprites to the table. His hat was a trophy. He tapped it with his left hand to make sure it hadn't mysteriously vanished. When he used both hands to put the drinks on the table he couldn't resist looking up to catch a glimpse of its long black tassel.

A beer would have been better for Francesca, something with punch to help ease her into the day, but there was no alcohol for sale in the café and taking a swig from the whisky bottle (no matter how surreptitiously) wasn't a good idea. She'd have to suffer sobriety.

'So, Abdul, why don't you tell me about your safaris?'

The sound of her words pecked at the thick atmosphere; she was almost surprised he'd heard her.

'You interested now, Mama?'

'No, thank you. I mean not now.' She was afraid of silence and needed conversation. 'How did you know I was staying at the hotel?'

He twitched.

'I thought it was strange that you knew my name.'

'Nothing strange. I have friend at hotel who tell me about you. I try and do business, that's all.'

His innocent attempt at commerce reassured her. There was no weird coincidence: she was only another tourist worth taking a punt on.

'I see. I'm sorry it's not for me. Perhaps another time.'

A fug of kitchen smells drifted in. Metal troughs filled with coals stood beside the entrance, and a mean, bony piece of chicken smoked on the fire. The room felt hotter. At least, it did to Francesca; no one else seemed to notice. She was surprised by a trickle of sweat – it felt like an insect barely glancing over her skin. Large dark patches formed at the armpits of her T-shirt.

'I was born on Zanzibar. Maybe I see you there.'

'That would be nice, Abdul. I was born in Wiltshire. It's not quite the same, is it?'

Wiltshire sounded as exotic to him as Ngorogoro did to Francesca. She didn't think for a moment that she'd ever see him again. A pity, really: he was gorgeous.

'I go now. I find work. *Asante sana* for Sprite. *Karibu* Dar es Salaam. *Karibu* Zanzibar.'

'Yes, thank you, Abdul. Goodbye.'

He left her sitting beside the giant green woman. As soon as he'd gone she checked for her wallet, a nervous reaction. It was still there.

# London

'The thing that worries me most about the trip is that new disease people talk about nowadays. What is it, dear? DVD? It's got something to do with legs, I think.'

'Deep-vein thrombosis.'

'Yes, that's the one. It'd be an awful shame to get pipped at the post by a clot, don't you think?'

'You'll be fine, Gran.'

'That's all very well for you, young man, but I'm sixty years your senior and varicose. Of course I worry.'

Carla Jackson packed for her trip with the help of her grandson; she was glad of his company.

'You should keep your toes wiggling and move around the aircraft. You'll be fine, Granny.'

Not seeing more of the boy was a big regret; another of life's unwelcome turns.

It was unusual for him to be alone with her – she couldn't remember the last time they'd spent time like this together. The reason behind his unwanted absence was his father, Tony, Carla's adopted son. He always said it was too far to come: 'Carla, it takes the best part of four hours to drive here. It's impractical to motor up and down the M1 just because you feel the need to mother us all.'

The journey length wasn't the issue: Tony's emotional

bond with his parent was more remote than his distant home. She knew, deep down, that he had always resented her. And he, in turn, felt as if his adoptive parents had duplicitously kidnapped him from his real life and traded it in for the bogus Middle England version. To live in the Jackson household was to do time in a chintzy clink. He hated life in a suburban home swagged with Liberty prints and expatriate mementos. But was that because he had not belonged, or because he had been another bourgeois rebel raging against perceived juvenile injustice? It was a modern fairytale, laced with an orphan's resentment, rather than the wickedness of his step-parents.

Carla saw Tony as a beautiful tragedy, a painful yet welcome result of a complicated miscarriage. It hurt her to know that he would always feel second best. He rarely called round with his own family. Carla knew that this guilt-saturated visit was a penance because of what had happened. He'd not shown up at the funeral.

Carla assembled her clothes as she would have done forty years ago – she preferred trunks to suitcases, always had. There were two, as old as their owner, covered in stickers from East Africa and Australia. A couple of faded, peeling scraps bore the Cunard legend. She'd not been on a trip by herself for years: her husband, John, had always accompanied her. She was sad he wasn't coming. He was missed, even though they'd not loved each other. Perhaps it was the lack of passion that had made their union a success. Carla kidded herself: they'd remained together because, above all, he was kind. There was nothing wrong with kindness, was there? Even though their marriage was sham and reeked of lavender, she knew that John had cared. It was a sympathetic, dynastic arrangement. She was an alibi, a prototype trophy wife whom he indulged; her wardrobe and trunks were evidence of that. And now he was dead. It was the past. All of that was done with. Perhaps it hadn't been much of a life for her appropriated child, but she loved Tony, truly. What more could she have done?

Apart from anticipated blood clots, she wasn't nervous. Quite the contrary. At seventy-four Mrs C. Jackson was setting out on another expedition to Zanzibar, the first in nearly forty years. She would see old friends again – if they were still alive. From 1959 until 1964 Mr and Mrs John Jackson had lived in a large house facing the sea. She'd heard the house was a hotel now, a luxury retreat with a swimming-pool and terraces.

'It wasn't exactly luxurious in my day, darling. Big, yes, and comfortable, but not luxurious.'

Her grandson feigned interest.

'It was bloody difficult to run. We had a dozen servants. Well, I did. Grampy John wasn't much interested in that side of things, he had the office to deal with. Now, how many tea-dresses should I pack?'

'Just pack T-shirts, Gran.'

'I knew you'd be hopeless. I'll have entertaining to do, I'll be meeting old friends again. They'll expect me to be dressed for the part . . . but what would you care about that?'

'Mmm?'

The teenager was texting a friend with his mobile phone. Carla claimed the devices were unhealthy. It was a lie: secretly she disapproved of the modern technology. It was confusing, she didn't find it easy to use, and that riled her as she'd always considered herself progressive. Ignoring the youngster's electronic interruption, she carried on regardless, checking for an old letter she kept in her bag. It was there.

'I can't tell you how all that dressing-up used to drive me mad when we were out there. It felt like every bloody night

11

we had some sort of do to attend. I spent my entire time desperate to kick off my shoes. I hate wearing heels in the tropics.'

## Ferry

The crossing from Dar to Zanzibar was easy. A relief because Francesca didn't have sailor's pins. An hour across the strait and the boat came to a halt; the local passengers were excited. Huge black fins broke the surface and plunged back out of sight. Whales. She strained to see, desperate to catch sight of them again. A rubbery head lifted above the waves, a titan riveted with barnacles. The old man turned slightly, as if inspecting the boat – Francesca was sure he was looking at her. The water made a deep *frump* as he sank back below. Another of the party screwed itself from the depths and hurled its huge form from the water. An enormous expanse of white belly seemed to hang in the air until it crashed back under the surf, rocking the boat in its wake. Gigantic tails reappeared and slapped the waves. Then they were gone.

Francesca looked at her neighbour, an elderly Muslim woman shrouded in black. They were equally excited by the spectacle, but their shared enthusiasm was hampered by lack of a common language. Francesca spotted another tourist sitting a seat back, a blonde girl wearing a sullen expression and the ubiquitous Northface rucksack.

'Wasn't that wonderful?'

The stranger looked at Francesca and groaned.

'The whales, weren't they fantastic?'

The disinterested blonde frowned. 'I don't know what the fuss is about. You're behaving like you've never seen a fish before.'

Francesca was stunned by the crushing response. 'You're right, I haven't.' She huddled back into her window-seat, gazing at the ocean. The whales were an omen, a sign of good luck. She wanted to see another before reaching the island. Thirty minutes later the boat docked in the busy Stone Town port. A score of porters and dozens of others were there to welcome the craft; they teemed towards those disembarking. A slender white woman with a lined face walked slowly through the fever; she carried a parasol.

'I take luggage?' A spindly man – the sun had devoured any clue to his age – looked hopefully at Francesca. She gripped the handle of her case. He smiled, the same broad mask of a grin she'd seen earlier. It was an amazing thing about the place: everyone had a radiant face. The small man was bare-chested, the remains of a ragged shirt flapped around him. His torn trousers were held in place with string, the sorry fabric a clumsy lacework of holes. It was a porter's uniform that might have walked out of a Victorian photograph; it charmed and shocked Francesca.

'No, thank you, I can manage.'

'You want taxi?' said another man.

'Where you go?' said someone else.

'Welcome, *karibu*.'

'Madam, let me help.'

'Taxi? Special rate.'

'Over here, Mama.'

'Watch out.'

Francesca tripped into the madness of jetty life, but didn't relinquish her case. Maybe she'd never see it again.

Mattresses, bicycles and cumbersome pieces of luggage were borne above heads. No sooner were these things in sight than they were gone, simply vanished into the morass. An immense tractor tyre was trundled up the gangway by four men.

Another ship had docked: it was much bigger than the ferry, rustier too. The passengers and luggage from both vessels converged. Latticed palm baskets filled with neurotic chickens, sacks with unspecified bulky contents, a few goats, motorcycles wrapped in straw, a forest of green bananas and sugarcane, and crates of all sizes were piled up beside the stacked corrugated coffers from container ships. There were two large steamer trunks, too, covered with bruised labels – relics, Francesca imagined, of another era, now filled with coconuts for all she knew.

Francesca pushed through the throng. She was nervous, but didn't like to show it. The sun defied belief; it felt like it could lift the skin from her forehead. She touched her face with her fingertips, as if soothing a wound. There was no shadow for shelter. The noises got louder. Bicycle bells pinged, car horns called for space. Shouts, blasts from lorries, more shouting. The heat was inescapable.

'*Hatari!*'

Francesca carried on, oblivious.

'*Hatari!* Danger!' A man pushed her to the side of the dusty track as a belching truck rolled past. All life was around her. It was like a carnival, except she wasn't joining in. If she walked like a crab she might see what was coming both ways. The immigration office was round the corner.

David had said the Emerson and Green Hotel was in the middle of Stone Town, only a ten-minute walk from the port. It might be in either of two directions, or three. She was feeling hassled, and what did he know anyway? Outside the port gates a dozen more taxis were waiting; she'd take one to the hotel.

'Excuse me.'

With two words and in nearly as many seconds she'd attracted four cab-drivers. There was stiff competition for her custom.

'Please, one at a time, calm down.'

Francesca gave up any pretence of knowing what she was doing and got into the first vehicle. Again, hiding behind her sunglasses seemed the best option. The driver grabbed her suitcase, placed his prize carefully in the boot, then followed her into the sweltering car.

'Where you go?'

'Emerson's, please. Emerson and Green Hotel.'

The car pulled from the rank, turned right and choked along the harbour wall. A tiny breeze helped lift the stifling atmosphere. At long last, this was Stone Town.

Carla Jackson proceeded through the scrum like a pro. She commanded respect. Her manner and age did it, as well as her parasol. She displayed the style of someone who owned the place. A man who looked older than her seventy-four years was waiting by her luggage. He was different from the other people in the port. It was his dress: he was cheaply but correctly attired. He wore a tie.

'Mrs Jackson,' he said, and held out an arthritic hand. 'How very good it is to see you again. *Safari nzuri?*'

'Yes, Mr Abeidi, a very good journey, thank you very much. It's jolly good to see you again, too. I imagine you were astonished to get my letter.'

He nodded and felt immediately foolish; he'd not meant to agree. 'I was surprised you knew my address, Mrs Jackson.'

'You were? I have it here ... see?' Carla opened her

handbag and showed him a yellowed scrap of paper. The missive was barely covered by a tatty, fragile envelope that blew open. 'I keep it safe here, Mr Abeidi.' She snapped her patent bag shut again, patting it as if to prove the point. 'And you look so well, Mr Abeidi, absolutely no different from the last time I saw you.'

The warm greeting was a charming fib, and pleased them both. They were silent for a moment, taking each other in. Her parasol felt heavy – she wanted to move on.

'Now, should we get a taxi or do you have a car?'

'It's here. You've not forgotten it, have you, Mrs Jackson?'

Cars weren't Carla's bag: they all looked the same to her, only in different colours. 'Good gracious, you've still got that old thing?' She had never been able to recall what it looked like even when she owned it. It was a miracle that he still did: keeping a car was an extravagance he could barely afford. He'd only managed to keep the vehicle by lending it to others for modest sums.

'Of course I remember. She hasn't changed either.'

It was another white lie: the car was a faint shadow in her memory. A black shadow. Her trunks were loaded into the back of the dented, antiquated motor.

As the split-screen Morris Minor pulled away, a porter retreated to the shade with a five-hundred-shilling tip stuffed into his pocket and watched the couple depart. The passenger had a ceremonial air about her; she sat rigidly upright and stared ahead. The veteran car was conspicuous as it edged out from among the Japanese four-wheel drives, taxis and handcarts.

Francesca arrived at a scrap of ground barely three minutes away from the port and beside an enormous white building. 'Is this it? Are we here?'

'No. This House of Wonder.'

She got fractious. 'I want Emerson's. Emerson's Hotel. I no want House of Wonder. Do you understand me?' The stilted language had returned. It made her angry yet she couldn't help it. It was her ignorance, not his. 'Emerson and Green, please. Can you take me there?'

The cab-driver got out of the car and collected the dusty red case. 'Follow me. Car no get to hotel, Mama.'

They walked past a small mosque and into twisting streets. It was Gothic, just as she had imagined Stone Town to be. It was another Venice, antique, crumbling and decadent. The colours were bleached out and it looked to be as old as civilisation. A small boy dragging a toy truck hacked from a one-gallon jerry-can varoomed past them. The cabby's flip-flops slapping on the lane was the only other sound; the heat seemed to amplify the noise. They walked past a few shops for tourists and locals: wooden doors opened into shabby dark interiors poorly illuminated with neon strips. A barber's shop with a cheap bead curtain had a sign outside it that advertised the Love and Peace Salon. Francesca caught a glimpse of pictures torn from magazines decorating a wall; Will Smith looked incongruous in the poor surroundings. The air felt heavier.

'We here, Mama. Five thousand, please.'

Francesca paid the driver and walked into the cool, tall, amber-coloured Reception area.

It was heaven, or as near to paradise as it is possible to be in a hotel. The enormous bedroom had a ceiling four metres high and a row of shuttered windows, closed to the street below but with slats open to the sunlight streaming in at an angle from above. The air was clogged with lavender light; she could almost smell it. A traditional Zanzibari bed stood at one end of the room – like a four-poster only with yards of mosquito netting. An occasional table and a large old wardrobe looked tiny in the theatrical surroundings. At the other end of the room stood a bath made of blue-painted stone. There was beauty in its simplicity; it was perfect. She could hide from the world in that bath; she could hide from herself in it if she cared to. It was a bedroom big enough to get lost in. She might stay there for the rest of her life; cocooned, safely escaped.

The whisky bottle came out of the bag first. Litre size – she loved that about duty-free shopping. 'No half-measures with these big chaps.' She poured some into a yellow tea glass and sank it in one. It was warm, but that didn't matter. She poured a second glass and sipped this time, then sat on the bed, kicked off her sandals, lit a Marlboro Light and shut her eyes. It wasn't sleep: it was the moment that caused it. Trying to picture Camden was impossible – to her relief, her mind remained blank. For a second she had difficulty remembering names.

Unpacking was easy: there wasn't much to pull out. 'Don't weigh yourself down, buy stuff when you get there,' had been David's advice. She pulled on a pair of Indian silk pants and a fresh T-shirt, then left her room ready to take a walk. Her first transit on a make-believe island. Zanzibar was magic.

In two twisted minutes she was lost. The labyrinth welcomed and disoriented her. That was a lie: it was a drug that clouded her head. She could feel the heartbeat of the place. Buildings crowded in from above, merchandise spilled out below. Brightly coloured *kangas* and coconut-palm mats vied with gap-toothed masks and anorexic totems. Flywhisks and ashtrays, goatskin drums, ebony elephants and cowrie-shell key-rings fought for space alongside plastic buckets and Masai bead necklaces. And the spices: everywhere the smell of cloves and cinnamon. Kitchen bowls were piled high with masala, cardamom, saffron powder (maybe it was turmeric) and a dust made from ginger. Vanilla pods and nutmeg, peppercorns and coriander added to the intense olfactory hash. The narrow lanes were an Outward Bound course designed to test the most dextrous. When least expected, bicycles and mopeds came whizzing round corners, the *ling-ling* of bike-bells a cue to back into the wall for fear of being knocked down. To begin with it is impossible to move safely around the streets of Zanzibar.

## Carla's Place

Malindi Villa is a mansion ten minutes by car from Stone Town. Carla had been there often enough in the past. 'What was it called then, Mr Abeidi? Can you remember all those years back?'

He needed no prompting: 'It had two names, like you, Mrs Jackson – Darajani Fort, and you called it the Place of Escape.' His voice had acquired a throaty echo with age.

The nearly forgotten names made Carla laugh. '*Palace* of Escape, if I remember rightly. Watch your memory, Mr Abeidi. I don't want you forgetting.' She was keen to see it again.

The ancestral Morris was parked to the side of the mansion. Carla walked slowly through the gardens to the front of the house. The grounds were pretty much as they had been back then; perhaps they were even better now. Palms, frangipani and thickets of bougainvillaea spread around pockets of jasmine, passion fruit and gardenias. The plants were the magic of the place: they were enchanting. It was very good to be back.

'Mr Abeidi, we must part company soon. I need a nap. Could we meet later for supper?'

'*Inshallah*. I'll be back at about twelve.'

'Twelve?'

'I'm sorry, my Swahili time. *Six*, Mrs Jackson.'

'That's more like it. I never could fathom two clocks. It always confused me and I'm far too old to learn it now.'

Swahili time and standard time: the same, but different. Daytime five degrees below the equator is pretty much the same in length whatever the time of year. Sun-up at six, sundown at six. The simple logic is to start your clock when the sun rises, so after one hour (seven a.m.) it is one o'clock. Eight a.m. becomes two o'clock and so on. When the old man said twelve he was correct, but getting Carla to understand something so simple had been impossible then and not an option now.

'Don't forget the confusion it caused, Mr Abeidi. We might laugh now but it caused tears then.'

Carla followed the two houseboys carrying her trunks. They were joking with each other. One tried to balance a piece of luggage on his head. The heavy case lurched off to one side and was closely followed by a squeal of laughter.

'Please be careful with that. Don't drop it . . . Yes, take them both to my room. Come along, no messing now. There's good lads.'

She looked for her companion, ready to raise her eyebrows

in mock-annoyance at the juvenile antics, but Mr Abeidi had slipped quietly back to his car.

## Creep

Francesca bumped into someone who didn't look hopelessly lost. He was a lot more purposeful than a tourist, swinging vegetables in a carrier at his side. He was surprisingly short, his cocky bravado overcompensated for his lack of stature.

'Excuse me, could you help? I'm a bit lost. I'm looking for Emerson and Green.'

'Yes, love.' He was happy to give directions. 'So, Emerson's, eh? Bit posh, ain't it? Nice, though. We're not far. I'll take you. *Hakuna matata.*'

Francesca was puzzled.

'Ain't you seen *The Lion King* yet?'

Francesca reddened and her chest lit up – it always did when she was embarrassed. They cut through the lanes and switched back, arriving at the hotel in a few minutes. She was grateful for his company. 'M'name's Keith.' She went to shake his hand that clutched the carrier bag, and they both laughed. Keith wasn't her type, but when he offered to take her out for a drink later, she said, 'I'd love to join you. Are you sure?'

Insecurity picked at her superficial shell of confidence. She felt as if she were an imposition. 'Well, only if it isn't any trouble. Would seven be OK, Keith?' Her tone was apologetic.

'Royal. I'll pick you up later, Fran. Ta-ra.'

She felt relieved to be back in her room: there was a feeling of sanctuary in the vast space. The bed creaked as she lay down to listen to the murmurings of the street below and catch the breeze from the ceiling fans. She'd read or nap, it didn't much matter.

Keith didn't keep her waiting. 'Where's it to be, darlin'?'

'I'm following you. You're the expert around here.'

Just two twists of the street disorientated her.

The unlit alleys felt blind and medieval. Getting lost in daylight was one thing, but at night the topography stretched and manipulated the town. The maze was both threatening and seductive. Ownerless voices echoed through the hot, sticky night. It was exciting, nervy and edgy. A relentless tinnitus of insects deafened the neighbourhood; some sounded like birds – they squawked. All the shops were shuttered and dead until the next day, adding to the sightless feel on the street, although sometimes a small louvred window accidentally spilt light into the tight, sleepy thoroughfare. Someone walked ahead, but the sound of his footsteps followed them ominously. At night-time the town was magnificently distorted; it was an adventure to be there with Keith. She felt safe.

Two icy beers awaited them at a small open-air Italian restaurant overlooking the sea.

'You on your holidays, then, Fran?'

'Sort of.'

'What's sort of?'

'It's not really a holiday. I'm here for three months.'

'You working, then?'

'No. It's time out. I'm getting away for a while.'

Keith was an expert in teasing information from people without revealing anything other than what he chose to about himself. He let Francesca know that he was single. 'Well, then, it's boyfriend trouble, innit?'

Francesca took a slug from the bottle. 'Something like that. What about you, Keith? What are you doing on the island?'

Keith said something and nothing. He was good at that. 'So, you're on your lonesome then, Fran?'

She opened up. What the hell? 'If you must know, my boyfriend was a prick. He dumped me because I didn't behave like a Fendi clutch bag.'

Outwardly she was glad they'd split, but in reality she was devastated. She'd been desperate for a boyfriend and felt a failure without one. All her friends appeared to be married, settled into familydom and doing things the right way. Children were hatched, mortgages shared and holidays taken in Cornwall, but it wasn't like that for Francesca. If her mother mentioned wedding bells one more time, she was liable to throttle her . . .

'Francesca, you've got to settle down,' she had said. 'You worry me. Is there something wrong with you?'

'No.'

'You'd better sort yourself out then, or you'll be left on the shelf if you're not already.'

Francesca's mother was glamorous, seventy years old and with a new companion whom she delighted in flaunting in front of her daughter. It was as if she were competing against her, proving that even though she was twice Francesca's age she was still capable of pulling. Francesca saw it differently: the old woman was attempting to cheat mortality and delude herself as to her attractiveness. The parent disgusted the child.

Francesca liked Keith, though. It was his yobbishness. He didn't behave like the ponce who'd left her. She perceived an

23

honesty in him that was appealing and made her feel relaxed. They got more beers.

'Don't know about you, darlin', but I'm starvin'. Can I buy you dinner?'

Francesca hesitated.

'It's not every day I get to take a lovely young lady out. Whatya think, Fran?'

'OK, then. That's very kind of you – but let me get the drinks.'

'Done. Oi! Waiter! Bung us a menu.'

More beer and a bottle of wine came to the table. The air was dense, still loaded with heat. Candlelight, crickets, waves stroking the shore below and Keith jarring opposite were the only things that disturbed the clingy atmosphere. His gingery hair stuck up. He'd tried to flatten it down but in the humidity it sprang back. Maybe he'd been in the army or navy. He'd got tattoos – the standard busty siren, a name, a serpent and Millwall FC engraved on his forearms. He slouched at the table, his head low, communing with the beer glass in front of him. His smile was wide and skinny and looked like it hadn't quite got the joke – including his own.

There weren't many diners – another couple, a table of four. The waiters chatted with regulars at the bar.

'It's nice to see a new face round 'ere.'

The beer had flushed Keith and slowed him down. Any semblance of charm was diluted by alcohol. He became monosyllabic and glazed; his uncomprehending eyes stared at Francesca. She played with an earring and sipped her wine. She would have liked to be back at her hotel with a whisky and a good book.

'So, fancy a bit of company later?' Keith reached across the table and stroked her hand. The sensation was repulsive and she pulled it away. 'No need to be hoity-toity.

You look like you could do wiv a bit of fun. What you say, then?'

'You've got the wrong person.'

The brute appeal was tempered by menace.

'So, what you goin' to do then? Shack up with one of them monkeys?' Keith nodded towards a waiter. 'Don't get me wrong, darlin', I'm not racist, nothin' like that. It's what they are.' He slipped his hand under the table and pulled at her trousers.

'Who the hell do you think you are? Get your hands off me.'

His vacant expression followed her as she stood up and walked out of the restaurant. She was shocked, tearful and lost.

The lane outside curled towards a streetlamp, and beyond she saw a large, expensive hotel. She went inside and ordered a drink. It felt like a refuge. 'And could you get me a taxi as well, please?'

Moments later the waiter returned: the cab was already waiting for her.


## Malindi Villa


'Bibi Carla, you have guest.' One of the trunk-carriers was at her door. He had called her grandmother.

'And do you know who it is, Ali?'

'The old man, Babu Abeidi.'

'Can you tell him I will be there soon? In five minutes.'

Carla sat at a large desk; she'd requisitioned it as her dressing-table. Sitting on it was a bottle of Chanel No. 5, night creams, two hairbrushes and a neat compact that was barely used. She'd brought her own ashtray too; she still smoked, not the same cigarettes as before – it was impossible to get Yenyidge Sobranie nowadays. Silk Cut was her brand. Carla dabbed the perfume in three places on her neck, left, right and front. Always the same order, always the same spots; they had been for ever. It tickled her that after years of repeated application she'd not got stigmata on her throat. A gin and tonic fizzed beside the scent; she took another gulp and another puff of her cigarette, careful not to smudge the damp lilac nail varnish.

Mr Abeidi sat in the main room; three enormous doors were wide open to the gardens and, beyond, the sea. A cool breeze shifted a curtain. That was why Malindi Villa had been built there: at night the gentle wind always came. It smelt fresh and was calming.

'Changed quite a bit, hasn't it?' Carla had surprised her guest by walking in behind him.

'The furniture has gone. Otherwise it looks the same, Mrs Jackson. The lights are different, I think.'

They sat on a couch facing outside, one at each end. Carla was reserved. Her string of pearls appeared to hold her together: she wasn't about to fall apart. 'I've asked Ali to cook for us here,' she said. 'I hope you don't mind, but I thought on my first evening it would be easier. We could eat on the terrace.'

A call to prayer spiralled up into the sky. It was loud; the mosque was amplified. After the first incantation came the sound of a siren from the town – faintly audible even there – and then whispers from other mosques, mournful chants that quarrelled with each other.

'Let's take that as a signal to eat, shall we?'

Carla had inadvertently got it right; it was the first day of Ramadan and the evening call to prayer was welcomed by the hungry devout. She hadn't realised it, though.

Dinner was delicate. It wasn't so much the food or the setting but the fragility of the participants that was arresting. Barely perceptible friction underscored their old age: it simmered beneath the polite enquiry amassed after four decades of separation. The meal was precise, stretching formally into the night.

Mr Abeidi went home and Ali cleared up. Carla was exhausted – the heat got to her. Tiredness tugged at her eyes so she splashed her face with cold water, which felt fresh. Lines filled with the vestiges of the lipstick she'd used earlier dug deeply around her lips, like a crimson graph recording the highs and lows of the evening with Mr Abeidi. She rarely used any other makeup; a dab on her lips was as much as she cared for. She took off her dress, sitting to do it, unbuttoning it all the way down the front. It fell open and she stood up to remove her bra. She looked in the mirror, trying to recollect the shape of her body in 1964. She was stooped now, loose and grey. Skin fell baggily around buttocks that had lost their dimples in the folds years ago; her toes were crushed – she'd worn court shoes for too long. Her flesh was draped like the sail on a dhow, wrinkled and well worn.

# CHAPTER 2: SHANGANI

## You Again

Francesca found an Internet café at the bottom of Shangani Street. It became a regular haunt: it was the cheapest way to communicate with David. Didn't all girls have a gay best friend? He was an outrageous love, and supportive like no one else in her clique. After his initial surprise, he had encouraged her safari to Zanzibar: 'Fran, you'd be a bloody fool *not* to go. There's nothing for you to stay here for, unless you count that wet ex of yours. And you're *not* going to do that, are you?'

'I'm having second thoughts, Davey. I'm a single girl headed to a Muslim country, for God's sake. It's not such a good idea, is it?'

'Too fucking right it is. I'd be there like a shot if I could. Imagine being trussed up by a Masai for the night. Have you seen those natural-history programmes? God! What if it's a whole tribe? Don't tell me you haven't thought along those lines, Fran. One night in a Bedouin tent is worth two weeks in Benidorm, don't forget it . . .'

'That's not why I'm going, David.'

'Read my lips . . . We are not talking relationships, Fran, think fabulous shags. I want to hear about you getting porked on a regular basis – or beefed. Silly me, no pork in an Islamic country. It'll be a different story in Zanzibar. Mark my words. First glimpse of that forbidden fruit and you'll be straight in there like an Ethiopian at a takeaway.'

To: Daveyboy
CC:
Subject: I've landed

Davey, im loving it. Told you i would be ok. Hated the Karibu Hotel, though . . . What in gods name made you think i wanted to stay somewhere DRY? And since when have you been an expert on Dar es bloody Salaam? You're a silly bugger sometimes! Ive been @ E & G's Hotel for the last week and im looking for my own place. There might be something in this neck of woods, perfect if it works out b-cos this is where i want to be. Ive been put on to a couple of people who are flat hunting for me as i write. Everythings laid back. You'd love it. Ive hired jeep & im hoping to travel round the island @ the weekend. Emerson (he's one of the hotel owners) told me of a fab place to stay on the east coast – its called Shooting Star Inn & is meant to be dreamy.

I'll tell you wots most striking here . . . its the people. No matter how poor they are everybody smiles. Its so refreshing & charming. The place is swamped in a kind of joy. Its so beguiling – im in a kind of heaven.

Ive met ALL sorts, said i wouldn't be lonely didnt i? I nearly got eaten by a vile cretin on first night, made my excuses and left. What a creep. B-cos Stone Town is so small i keep seeing him around. Don't you worry, i

can look after myself. Dinner tonight with a new ozzy gal-pal (she's on hols & doesnt know the place – i feel like an old hand now!) we're going for a CHINKY!!! Can u believe it? Halfway around the world & im eating sweet & sour prawns. I still haven't got to grips with the streets. Im always getting lost. But my Swahili is coming on! Tutaonana baadaye (see you later). Not bad eh? Send my love to everyone,
XXX Fran

She paid five hundred shillings to the guy on the desk. He knew her now; he was always cheery, even when the servers were down. She left the air-conditioned café and stepped into the furnace outside. It had rained earlier, a huge downpour that lasted an hour. When it rained like that the air temperature dropped slightly, until the mercury soared once again with the extra humidity. Now it was sticky. Francesca walked back to the hotel, hopeful of a message about a flat. She cut across the House of Wonder, a massive building that had once been a palace. It looked grand and colonial, and way too big for its setting. Two large cannon sat in front of the pompous edifice, phallic *émigrés* pointlessly aimed at the sea. The building was elegantly imprisoned by dozens of slender white columns – local mythology had it that a slave was inside each one. Scores must have died in its construction.

'*Habari?*'

'Yeah, hi . . . *nzuri*,' she replied, without looking to see who was speaking. Everyone said '*habari*' or '*hu jambo*' or '*mambo*' or something. To begin with she'd say, 'Hello,' back – but spent hours doing so because the greeting inevitably led to a series of questions. A simple exchange could take a few minutes and spending time with everybody soon added up. Then there were the beach-bums peddling dope: they might keep you for a further quarter-hour as you patiently explained that hash made you sleepy or sick and 'No, I'm really not interested.' To avoid the minutiae, she started to play dumb, giving a little wave, a big smile, then pressing on. It was quicker that way. She didn't realise her brusque behaviour was deemed offensive, and that it was bad manners not to engage in the elaborate civility. Island time had yet to catch up with her: she was still on a North London rhythm, even though a week had elapsed.

'Mama Francesca . . .'

She thought she recognised the guy. Where the hell had she met him? Market, probably. He was familiar, tall and good-looking.

'Francesca, I say I come to island. And now I find you.'

It was Abdul. He'd turned up. 'Blimey, what on earth are you doing here?'

'I do no business now. Dar es Salaam is quiet, I think I come and see you.'

Francesca became coquettish, but was too boyish to carry it off; she was partly urchin at heart. His expression hovered somewhere between irritation and bewilderment: he was an enchanting enigma, a sexy riddle. Francesca was conscious of being just a little too excited at seeing her new friend. She attempted to sound cool and rein in her obvious interest. 'Are you OK, Abdul?'

'Fresh.'

'You look a bit out of sorts.'

His expression didn't change.

'Do you want to join me for a drink, Abdul?'

'Is not possible yet. For Ramadan.'

'Yes, you poor thing, no wonder you look down.' Francesca thought of Ramadan as a punishment rather than a holy month: she couldn't imagine why anyone should be deprived of food and drink, especially alcohol. 'Well, I'm going for one anyway. Come along for the ride and tell me what's been happening.'

They changed direction and walked along the harbour-side to Mercury's, a restaurant named in honour of Zanzibar's most famous son, Freddie. Francesca liked it there: it was friendly, buzzy with both locals and tourists, and the pizza was good. At home it was difficult to find a place where a woman drinking solo wasn't seen as either a pariah or a tart. In London she never felt comfortable drinking alone, especially in pubs, but it wasn't an issue here; she wasn't made to feel like a freak.

They sat on a swing at the side of the bar, Francesca with her drink – she'd mischievously sneaked rum into the Coke – and Abdul without his. 'I'm glad you found me, Abdul.'

She meant it. The man was attractive – not handsome in an ordinary way, but refined. His quicksilver face went from cloudy to bright with no perceptible change in expression. She'd noticed these barometric variations on their drive in Dar es Salaam. He looked deep, she was a sucker for the sensitive type. Her last boyfriend, Gary, had been sensitive, but what a jerk he was. Faggot! The dopey idea was an amusing revelation. It stood to reason, didn't it? He was a label queen, lousy in bed (on the rare occasions they had fucked) and had more shoes and skin-care products than she did. It made sense now.

'Where are you staying, Abdul?'

'I stay with my mama.'

She had thought he might be staying in a hotel – not all of them were expensive, surely? 'Does she live near here, Abdul?'

'Is in Mombassa.'

'I thought Mombasa was in Kenya.'

'Is ten minute with *dala dala*.'

She learned that this Mombassa was a suburb on a local bus route. 'Is business any better here, Abdul?'

He was noncommittal and shrugged, then looked wicked. A surge of excitement, a speckle of expectation gnawed at her. He flirted stealthily and she couldn't help but respond. She reddened, captivated by his body language and proximity: he was almost touching her.

'What you do later, Mama?'

'I wish you'd quit the Mama thing, Abdul. It really gets on my nerves. I'm not a mama.' She was a little too snappy, defensive and pettish. 'I don't have children and I don't have a husband. I'm not a mother.' Lighten the conversation, Fran, she thought. 'Call me Francesca like everyone else.' She smiled, hoping to soften her bite.

'Is OK, Francesca. So tell me, what you do?'

She bit on her frustration and took a deep breath. How was he to know? 'I'm going with a friend to Pagoda, it's the Chinese restaurant near the old post office. Would you like to join us?'

He considered her invitation and visibly flexed, engrossed by some hidden complication. Francesca knew instinctively what it was. It was the first time her *native* intuition had worked. He couldn't afford it. 'Please, be my guest, Abdul. Meet me there at eight?'

'I like that very much. I like to see you later, Francesca . . . Very much.'

He stared at her. It was a delicious lechery. She felt demure – it was a strange experience for someone who believed chastity extinct in herself – and blushed. 'Eight o'clock, then? See you later, Abdul.'

Francesca stood up to leave, then returned to the table to retrieve her purse, cigarettes and lighter. 'Oops, silly . . .'

She felt foolish, giddy and excited. 'See you later, then, Abdul.'

He smiled.

Francesca mastered the route back to the hotel by memorising strategic street corners; she didn't vary her way because the labyrinthine town inevitably spat her out in some alien quarter. Back at the hotel a message was waiting for her at Reception. 'Flat in Shangani district, two bedrooms, kitchen, baths, etc., top floor. Rent $350 per month.'

Francesca called the number on her mobile: she'd got connected to a local tariff the day after her arrival. 'Is that Mr Hilal? Hello, Francesca here. I've just got your message. You have a flat for me to see.'

The man explained the location; it sounded ideal. An appointment was made for her to view the property an hour later.

A small blue door led into a narrow courtyard. At the back a grey door opened to a staircase. 'The flat is on the top floor, Mrs Francesca.'

Hilal spoke good English, but she decided not to correct him on her marital status.

'This here is an office.' They were on the first floor passing a louvred door with a heavy lock. 'This is not used at weekends, just weekdays. Come, one more flight.'

Large double doors opened into a huge light hallway; two big bedrooms, a large sitting room, two filthy bathrooms and a grubby kitchen completed the flat. The size of the place was good, but it was covered with an inch of dust and there was no view from the unglazed windows.

She was taken up another steep staircase. 'And this is the

tearoom, Mrs Francesca.' A padlocked grille was unlocked and flung open.

It was like climbing from a galleon's hold on to the deck. Francesca walked on to a covered wooden terrace that looked towards the sea, the old fort, the House of Wonder and across the rusty, cubist rooftops. Voices rattled from the street below; pigeons gurgled. It was a traditional Zanzibari tearoom – an open-air space set on top of more affluent buildings to catch the breeze. She'd fallen in love. The Shangani house tearoom had been in her dreams: it was a private heaven looking over the Stone Town paradise.

'I'll take it.'

Her decision was a surprise to them both: so abrupt, so definite and so . . . final. No negotiations. It was settled on the spot; she was the tenant Hilal must have fantasised about. Three months up front in hard currency and she'd move in that afternoon.

A flashing sign pointed to the whereabouts of Pagoda's entrance; it was down an alley. Francesca walked to the door with the Australian girl she'd met earlier but didn't catch sight of Abdul.

'Hello, Francesca. Why not you see me?'

He was there, invisible one moment and standing in dim light the next, like a trick. He wore a brightly coloured shirt.

'You're dressed for the occasion, aren't you? Is it designer?'

The silly comment mystified Abdul.

Francesca wore embroidered green Indian silk trousers and a yellow silk top. She'd inherited her father's wiry body; she wasn't sleek and busty like her mother. Her slightness was disguised by the bright, loosely fitting clothes.

'I can't believe a daughter of mine can make herself so shapeless. Won't you try a little harder? There must be something you can do. I mean, why don't you make more of an effort, darling? You've got lovely feet and ankles. Wear a skirt, for goodness' sake, let people see your legs.'

'I'm happy like this, Mother.'

'You could have fooled me. No one's going to take a second look at a pink bin-liner. Tidy yourself up – no wonder you can't get a man.'

Her mother maintained a manicured 1960s precision flair that manifested itself in lengthy makeup procedures and starched coiffures. Her peroxide hair was complemented by a platinum-card mentality. 'I wouldn't be seen dead without my face on. You could do a lot worse than take a page out of my book, especially at your age. You're not twenty any more, mark my words, Francesca.'

'I'm not you, Mother. I'm fine the way I am.' That was a lie: she hated the way she looked. Her face was full of imperfections and she'd spent years mapping each one. To Francesca's mind it had been built up with ill-fitting jigsaw pieces, yet she couldn't see how, when added up, they coalesced to make an individual, startling beauty.

The trio walked in, Abdul proud and cocky, as if he were Pagoda's best customer. Francesca was dwarfed by his presence. 'Is it OK for you to eat now, Abdul?'

'Yes.'

'And drink?'

'*Hamna tabu.*'

The other girl looked dopey, unsure of what had been said.

'It means "no problem", Gilly.' Francesca winked at Abdul: she was showing off in front of the new girl. 'You lead the way,' she told him.

The restaurateur greeted them at the top of the stairs, courteous to all three. On the top step Abdul lost his bravado, wilting under the unfamiliar attention, out of place and unsure how to deal with relaxed formality. For a moment he looked childlike. Francesca said nothing and ushered her companions through to the dining room.

It was like walking into an extra-large living room: an ultra-surreal lounge, over-decorated with satin curtains and silly pelmets. It felt incongruously suburban.

'Well, I'd say this is fine.' She hoped to cover Abdul's funk with a stream of chatter. 'What do you think, Abdul? Do you like it?' The roles were reversed: a week ago she had hidden behind his self-assurance; now she was able to reciprocate. 'Wine or beer, folks? Hell, are you guys *allowed* to drink beer during Ramadan?'

'Me, yes. Some others, no, they can't.' Abdul, like many younger Zanzibaris, drank moderate amounts of alcohol. It was an irreligious habit that hypocritically adhered to the conventions of holy month.

Abdul took a menu and studied it like the Qur'an. His finger followed a culinary prayer down the page, as if each dish contained a parable or a secret. His intensity vaguely irritated Francesca: she wanted his attention, and butted into his train of thought: 'Let me get the drinks, will you? I'm dying to test my Swahili.' She summoned a waiter and ordered; he understood what she wanted. 'Not bad, hey? That was my first time with the new lingo.'

Gilly seemed impressed. Abdul continued earnestly to examine the menu. The waiter returned with a single glass of white wine.

'Oh, no, no. I wanted a *bottle* of wine, three glasses. I'm sorry.' Her chest reddened and so did her face, even though there was nothing to be embarrassed about. It was at moments like these that Francesca felt unsightly, as if she were a gargoyle rather than an interesting woman carrying not quite enough flesh. In her mind she was a beacon of unprettiness. Abdul also made her self-conscious.

'Are we ready, then?' Francesca over-compensated for her embarrassment and his discomfort by governing the table. 'Is there anything you like? The crab claws in black bean sauce sound good. We'll share, shall we?' She would rescue the novice and her own sense of self with her suggestions. Was she doing this for him, or for Gilly's benefit? The drink and awkward situation made her garrulous. 'Abdul, I think the chilli chicken will be good. What do you think?'

She wasn't really asking. When she was anxious, her questions came out mostly as statements, a trait that annoyed her friends back home although no one ever mentioned it. When she was bloody-minded she unconsciously bullied those around her. It was paradoxical: Francesca was the one who felt unsure and set upon; she'd be appalled to understand that her friends sometimes felt like that because of her. Abdul agreed with her choice, put down the *hadith* – secretly enlightened – and blew into his hands. Gilly ordered, too, and they were done.

'Wine's not bad, is it?' Francesca gulped at her glass; the other two sipped. 'Better order another, what do you say?'

No one said anything other than Francesca to the waiter, and then it was in bad Swahili. More wine was brought to the silent table.

The combination of three at dinner was wrong: one or other or both of her friends felt out of place. It was too intimate.

'Abdul arranges safaris. Would you be interested?'

Francesca hadn't anticipated Gilly's enthusiastic response. Interested? She was, very. 'Yeah, I'd love to go on one. Have

you seen a lion? I'd love to see a lioness . . . and cubs . . .
It sounds amazing, Abo. Weren't you scared? You've got to
be really quiet doing that, I bet . . . That's fierce, Abdul! Is it
really that big? You're so lucky, I'd love a job like that.'

The attention she paid him piqued Francesca. Gilly could
organise a trip with any number of agents, why employ
Abdul? Unless she was making a pass.

The food arrived and Gilly continued to flirt harmlessly
with Abdul. Francesca interpreted it as a direct challenge
and took another slug of wine. She was getting pissed and
jealous. 'I'll order another bottle, shall I?'

The question was pointed: Francesca was going to salvage
the situation. She would attempt to bring the focus of attention back to herself, but had no need to: it was done for her.

'Awright, girl? It's like you've bin avoidin' me.'

Keith greeted her across the table, exuding all the warmth
of a congenial hoodlum. Gilly turned abruptly from Abdul
and smiled at Keith. Her sudden interest in him suggested she
found the contradictory combination compelling. Francesca
held her breath, sobered up, and replaced her drunken smile
with a frown.

'Out on the town, then, girls?' He directed his conversation
exclusively at the women.

'We're going home soon,' Francesca said.

'What? So early? Come off it! It's Friday night, innit? Time
for a few more drinkies. Whatya say?'

'I'm going home soon.'

'Well, I'd be up for it,' said Gilly. 'Sounds fun. Don't be a
spoilsport, Fran. C'mon, let your hair down.'

Francesca tried to communicate with her eyes. It didn't
work. She'd already needled the other girl with her heavy-
handedness. 'We should go home, Gilly. It's late. You
shouldn't be by yourself in Stone Town. Not at this time.'

'Don't be a wuss, Fran. I've got Keith to look after me,' Gilly said. 'You're strong and brave, aren't you?'

'Nothin'll happen to you, girl – well, not unless you want it to.'

'Keith! You're too much. But don't go getting dirty thoughts – I'm a good girl! I'm raging for a drink, though. Where d'ya know that's got music?'

Francesca was impotent. Her gambit to stop Gilly taking up with the shyster had failed. Perhaps she should tell him to fuck off; it would be language he understood. She thought better of it, deciding instead to instruct the girl on what she should do. It was for her own good – she wasn't being bossy. 'Gilly, you must stay here with me. I mean it. Don't go out later.'

'Francesca!' The girl scowled at her. 'Just because you don't want to go out and have a good time there's no need to fuck up everyone else's evening. You're really selfish, you know?'

Francesca stared at her new friend and felt her lip twitch; a precursor to tears. She mustn't cry.

'You need to take a long hard look at yourself some time, Fran. Keith, I'm up for it. Where are you taking me?'

Keith had watched the exchange with what appeared to be satisfaction. His thick jaw framed a thin smile. 'I s'pose that settles it, ladies. Gilly, if you'd be so kind . . .' He pulled back the Australian girl's chair.

Gilly grinned at Abdul, a what-the-hell expression of resignation, then glanced at Francesca as she put down her share of the bill. 'See ya, Fran.'

Keith looked back at her over his shoulder and sneered: 'Francesca, I'll leave you wiv Mowgli 'ere.'

The thug and the tourist left the room. Francesca remained seated, spiked by younger girl's betrayal; her crack at helping had been repaid with a slap in the face. What was wrong with people? Why couldn't they see she was right? It made her angry when others ignored what she saw as sound advice. Francesca felt isolated, even more alone in Zanzibar than she was at home.

Abdul employed the detachment of a UN observer. It was only as Keith left that he gave anything away: a shot of hatred.

'Abdul, I'm sorry.'

'Is OK, is not your fault.'

'He's a shit. I'm sorry he was rude to you.'

Abdul had been ignored throughout the encounter. He blew into his hands again. 'I say is not your fault, Francesca.'

'Let's have a drink now they're gone, just the two of us.'

'You have drink. For me? Is fine without.'

She ordered a glass of wine, rested her chin on her fists and waited for Abdul to say something, anything. He looked as introspective as when he'd read the menu. His thought process was devotional. The silence at the table seemed penitential. 'This is too weird, Abdul. Come on, let's go.'

He agreed, and led Francesca out. They walked down the stairs and past a cheap fountain that sobbed rather than spurted. As they left the restaurant his confidence returned. The clingfilm was unwrapped and he could breathe again.

They strolled through the stifling alleyways and returned to Francesca's new flat. The small blue door on the street was locked and her key wouldn't work properly. She twisted at it, skinning her knuckle on the metal doorknob. Panic scuttled up inside her; this was ridiculous. She tried again, then rattled the door. Eventually the night-watchman let them in. The old man's eyes were partially glazed with cataracts and his mind was evidently furred up with thoughts that had nothing to do with latecomers seeking access. He was lost to dreams. Francesca wanted to berate him, blame him for her inadequacy and lack of keymanship; luckily her lack of Swahili prevented an outburst. She led Abdul to the grey door and the bottom step.

'So, this is it, the stairs to my new home. Would you like to come up?'

Abdul stood by the door surveying, rather than looking at, the property. '*Hamna*, Francesca. I must to go home now. *Lala salama*. Goodnight.'

'*Lala salama*. Goodnight? That's so sweet. *Lala pajama*. Tomorrow, then?' She was vexed; she had wanted him to see her new place . . . She'd wanted him to look at her.

Abdul vanished into the darkness leaving Francesca to climb the stairs to her flat, unable to shed a stubborn melancholy.


# Returning


Carla spent the first few days in the Malindi Villa sleeping, supping gin and tonic or quietly meandering in the garden until the sun spun to another quarter and the heat or night drove her back inside. She'd tried to capture fragments of another time with the devotional visits of Mr Abeidi as they picked at the past from the safety of a red silk sofa.

'It's the prerogative of old age, Mr Abeidi. I'm happy staying at Malindi doing nothing very much for the while. It's so nice to be able to breathe the place in again.'

Carla said the journey from Heathrow had exhausted her and that she didn't travel so well any more. That made her laugh: she'd described herself like one of her vintage wines.

But today would be different: she was planning a trip. She stepped into the passenger seat of the battered Morris and groped automatically for a safety-belt to find herself pinching air instead of webbing. Of course the car didn't have belts – it never had.

'This car is over forty years old, Mrs Jackson.'

Mr Abeidi and Carla drove towards Stone Town.

'Only forty? It's not much more than a baby, then.'

'Maybe, but very old for a car. It still has the same registration. I think that it is the only one in all of Tanzania.'

'I'm sure it is – now, mind the bicycle, Mr Abeidi. Stop getting distracted.'

The old man drove the car between a phalanx of cyclists and handcarts. A *dala dala* overtook them all; thirty people were crammed into a vehicle that would have been crowded with ten.

They parked the car under the enormous branches of an immense banyan tree near the port.

'I'm glad that tree's still here. And they're still building boats?' Three men hammered at the skeletal beginnings of a tender in the shade of the ancient tree, a big boat, twenty feet long. The tree easily covered it.

'Shall we walk to the palace museum, Mrs Jackson?'

'No, not yet. Let me go back to the streets first.'

She fixed her parasol and linked arms with her companion. They proceeded like a couple of elder statesmen. The place had changed – it didn't quite dazzle in the same way. The streets were recognisable, but the walls had lost their perfect whiteness. So many tourist shops. 'Gizenga Street? Wasn't this Portuguese Street, Mr Abeidi? What's happened to the tailors?'

'They're not in this part any more, Mrs Jackson.'

'And don't they paint the walls now?'

Impressive greying flanks loomed above, the flaking plaster stained with decades of weather and neglect. A building had begun to collapse in on itself. The basement walls could barely contain the crumbling upper storeys and required a Giacometti scaffold of mangrove branches to retain the heavily pregnant frontage. It was inadequate: the ancient house was beyond repair and doomed. Carla noticed an old streetlamp – she remembered them from before because they had been made in Brighton – but now it was a blind, useless, rusting gibbet.

'Mr Abeidi? Wasn't this Patel's?'

They stood in front of a tourist shop selling cheap African masks and spices wrapped in palm-leaf boats. It was a dusty, sad emporium, and looked as if the stock had never sold.

'What a memory, Mrs Jackson. Yes, it was.'

'It was my favourite shop. I must have spent hundreds of shillings on records here. You know, I've still got them all. Ella, Oscar Peterson and – who was it? Bugger.' Carla rested her hand on her heart as she thought back. 'Milt Jackson! Now how could I forget a name like that?'

She hadn't played any of them since leaving Zanzibar. They brought back too many memories, reminiscences that, like the half-forgotten discs in the attic, were safer left hidden in the back of her mind.

# December 1963

'Won't be long, Johnno. Popping to the jeweller's to pick up my watch.'

'Can't Sima go for you?'

'I'll do it. I might call in for a snifter at the Africa on my way back.'

It was unusual for John Jackson to be home for lunch; normally he'd eat at the office or in a restaurant.

'Drinks later with the East German fellow, what's-his-name. You know, the big chap. Don't forget Lar. Eight thirty.'

Carla hated drinks with official German chaps as much as she did the sun at this time of day. They were still the Hun, East or West – she couldn't help it. 'You don't just *stop* being a Nazi. Why should twenty years make any difference?'

Johnno knew how she felt: they'd killed her brother. She called for the car. 'I'm going to de Silva's.'

Carla's new driver parked the shiny black Morris Minor on Main Road outside Ranti de Silva & Sons. The sign outside left no one in any doubt as to what they'd find inside: 'Manufacturing Jewellers & Gem Merchants: engravers, ivory-carvers, watch-repairers'. Carla's watch was in for cleaning; the second time that year. Stupidly she'd worn it at a beach party and got sand in it again. 'Is it ready, Mr de Silva?'

He went to a workshop in the back. Carla leaned on a glass cabinet admiring the stock. A watch caught her eye. 'This is new, isn't it?' she said.

The jeweller poked his head out to see what she was referring to. 'The latest Rolex, Mrs Jackson. It's a bit pricy, I'm afraid, three hundred and fifty shillings.'

'Is it really? I'll tell Mr Jackson. Perhaps if I'm very good it might just end up as my Christmas present.'

De Silva returned with her repaired watch.

'Don't wrap it, I may as well wear it now.'

Her mother had had it inscribed on the back: 'Darling Lar, bon voyage 1959'. She wasn't given to originality.

'It seems my watch has taken to measuring other times as well as the hours and minutes, Mr de Silva.'

'I beg your pardon?'

'It's started to measure years, and five have gone already. I can hardly believe it.'

'What's that, Mrs Jackson?'

'I've been here five years. Goodness, it could be fifty. Funny, really . . .'

The watch was too grand to wear every day, platinum and diamonds, but the clasp was nice: it made a satisfying click when it was done up. Carla called it her car door.

She left the shop and asked the driver to take her a hundred and fifty yards to the Africa Bar. It wasn't laziness: she couldn't walk in the heat. Wooden doors with heavy brass studs led into a cool marble lobby. The main bar was ahead, a smaller one to the side. In the middle of the lobby there was a fishpond, also marble. The doctor's son was there, terrorising the fish and frogs. He was bitten by a small turtle and started to cry.

'How many times have I told you to be careful, Ramil? Those turtles are little buggers – whoops, I mean *beggars*. Now, let's be having you, soldier, let me see your hand.'

Ramil sat on Carla's knee and proffered his bleeding finger.

'This is *very* serious. I'm going to have to operate, Ramil.'

The boy looked worried and sobbed.

'It'll have to come off. Are you ready?' Carla plunged tickling fingers into the child's ribs and he let out a squeal. 'Stop that, Ramil. I can't take your finger off if you're laughing. This is a serious business.'

He yelped. A ticklish, squirming, giggling boy replaced the crying, bitten one. A dab with a spit-dampened handkerchief revealed that the bite was tiny. 'Run home and get your mummy to clean it for you properly and . . .' Carla whispered like a Russian spy with a message '. . . here's fifty cents. Don't tell *anyone!*'

Ramil scarpered, and Carla went to the bar.

Felix Gomez was on his stool, the only one in the main bar. Carla sat in a cane chair and ordered a whisky sour. She didn't normally drink so early but she was bored, needed a bit of life. A zoological jigsaw surrounded them. Twenty-seven impala heads, some with horns, a buffalo bust and a scowling cheetah's face hung on the walls. Four elephant feet propped up a coffee table and a flattened lion lay exhausted of its insides beneath Carla. A gorilla's hand fashioned into an ashtray was used for peanuts instead of butts. Carla couldn't bear the thought of eating anything from it.

'Quiet today, Felix?'

He grunted. The miniature Goan held enormous grudges and had been in Zanzibar for ever. It was odd that anyone used his place. It wasn't for lack of choice – God knows, there were plenty of other bars. But this was *the* place. Everyone came to the Africa Bar, tourists and ex-pats. It was the bee's knees to them all. John said he'd once seen the old Sultan in a private room at the back, but Carla found that hard to swallow. She wanted to know if the adjacent bar had any customers.

'We've been quiet all day, Mrs Jackson, it is Ramadan.'

She'd quite forgotten. She tapped a cigarette and fed it to her mouth.

A waiter brought over her drink and the day's newspaper.

'Could you put the fans on? There's a good chap.'

*East African Herald*, 11 DECEMBER 1963: Zanzibar
Full independence was officially declared in Zanzibar yesterday. After 73 years of British protection, outgoing British Resident Sir Julian Parrish handed over power to

the new Zanzibari government. The new Sultan, Sultan Rashid Ahmed, presided over the ceremony.

She knew the Parrish chap quite well: he was always popping round to the house for a drink. He'd said that independence was the best thing for the place, although Carla was unsure. She didn't like change, and saw no reason for it now.

When the idea was first mooted, John asked: 'Julian, how's this independence business going to affect us then?'

'It won't, Johnno. You'll carry on with business as usual.'

Carla was unconvinced. 'Are you certain? I mean, look what happened in India, darling. There's been nothing but trouble ever since.'

'Lar, you have nothing to worry about. You and John will be perfectly safe here, doing what you always have done.' Julian pointed at his empty tumbler. 'Talking of which, my glass is looking a tad empty. What say we have another before dinner . . .'

Carla went to fix more drinks and was followed by the reassuring laughter of John and Julian.

Felix was too engrossed in his crossword to be any fun; unfortunately he wasn't in the mood for gossip. Carla admired her new lipstick colour; the end of her cigarette was cherry red. The room was silent apart from the swish-swash of the fans and Felix clicking his ballpoint pen in and out. She pouted; an unconscious action. Those who knew her well would have realised she was bored: it was her signal. 'Well, that's me done, Felix. I'm off. I might be back later. I'll need to escape from another of Johnno's bloody dos.'

'As you like, Mrs Jackson.'

He didn't look up and Carla didn't look back. She clacked

elegantly across the marble floor in lizardskin shoes with pointed heels and climbed smartly into the back of the Morris. 'OK, buddy? Put your foot on the gas and get me outta here. Time to drive me home.'

Carla was below average at impersonations. Her Yankee accent was lamentable, not that the driver would know the difference between that and her conventional crisp tongue.

'You got it!' came the faultless Bronx reply – the result of watching countless American films at the Sultana cinema in Malindi district. The car took off slowly.

Carla was pleased: the new fellow, Mussa, was bright. 'You liked my little joke?'

'Yes, madam. I liked it very much.'

# Francesca's Stone Town

Francesca engaged a cleaner on the recommendation of the boy in the Internet café. The ebullient, toothy woman's command of English was as bad as her employer's Swahili. Luckily, Fatima needed to be told nothing. She powered around the apartment, scouring, removing cobwebs and attacking both bathrooms with a miasmic acid. She swept everything over and again with a broom built from a long bundle of slender twigs tightly bound together. A trendy Londoner would have displayed it as an *objet d'art* on the wall. Francesca asked for more brushes. 'I want ten of these, Fatima.'

She slipped back into moronic-speak with the cleaner and showed ten splayed digits, then pointed to the brush again. Fatima took three thousand shillings, and returned a little later with the unlikely wholesale purchase.

The next day Fatima found the brooms stacked in a long line down one side of the hallway; she took one and started the tedious job of sweeping away the dust. Francesca pulled the brush from her. 'No, Fatima, those you leave alone, OK?'

The cleaner had no idea of what Francesca was talking about.

'These are *special*, I like them there. Here, this is your broom. *Not* these.' She handed over yesterday's besom and placed the new one back against the wall. 'Don't touch these, OK?' She shook her head slowly from side to side, and wagged a finger as if she was chastising an infant. To her mind the regimented, simple display of rural domesticity was artistic: a similar arrangement had been featured in last month's *Marie Claire*.

To Fatima's mind it was a line of brooms. 'Crazy *mazungo*,' she said, and laughed to herself for the next two hours.

TO: Daveyboy
CC:
Subject: a flat and balls

Davey, i've got it! The perfect flat smack bang in Stone Town in an area called Shangani. Its near Kenyatta Road. Kenyatta is the main drag, well the post office is on it and so is the offy (thank you god). I discovered the market, great for fish & veg, but the meat looks a bit dodge – i saw a bloody antelope in there the other day. Ok it might have been a goat, but it looked more gazelle-like to me . . . Ive got a tearoom on the roof & the views are incredible, i can see forever. Its the place i had in my dreams, you know ive always been a secret poet. I only wish you could see it. No address @ the mo cos theres

no postal service as such, so best communicate by email,
i will get a p.o. box # later, that's what the locals do. The
chinky meal went sour, the ape i told you about showed
up and whisked my ozzy friend off, i only hope she's ok
as i haven't seen her about since. I still haven't driven
around the island, too busy cleaning the flat out and
nesting.

Heres one for you . . . testicle mauling seems to be
a national pastime here. EVERYONE does it. Cocksure
/prickcentric nobrite if you get my drift. If theyre not
scratching their goolies theyre tugging at the python.
Rethink! Nose picking is the second most popular sport! Its
all groping & burrowing over here . . . Ramadan @ the mo
so im all covered up, i cant wait to get a suntan, maybe
that place on east coast? I met a sweet guy called Abdul,
ONLY a friend, so don't go getting any thoughts cos that's
the last thing on my mind right now. Hope everythings ok.
Kwaheri and love
XXXFran.

The rains were more frequent now, stupendous down-
pours that switched themselves off as easily as they did on. It
never seemed to rain at night; mornings at about eleven were
the most favoured moments. Enormous curtains of water
hammered on rusty corrugated-iron roofs and spurted below
into fast rivers that had once been alleyways. Francesca got
caught out twice on Gizenga Street and tried to shelter in a
shop doorway on an extra high pavement. The shop was
closed and she got sodden. She squelched her way back to
the flat and sat dripping over Fatima's clean floor. There was
a new bottle of whisky in the fridge and she poured herself a
decent glassful. She didn't want to get a cold – at least, that
was her excuse.

It wasn't something she liked to admit, but Francesca felt muffled by loneliness. Ostensibly she was an independent spirit: striking out, fending for herself, not needing to depend on the hospitality of strangers. Privately she suffered, and felt like a dim-witted art student who'd arrived to live like a pauper in Paris in the naïve hope that his art would somehow improve with poverty. She knew she was being a jerk, playing at finding palmy days.

She'd taken to going to a local café for early suppers. It was grotty and had a parrot that spoke English. 'Evening, chaps,' the blue bird chirruped. 'Bottoms up,' was another peculiarity. 'Get them in, Felix,' it had a British provenance. It was a camp parrot. The food was uniformly dreary, although an advertised dish of crab's legs amused her; she presumed they meant claws. The last meal she had had there was a fetid pilau, preceded by a bowl of greasy, unidentifiable soup; she hoped the parrot might have been added to the pot. She was disappointed: it hadn't.

Crossing the street to go home, she noted a familiar silhouette in a doorway. 'Abdul!' The tall skinny one slunk out of the early evening. She was pleased to see him. 'Would you like to have a drink with me?'

In the bar she fell upon him, talking about anything and nothing, pleased to have a chum, a drinking buddy, and desperate for the companionship. 'God, I can yack for Europe when I put my mind to it. What have you been up to?'

Abdul flicked on his intense look. '*Sawa sawa.*'

'You must have done something. How's business?'

'Is quiet, no tourist. Me, I try, but no one come after New York attack. That is life.' He glugged from a Kilimanjaro beer and looked towards the road. He seemed unsettled. He cupped his hands round his mouth and puffed into them as if he was cold.

'You have car, Francesca?'

'Yes, I've got a hire car round the corner.'

'Then let us go.'

The Jeep was parked beside the entrance to one of the decrepit mansions that lined the waterfront. Plaster flaked away from the walls and the once grand door was stripped of the vast brass rivets that would traditionally have adorned it. They were probably decorating a portal in West London now. Ranks of neatly drilled holes were the only clue as to what had been there before. The wood was daubed with graffiti: 'Bin Laden area'.

Francesca wasn't sure if it was a sick joke. 'That's a bit unnerving, Abdul.'

'Not for you to worry about. You OK here with me.'

His tone implied that the painted message might be genuine.

'Well, I hope I'll be OK. My mother would be only too pleased to say, "I told you so," if I got into trouble.' As she spoke she realised how fatuous she sounded. Abdul said nothing more.

Earlier in the day she'd spoken to an American student in the Internet café. He was a novelty, primarily because he was someone new to talk to, and secondly because after the World Trade Centre tragedy there hadn't been many American visitors anywhere. He was convinced that members of al Qaeda were on the island, although this news puzzled Francesca. How could he be so well informed? He said: 'It stands to reason. Some of these guys are bound to be, like, Islamic fundamentalists. They have a monopoly around here.'

Francesca was unimpressed by his insight. 'You need to relax. Ever heard of born-again Christians? The States are full of them.'

He didn't get her point.

'All I'm trying to say is that there are extremists all over the place,' she explained. 'The Oklahoma bomber couldn't have been more American. You certainly don't need to be Islamic to take a reactionary line.'

Abdul drove her to a small bar near the airport. A high wall surrounded the compound, and disco Tarab thumped across the space. The musical fusion of Arab-influenced tunes, spiced up with a pounding disco beat, sounded faintly naff to Francesca. Abdul enjoyed it, though; he sang along to most of the numbers. 'This is place where I like. Beer's cheap.'

Francesca liked it too: it fulfilled her romantic notion of where she should be hanging out. She also enjoyed the attention Abdul paid her, and her status as the only white woman in the bar. Abdul was proud of her, she felt like a trophy, something special. Plastic chairs and tables lined one wall – they had taken a cheap retirement from a more salubrious establishment. She made her way over to them and was greeted by the same smiles that followed her everywhere on the island; they seemed even more powerful here. An *umbra* danced by himself in the dark. A neighbour at the next table told her, 'It's the beer dancing, not the man,' and laughed.

Francesca drank two to every one beer Abdul had. She was getting tipsy and voluble.

'Mama Francesca . . . you drink too much.'

She seized up, her face darkened. 'I beg your pardon?'

'I say you drink very big.'

Her splashy party spirit evaporated. 'No, before that, what did you say?'

It was obvious Abdul didn't understand the sudden change of mood.

'Quit the mama thing, will you?'

Her voice was metallic and empty.

'I'm not a mama, never have been. Don't you get it?'

To him it was only a form of acknowledgement.

'I am not a mama. I've told you a dozen bloody times, I'm not a fucking mama. Now, if you don't mind, I'm off.'

The speediness of her switch took them both by surprise. It was a fleeting conversion to misery from which she was unable to back away. They went to the car. Francesca stalked ahead. 'I suppose you'll want dropping off.'

'Is OK, I get *dala dala*, Francesca.'

'Fine, then. No thanks for the drink. Goodbye.'

She drove away quickly, knowing she'd been too abrupt again, too emphatic. She was weepy. God, how she hated herself when she got into this state. His tall silhouette was caught in her side mirror: he was lit and relit by passing cars, an unlikely standing-stone, plaintive and alone. She looked ahead – tears stung her eyes – and attempted to concentrate her rage in her driving. Abdul wasn't lonely: the real loneliness sat in the driving seat. It wasn't Abdul who was detached from his surroundings; she was. She missed London. Back at the flat she headed straight for the fridge. Out came the whisky. Voices echoed up from downstairs. All had purpose, were tinged with enjoyment, maybe. Why did everyone seem happy? What did a penniless beach-bum have to celebrate? It was as if they were laughing at her. And even though it was late, the singsong and squabbles of children came wafting up to haunt her. It was nothing a stiff drink couldn't mend.

Next morning a loud knocking woke her.

'Franny? Hello, Franny? Is Fatima here. You let me in?'

She'd fallen asleep on the sofa and had a hangover from

hell. She unbolted the door letting the cleaner in to clatter around the kitchen.

'Stop making such a noise, Fatima.' Francesca put a finger to her lips and hushed. 'Do the washing or something, but keep it quiet.'

The cleaner left the dishes and went into the bathroom to scrub at clothes that had soaked overnight in a bucket. Francesca crept into the kitchen to make coffee. She was feeling remorseful: she shouldn't have taken out her misery on Fatima. There was a lot she shouldn't have done. Why had she drunk so much? She was out of control. Francesca wanted to see Abdul: she needed to explain last night to him and apologise for being drunk, but she couldn't until she met him on the street again. Frustration compounded her hangover. Nothing was easy in Zanzibar. She left Fatima in the flat, found the car and drove. Maybe she'd see him by the roadside.

Negotiating Stone Town was hazardous. If it wasn't pedestrians, it was bicycles or motorbikes she needed to look out for, hundreds, thousands of them. Why it was any worse than driving in Camden she couldn't imagine; it should have been a cinch by comparison. Maybe it was the hangover or perhaps she'd slowed down. She couldn't face driving through town so set off up Kenyatta Road past the law courts. She'd skirt to the East Coast Road through the new suburbs. It was downbeat. Shabby apartment blocks lined one street; they belonged in the East End of London. But there was a difference between the Stone Town flats and their foreign cousins. Naïvely Francesca thought tropical broken windows, open to the heat and the dust, were home to a *sunnier, smilier*, more *natural* poverty. The blocks gave way to humbler dwellings, but a hundred metres behind them she could see the tiled rooftops of more affluent homes, satellite dishes pointing upwards to catch CNN and the BBC World Service. A shanty town of mud huts stood near the rubbish dump. Makuti palm-leaf roofs sat upon tumbledown walls. On top of one roof there was a wire contraption: the householder had optimistically fashioned an antenna from coat-hangers. There was something both endearing and appalling about it. The invention was joyful, yet its inadequacy was heartbreaking.

In ten minutes Francesca was driving past a sprinkling of coconut palms and banana plantations. Even though it was busy, her foot went down. She was impatient to escape those on the road. The smiling chatter of idling cyclists was bawdy abuse – they were laughing at her, of course they were. Her self-absorption and insecurity interpreted everything as a personal slight. The sun shone, the music was loud. *Gorillaz*. Damon was perfect road music. A sign for the Jozani forest pointed right: she followed, leaving the amiable traffic far behind her.

'At first acquaintance the forest is mysterious, humid, riddled with frogs the size of peas, whispering pines and palms that are truly exotic. It is also the home of civet cats, gazelle, rare Zanzibari leopards, any number of birds, and a panoply of snakes (including python).' Francesca closed her guidebook, understanding she would see none of the latter. Perhaps it wasn't the best place to be with a hangover.

A guide took her out of the rainforest into dry forest. This was a misnomer, it was scrub, but at least Francesca got to see animals. High in the tree was a red Colobus monkey. She was quiet, as serious as David Attenborough might be, so as not to scare them. The monkeys appeared everywhere. An extended family of miniature primates came hooting out of the trees and somersaulted into the bushes. They were hardly shy – or, at least, the ones she found weren't. The crazy, ostentatious creatures had borrowed wigs from Andy Warhol. They were charming, even with matted arses, a dick that looked like an acorn and caterpillar nipples, and shot off the end of the cuteness scale. Why did wildlife always look so manicured in photographs? In her limited experience it invariably wasn't.

She looked around for another hour and headed back to town. She was going to find Abdul.

## A Beach Then

'Ask Mussa to get the car ready, I feel like a drive.'

Carla wasn't talking directly to anyone: she had made the announcement as she peered through a slatted window and pouted at the sea. She turned to see if the message had been heard and saw Sima nipping from the room and down the long corridor. Carla called after her: 'Can he be ready in half an hour?'

'Yes, madam,' the girl shouted back.

Carla changed into a floral cotton dress that nipped in at the waist – her best feature, she thought – sandals and a hat, no stockings. Maybe a picnic would be a good idea, something simple. She walked into the kitchen and asked the cook to prepare sandwiches and fruit. 'Don't bother with a hamper, Hammid, use the greaseproof. It's only for me.'

'You want water, madam? I put some cold in Thermos for you.'

The lot went into a small, locally woven shopping basket – Sima liked to call it a Zanzibari briefcase. Carla walked to the front door with the bag and found Mussa waiting. 'Could you take this from me? There's a good chap.' She handed it over. He let her into the car, then got in himself.

He turned to look at his passenger for directions. 'I thought we might go to Mtoni,' she said. 'The beach is nice there.'

The drive from Shangani along the harbour was beautiful, past the House of Wonder and the Sultan's palace, both so gleaming white that Carla needed her sunglasses. Dhow builders were sanding an almost complete vessel in the shade of a huge banyan tree. A liner was in port; its funnels dwarfed the harbour buildings. Three dazzling columns from an incomplete Greek temple appeared to stick surreally from the sea. They cruised past the Sultana cinema and on to the pretty road that led north to Mtoni. The coconut palms formed a dense forest of skinny trunks and cartwheel hats, the lot swaying in unison. They were tropical rockets; their vapour-trail trunks careered skywards before exploding into a shaggy green head. It was quiet today: the road was empty.

'Open your window, Mussa. Let's get the wind in here.' She could see his eyes in the driver's mirror although he didn't look back at her.

'Is that better, madam?'

'Much.'

Her hair had always been such a thing – in London, anyway, and in Africa, too, for the first couple of years. It didn't matter so much now; she was happy for it to be ruffled instead of coiffed – it made her feel real. Any small freedom was better than the regimented life she lived with John. A curly blonde strand blew into her eyes.

'Your English is very good, Mussa.'

'Thank you, madam. I was taught as a child, when I worked for the Parrish household.'

Mussa and Carla walked down a dirt track that only just made it through the densely crowded vegetation. Its shade was a delight, protecting the pedestrians from unforgiving sunlight. Picture-postcard palms fringed the slip of beach that fell into the ocean. It was Carla's hideaway. She thought that no one apart from herself ever went there. 'Here will do nicely, thank you, Mussa.'

A travel blanket was unfolded for the solitary picnicker and her lunch. It was placed on the white coral sand. Lying on it was as comfortable as a bed: the fine grains altered to the contour of her body. It was perfect isolation; she wanted music to fall asleep by. The day would improve no end if she could nap while listening to Dinah Washington, Tony Bennett, Chet Baker . . . 'My Funny Valentine'. She began to hum.

The driver started back to the car. Carla looked up, conscious of him leaving. 'You don't have to go, Mussa.'

He didn't seem to know what he should do.

'Cook's made enough sandwiches for a regiment. Share them with me.'

'I can't, madam, it's Ramadan.'

'Join me, go on. We'll hide the food – I'm not hungry, anyway. We'll have a holy-month picnic. Our Muslim picnic . . .'

She put the food back into the basket; the rug was empty.

Carla had an infectious laugh – it could be heard at sea. If she found something funny enough she'd cry. This annoyed John, especially if it happened at one of his functions: 'Lar, please calm down. I've got some very important people here.'

'Johnno, if I can't laugh, what the hell can I do?'

Carla was laughing now on the beach. It was a cheerful, inclusive sound. Mussa laughed too.

'Don't just stand there, sit down with me.'

The request was unusual; he appeared unsure of the etiquette and sat stiffly at one end of the rug, averting his gaze to his lap.

'If we're going to accompany each other on an imaginary picnic we should at least speak to each other.'

'Yes, madam.'

Carla was looking straight at him. 'About anything other than food, that is.'

He looked up, and seeing her smile, relaxed.

'It's beautiful here. Have you been to this place before, Mussa?'

'Yes, madam, many times.'

'So I'm not the only person to hide on these sands.' Her words betrayed disappointment that the beach wasn't entirely hers. 'Tell me something about yourself, Mussa, tell me a secret.'

He was unused to such talk, not only with a *mazungo* woman but with any woman. 'I don't have secrets.'

'There must be one. It would be terrible if you didn't have any. Let me guess. This place. Right here. I bet this is one of your secrets, no?'

'You can read minds, madam. You're like a witch-doctor.'

'I promise you I'm not. But I know that this is one. It's one of mine too.'

They didn't see the clouds form. It began to spot.

'Bugger, it's going to rain.'

As she spoke the pregnant sky let its load drop.

'Quick, Mussa, help me.'

They gathered up the travel rug and food, and ran to a tree. Its shelter was inadequate; the rain soaked them.

'We might as well have gone straight in, Mussa, clothes and all.'

The warm rain pounded the trees and kneaded the sand.

'Shall we?'

'Shall we what, madam?'

'Go in.'

Mussa didn't understand.

'Come on.'

Carla kicked off her sandals and ran into the ocean. Her dress floated around her like a chintzy lily-pad. 'Mussa, come on, it's wonderful.'

He stood still, nervous in case anyone should see.

'For God's sake, come and join me. You'll not get any wetter standing there.'

Mussa looked around: there was no one else on the beach. He undid his shoes and walked to the waves. They licked at his feet and the turn-ups of his trousers.

'Come on, Mussa, join me – it's fantastic.'

He ran into the sea fully clothed, as delighted as Carla.

# CHAPTER 3: WHISKY SOUR

## Meeting

TO: Daveyboy
CC:
Subject: tourist spotting

Davey, Forodhani Gardens is the business. Its a great
social place, im always bumping into someone – like
the Masai boys; they're fun wouldn't you like to know!
Everyone shows up at some point; all the locals & some
tourists. You should have seen the sorry bunch last
night . . . A gaggle of backpackers doing a pan-African
tour on one of those lorries . . . One bloke was wearing a
dhoti that was so baggy he looked like he'd shat himself!
Anyways, sarong man made a big point of deliberate
limping around the stalls – giving the impression hed
sustained a major sporting injury, you know the type
of thing: a broken hip after an energetic game of pool,
or a crushed tibia after a rough game of darts. As soon
as he limped away & thought no one was looking his
natural walk came back! There was NOTHING wrong
with him at all . . . I reckon he felt too much like a
woofter in his frock so had 2 toughen up his image . . .

Talking of poofs, how you doin? Miss you like mad. E me soon.
XXXXXXX Fran

The fires and storm lanterns in Forodhani were seductive. At sunset the call to prayer slipped into a red sky and traders set up food stalls along the harbourside. Trestles were laden with squid and curly octopus, small lobsters and huge prawns, tuna kebabs, miniature skewers of beef and chicken satay, kingfish, marlin, chips and bowls of salad. The golden lamplight made the food appear even more attractive. Cooking smells from three dozen barbecues scented the air, inducing hunger even in those who felt full. Silhouettes vanished into the darkness after buying a supper doused with *pili-pili* while optimistic stall-holder faces peered from the yellow glare for more customers.

Francesca developed a taste for Zanzibari pizza, a savoury 'crêpe' filled with chopped meat, spices and egg. The kitchen she liked most was at the far end of Forodhani, near the ice-cream hut. She sat at a simple plank table near it. The food was delivered on a flaccid paper plate and accompanied by a cocktail stick with which to spear the greasy snack. There was a definite knack to balancing and devouring the 'pizza' without making an almighty mess.

Francesca considered her options: either hang around Forodhani Gardens a while and maybe Abdul would show up, or go home alone and read, or go out for a drink, a grown-up drink. The Serena Hotel was the best place for that: it was where she had escaped to after being harassed by the lout on the day she arrived, and was easily the grandest place in Stone Town. A large terrace hooks around the pool and looks out to sea. Large rattan chairs sit outside between monumental pillars. The waiters – dressed in tightly belted white tunics and brightly coloured waistcoats – effortlessly ply between the tables in the bar and on the terrace. They pad, rather than walk, in sneakers. Francesca sat outside.

'Would madam like cocktail?'

'That's a lovely idea, yes, please. Could I see the list?'

She decided on a whisky sour.

'That is popular drink tonight, madam.'

'Really?' Her interest was a pretence.

Francesca lit a cigarette, sank into her chair and stared into space. The bar was quiet: only one other person sat on the terrace, an old white woman, a couple of tables away. The waiter returned with Francesca's drink. Lifting it, she caught her neighbour's eye. 'Cheers,' said Francesca.

The woman nodded and lifted her own glass: 'Bottoms up!'

Francesca had no intention of being cornered by a geriatric on holiday. Perhaps she'd taken shore leave from a cruise, but there'd not been any liners in the harbour. Francesca watched her furtively. There was something about her manner, a confidence that didn't necessarily go with her age. She was caught spying. She reddened and felt stupid.

The woman spoke: 'Would you like to join me for a drink?'

It was the last thing Francesca wanted. 'I'm fine by myself, thank you anyway.'

She hadn't convinced her neighbour. 'Go on, I insist, a quick one until your friends arrive.'

Francesca felt obliged to join the biddy. Ten minutes would do the trick, then she could leave to find her fictitious companions.

'Carla Jackson.' The old woman put out her hand.

Francesca took it and answered primly – as if visiting someone else's grandmother. 'Nice to meet you, Mrs Jackson. I'm Francesca Wade.'

'Goodness, you are old-fashioned. Call me Carla, or Lar. Everyone else does.'

The old woman was sassy, and had surprised her guest. Francesca joined the table unsure what to say; she felt awkward with the unexpected company. It wasn't that she was rude, she felt unnaturally shy and clammed up.

Carla steered the conversation. 'Are you on holiday, Francesca?'

'I'm here for a few months, actually.'

'How exciting. Do you know your way around yet?'

'No, not really, I keep getting lost.'

'Don't worry, it happens to everyone. You'll fathom it out soon enough. Do you know many people in Stone Town?'

Francesca fibbed: 'Some. Are *you* local?'

Carla sipped from her glass. 'Not exactly *local*, darling. No, not now, anyhow. I used to live here a *very* long time ago.'

'You had a house here?'

'Oh, yes.'

'A holiday home?'

'No, it *was* my home.'

Francesca wanted to know more. 'Was it in Stone Town, Lar?'

'It was right here.'

Francesca was puzzled.

'We're sitting in it – this place, the Serena, darling. This used to be my house. Changed a lot now, of course. That bit there is totally new and we didn't have a pool. The other side of the building was where the cable and wireless chaps operated from.' Carla shuttled to her past. 'Good God!

Enough of that. You don't want to listen to an old woman droning on about her history.'

'Yes. I mean, no, you're not droning. I'd love to hear more, Lar.'

'That's kind of you, but I'm sure you'd much prefer to find your chums. Are you meeting them here?'

Francesca changed her mind about escaping to meet non-existent friends: she wanted to stay, she liked the company. 'I'm here by myself.'

'You are? Then let me get you another. What's it to be? A whisky sour? How funny, that's my drink too.'

Francesca hadn't expected to befriend a dowager. *Old* wasn't her thing. She'd not made a conscious decision to exclude pensioners from her life: it was simply that she didn't know any except those in her mother's circle, and she made a point of not knowing them. If she was honest, old age depressed her. She had a horror of mutating into a skinny version of her overly made-up and curvaceous parent. In London she'd been too busy with her career and friends or the pursuit of boyfriends to take any interest in OAPs.

Francesca considered the woman sitting before her. She was chic without much makeup or jewellery, projecting an old-fashioned confidence and glamour that belonged to another era, some indefinable time before Francesca was born. She thought everything must be simple for those of grandmothering age. What did they have to worry about, other than mortality? Their time of life must be easier. Having a closet-queen boyfriend or a neurosis about an ill-fitting face surely didn't figure in an old-timer's almanac. It couldn't be that complicated.

'Do you smoke, Lar?' Francesca offered a Marlboro Light.

'Thank you, darling, but I'll have one of these. I've been meaning to give up for years. A bit late now, isn't it?'

Carla's chatty, intimate manner had put Francesca at her ease. The two women worked at their drinks.

'How long are you here, Lar?'

'I'm just like you, my dear. I'll be here for a while, provided I don't drop down dead.'

'Unlikely, isn't it?'

'I'm seventy-four. I'd have thought it more likely than not.'

Francesca was impressed. Carla's appetite for whisky sours and Silk Cut would put a younger person to shame. Her face was wrinkled, but she didn't look *that* old. 'I'm amazed. You don't look anything like it.'

'Thank you, but I'm still funny about notching up birthdays, even at my great age.'

'Get on with you, how could you be?'

'And what would you know about it? I imagine you were an irrational mess when you were approaching your thirtieth.'

Francesca went for her drink.

'Goodness, that was rude of me. I'm sorry. I should watch the whisky. You'll find that's my nature, I'm afraid – always speaking out of turn. I don't mean half of it. It's silly of me. Why, you don't even look thirty.'

'I'm thirty-five, Carla, and, yes, you're right, the idea of hitting the big three-oh freaked me. I felt so . . . past it.'

They drank more whisky and sat talking for another hour. As they left the bar they promised to meet again.

'Perhaps you might come to my villa one night for dinner?'

'I'd love to do that, just name the day.'

Francesca returned to her flat, crept up the steep stairs to her tearoom and looked across the scruffy tin roofs to a black sea. She'd have another drink before bed.

# Abdul

Abdul was twenty-nine. At least, he thought he was. He was in the habit of claiming to be the same age as the person he was speaking to – within reason. Maybe he was thirty-one, but definitely not younger than twenty-eight. What did it matter? Once, he'd maintained he was thirty-nine but he wasn't believed. He should ask his mother. Perhaps he was thirty-three . . . Abdul's mother had forgotten how old she was years ago. One of eight, he was the second eldest child and eldest son. It was a responsibility, not unlike being a parent himself. His father had deserted his mother years ago and she had remarried. When her last husband died she was left with a large brood of half-brothers and sisters. Because of this, all things paternal in the household naturally gravitated to Abdul: sorting out familial squabbles, the electricity bill (they'd overridden the meter for years and been caught out), money for food and rent, even the politics became his inheritance. It was tough: there was never quite enough to go round. Returning from Dar es Salaam was as much about looking after his family as it was the tourist trade collapsing. It was an obligation, a prison; he couldn't escape it. That was the attraction of Francesca: perhaps she would be the answer and help him change his situation.

Mombassa district is part of the new town. Abdul's mother had lived there since she was sixteen and already in the family way again with him. It was an ugly neighbourhood, consisting of concrete tenements, some middle-class housing and older, neglected terraces. Other than its lack of aesthetic there was nothing much wrong with the place. It was poor,

71

but where in Zanzibar wasn't? The water worked, mostly, and if it didn't there was always a communal well; power-cuts happened sometimes but not frequently, the streets got swept and there had been no serious outbreak of disease for a while. Malaria was a problem. With that there were three options: buy drugs (expensive); get local bush medicine (cheap); sit it out. The last time he got it Abdul had made his own medicine and was fine after a few days. When his aunt was ill the family pooled money for drugs: she had needed them.

He sat in the Forodhani Gardens doing nothing much except brush at flies and look out to sea. He'd not done any business for weeks, not since September. The tourists stayed away because they were too nervous to travel. It was the same for everyone. With no tourists there was no work. There was talk of hotels closing. The men who ran the curio shops on Gizenga Street gathered in small groups near the fort to sit in the shade, hopeful the *wazungo* would come back and start buying their trinkets again. Abdul sat resigned and trance-like in the shadow of a tree. Ramadan hunger compounded the problem. It was hot and silent, except for the caw of crows and the whir of mopeds. The town was menopausal: it was changing; it was flushed and bothered.

Abdul flicked aimlessly at his mobile. They weren't uncommon on the island, but having airtime credit was. He used his for rare incoming calls only. A tourist had given him the old Nokia. The aerial was broken, but the handset was still in working order. The heat intensified, and a bead of sweat ran towards his shirt. It was too hot for birds to fly. If he remained motionless he might be lucky and catch the end of a breeze. He was as still as a lizard – sleepy too. His lids dropped, shuttering his eyes.

'Hey, you, I was hoping you'd be here.'

Francesca had shown up.

'I wanted to say sorry for the other night. I shouldn't have been so snappy. Are we still friends?'

He turned to look at her with a face that gave nothing away. He nodded.

'Good, can we meet later? My treat . . .'

'Maybe that is nice, Francesca.'

She sat down in the shade beside him. The small distance between them falsely suggested easiness and a relaxed intimacy in their fledgling friendship. 'Is that a new phone?' It was a condescending question: the phone was patently old. She'd meant was it new to Abdul; the enquiry was innocent. He knew she wouldn't comment on a tatty phone belonging to another *mazungo*. It made him resentful, but she didn't notice.

'Give me your number, Abdul. It'll make life easier if I can ring you.'

Abdul programmed it into her phone. His finger shirked from the digits, as if it had received a small electrical shock after pressing each button. He cricked his finger joints after the procedure, then bit his lip.

'So, tonight? Why don't you come to my place? I'll cook.' She was determined to get him there, not only to alleviate her loneliness, but for something else. She was anticipating more than company: nervously she had planned his seduction.

## Carla's Run

'Mr Abeidi, I missed you at the Serena last night. I hope everything is OK?'

'Forgive me, Mrs Jackson. I was feeling unwell. Did you get my message?'

The two elderly friends sat on a veranda in the Malindi Villa, crumpled-tissue-paper figures nearly blown away with the breeze. Two empty china cups were sitting in front of them on saucers.

'I picked it up on my return. I was worried for you, but you seem shipshape today.'

'I feel a little better, thank you, Mrs Jackson.'

Mr Abeidi felt guilty: he'd not been wholly truthful with his friend. It was true, he hadn't felt well, but his reason for not joining her had been his overwhelming fear of entering the hotel. They began sipping at sugary tea poured for them by the houseboy, Ali. Darby and Joan, black and white, older and old.

'After you didn't show last night, I stayed on for a drink and met a young woman. She reminded me of someone from all those years ago.'

There was silence.

'She jolted something in me. My memories clicked back into place. She's running away, Mr Abeidi. She's come dashing to Zanzibar to get away from a man in London. She said she felt caged. Her freedom had been taken away. I'm not sure if I entirely believe her, but that's not the point.'

Her friend didn't say anything.

'Well, doesn't her situation remind *you* of anyone?'

Carla trawled her memories; the old man visited his own.

'It was me! Can't you see that, Mr Abeidi? In a funny, reversed sort of way, it was me!'

He seemed distracted by other thoughts.

'I was just like her, all those years ago, the one who needed to escape. I was locked up. That funny girl and me, we're similar.'

His eyes were magnified to preposterous dimensions by thick spectacles. 'I think, Mrs Jackson, you will find that it was *me* who was trapped.'

Carla fidgeted, mystified by his words. What was he saying? She hadn't forgotten what it was like then; she'd not misremembered those painful years shuttered in a breathless marriage. She'd been suffocated with niceness, trapped by convention and stifled by a good marriage. She'd been a *prisoner* all her married life.

He looked at her, his leathery, pleated face held in place by the goggles. 'It was me who was imprisoned, Mrs Jackson. I was the one who was locked up. And you're right, you did do the running, but you didn't stop. You managed to escape.'

Carla gazed at her tea-sipping companion. He slurped a little: his teeth had gone the same way as hers, except he'd not renewed his. She was quiet for a beat. Then: 'What are you saying to me? Are you saying that it was you who did the suffering?'

'Yes, that is exactly what I said.'

His defiant words surprised her nearly as much as the hollow, brittle tone in which they were delivered. Carla was baffled by the revelation and didn't want to proceed with that line of conversation. She didn't know what it would wake up. She manipulated the subject. 'I said to the girl it would be jolly to meet again, but I dare say I'm too old for her. She won't want to spend time with me.'

Mr Abeidi nodded, perhaps meaning good idea, go ahead, meet your new friend again, or affirming that, yes, she *was* too old to spend time with a younger woman. The nuance wasn't lost on Carla.

'What say we go for a short drive, Mr Abeidi?'

The journey would distract them from a conversation that might prove too raw.

They motored gently to Mtoni. 'God, hasn't it changed? Where have all the palms disappeared to? And there's a hotel on the beach now.'

The vintage Morris pulled on to the gravel forecourt of the Mtoni Marine Centre. The dust track to the secret beach was long gone, vanished with the coconut forest. There were a couple of administrative buildings hard by the road, and a new path led towards the ocean and hotel accommodation.

'Shall we, Mr Abeidi? It's been some time since we went down this road.'

He looked hesitant, but followed Carla, evidently hoping that her authority might in some way shield him from the alien environment. They walked along the gravel and came to a large bar and dining room covered by an enormous *makuti* roof. The vaulted, towering structure was an unlikely seaside cathedral. Tables led from inside to out, spreading among the remaining palms and on to the beach. There were sun-loungers and a couple of tourists. 'I don't think this is a secret any more. It's been discovered.'

'Mrs Jackson, you forget. It was never lost.'

Carla wanted lunch but hesitated because of Ramadan. 'Would you mind terribly if I had a little to eat, Mr Abeidi? I'm afraid it's not a Muslim picnic this time.'

He was also hungry.

'But don't you have Ramadan today?'

'No, Mrs Jackson. Because I'm not so well it will be fine for me to eat.'

'Then you must be my guest. It's my privilege.'

Older and old were shown to a table beside a palm tree and sat down in its mottled shade. He stared at the cutlery in front of him. The utensils were confusing, abstract riddles because he was unsure of their sequence. Carla ordered, and when the food arrived she started to pick delicately at it with her fingers. Mr Abeidi followed suit happily.

A girl came out of the ocean and flopped down on a sun-lounger. Her boyfriend took no notice of her.

'Mr Abeidi, don't you think that gentleman has chosen his girlfriend rather carefully?'

Carla was right: the truncated couple were exactly the same height, except she was curvy and he chubby. The girl stripped off her bra and lay in the sun; her nipples gazed heavenwards. Carla looked sharply to Mr Abeidi. He wasn't interested in the display of flesh and modestly diverted his attention elsewhere. The stout, pink, doughy man was a diminutive vision of anxiety. He kicked his miniature feet against the legs of a sun-bed. A mobile phone rang, the sound as loud and vulgar as its owner.

'Keith, won'tcha get that or are you going to let it ring all day?'

The diners tried vainly to ignore the self-important display.

A waiter cleared the table. The food had been a distraction, and now it was gone Carla felt exposed. 'Mr Abeidi, did you really suffer?'

The old man weighed the question for a little time. 'Yes.'

'I'm sorry. I had no idea. I was so caught up with what was happening in my life then. I thought it was only me.'

'Mrs Jackson, you left me here in the revolution – of course I hurt. I hurt very much.'

Carla leaned across the table and touched his hand, as she'd touched her heart when trying to remember the past. 'It wasn't my fault, Mr Abeidi. It affected everyone, not just you.'

'Revolution? You think it was all about revolution, Mrs Jackson? How could you?'

He held on to the sides of the chair, steadying himself against an emotion that was better left dormant. 'Why do you think I stopped writing, Mrs Jackson? Because I couldn't be bothered? It was because I couldn't bear to.'

They sat in silence as the odious man on the beach carried on talking into his mobile.


## Francesca's Dinner


She heard clunking on the stairs before the tap at the door. She knew it was Abdul.

'*Karibu*. Here it is, welcome to my new home.'

Abdul walked into the flat. Francesca had made various homely changes, not that Abdul knew any better.

The line of brooms was mentioned: 'What you do that?'

'I like them. They're my sculpture.'

Abdul smiled. It was a relief: he could look formidable.

'And this is the living room and up those stairs is my tearoom. It's not seen much tea so far. Fancy a beer?'

They looked across the rooftops. The muezzin sang the faithful to prayer as the sun shot below the horizon – it always ran the last bit, never sinking slowly. It got dark, and Francesca lit storm lanterns, placing them on a large raffia mat. Two simple benches were covered in cushions – they were higher than a normal seat so that you could more easily admire the view. In the harbour, lights from moored boats winked at passing dhows carrying torches to tempt squid. The streets were unusually quiet, the silence broken only by a murmur of faraway men and a distant motorcycle. Bats swished around the building, in and out of darkness, silent unless you had young enough ears.

'Popo,' said Abdul. 'Popo Bawa!' He started to laugh nervously. 'But maybe not tonight, Francesca.'

She had no idea of what he was talking about. She asked him to explain.

'Popo Bawa is man who comes to hurt you.'

'What man?' She was faintly alarmed.

'He man that come like devil to your house when you sleep. He like bat.'

'Do you mean a vampire, a creature that sucks blood?'

'Is story of man who comes in the night and have sex and hurt and sodomise. Popo Bawa live on Pemba Island and sometime he fly to Zanzibar.'

Francesca assumed he was talking about the local mythology.

'Many people here, they are afraid of Popo Bawa.'

He created a strange thrill with the beginnings of the macabre story, teasing her with a half-told tale of something she couldn't understand. 'I'm sure that's nothing but a bad fairytale, Abdul. How the heck could Pompom get up here?'

He looked at her as if she'd just asked the most ridiculous question.

'Well, you're here to look after me. Ghosts don't scare people in pairs now, do they? You've got to be by yourself to be haunted.' She was attracted by the idea of being a confidante to something she assumed secret, yet annoyed because she didn't know what the secret was. She felt stupid.

'I hope you're hungry. I've fried fish and made rice. We'll eat up here.'

Francesca had created her own version of native cuisine. In the market she'd bought a stainless-steel platter, like the ones she'd seen used in India. On to this she piled basmati rice, cooked with saffron, cardamom, cloves and cinnamon bark, two perch, fried in massala, then decorated the whole with freshly chopped red chilli and coriander. She brought the dish upstairs.

She'd impressed her guest. 'How you know this is traditional Zanzibar way?'

It was pot luck. Francesca had no idea that this was customary, but she'd eaten enough fried fish and rice to know it was a staple diet. The platter was placed in the middle of the mat and they sat down to eat with their fingers. The technique could be elegant – at least, Abdul's mastery of it was: he twisted small amounts of fish and rice between his thumb and first three fingers, keeping his little finger curled into his palm, then rolled the morsel into his mouth. Francesca grappled clumsily with the food, sticking her fingers into her mouth and dropping rice along the way. Abdul ate with only his right hand; Francesca used both. He told her politely to desist, which made her feel coarse beside him; this was the type of criticism her mother made: 'You should have gone to finishing school, Francesca. It might have been better for you than college.' That was her mother's grandiloquence. She didn't have the money for upper-class frivolities, although she liked to delude herself that she did.

'I've made a pudding, too, shall I bring it up?'

'That will be nice, *chakula kizuri sana*.'

'Thank you . . .' She hoped he meant that he had enjoyed her food. 'I'm glad you liked it.'

She returned with chopped pineapple and a jug of syrup. She'd simmered cardamom, cloves and a dried red chilli in a little water, removed the spices and added rainforest honey to the reduced, spicy liquid. The honey was her idea of heaven, something local, perfect and delicious. She went to pour the tangy mixture over the fruit.

'What that is, Francesca?'

She explained the recipe.

'I think that is not good.'

'What do you mean "not good"? It's delicious.'

'You must to be careful with honey and things like that.' Abdul held the small glass jar to the light, scrutinising it as a doctor would a urine sample.

'What could possibly be wrong with it?' Francesca took a swig of her whisky and Coke. She had stealthily poured an extra large one in the kitchen, deluding herself that Abdul wouldn't guess there was more than Cola and ice in the glass. She was conscious of her drinking, embarrassed by it, feeling the need to keep it secret from him. 'Now, what could be scrummier than my spicy honey?'

'This honey, it destroy you.'

'Uh?'

'I tell you this honey can kill if taken wrong.'

'Abdul, what the hell are you going on about?'

'If man he drink honey like this from bottle he die. Is true, I know. And if he mix honey and lime then him die too. I don't think this good.'

Francesca was being given a crash course on Zanzibari superstition and magic.

'Where you get honey?'

She described the place: it was a shop, just a minute from

the market, with dozens of brooms and brushes outside. It was these that had initially attracted her. Dried animal skins dangled above the brushes. She'd thought they were goat, but one was stripy. Inside, the apothecary's shop was dark, dusty and peppery. Troughs brimmed with strange bark; a sack covered abstract lumps that looked like spare body parts. A Victorian glass cabinet carried an eccentric assortment of items, including a remedy for gout alongside small glass jars of what she thought might be pickle. The honey was produced from a room in the back and presented to her in an old Safari beer bottle. Several varieties were offered, but she took the first on the understanding that it was from the Pemban rainforest – where bees gorge themselves on clove flowers. She'd dipped her finger into it as soon as she'd got home and could attest to its exotic provenance. It was nectar for humans.

'That is shop of local medicine, Francesca. They sell magic thing in there.'

'So I've bought voodoo honey? That's too fantastic! Sainsbury's will snap it up and get Jamie Oliver to do a crispy chicken with witchcraft honey glaze. Davey would die for this.' Francesca spoke her thoughts aloud. The idea of foodstuffs drenched in the occult seemed too far-fetched and wonderful.

Abdul looked serious. 'Is not joke, Francesca. Like Popo Bawa and these things you have to be careful.'

Francesca handed him a dish of pineapple, scooped herself a bowlful and poured the magical honey over the top. 'It's OK, Abdul, don't worry, you're not getting any voodoo juice.'

She took a peppery-sweet, self-congratulatory mouthful and shut her eyes involuntarily.

Abdul looked on, astonished to see that Francesca didn't

drop down dead on the spot. He continued eating regard-less.

Francesca manoeuvred herself beside Abdul, not too close but near enough so that their arms touched when they picked up or put down a drink. He was mesmerising: there was something edgy and raw about him that she found intoxicating. Francesca felt a chatter of nerves: maybe she was too obvious. Perhaps the honey was working its spell. It was Abdul's presence that discomfited her. She wanted to get close to him and touch his face, but was unable to do so. Her concentration was broken by a question.

'Why you don't like being called Mama, Francesca?'

She'd been taken off-guard. 'I just don't, that's all.'

They sat quietly in barely moving air. She lit a cigarette and played with her shell necklace. It was an easy silence, a secure and comfortable hush.

'I can't have children, Abdul.' She had surprised herself. Her voice came out calm and assured. She'd not got frantic as she usually did with this subject. The night seemed even quieter now. He studied her as he had the menu in the Chinese restaurant.

'No, I can't have babies, Abdul, and that hurts me. That's why I don't like being called Mama.'

The muezzin called to the righteous again, coughing his notice to believers down below.

'Francesca, I am sorry for to call you Mama.'

'You don't have to be, Abdul.' A small sad smile sniffed out of her. 'You weren't to know. I was stupid to get so upset.'

There was something new between the two of them, an intimacy achieved through the sharing of an intensely personal admission. It was as if her tribulation had lifted in some way with her disclosure. At that moment, she was genuinely happy in his company; her guard had dropped.

'It time for me to go, Francesca. *Asante* for food. I like very much.'

She flinched at the idea of him leaving. She'd do anything for him to stay. 'Don't you want another drink?'

'No, I must home now.'

Francesca searched for delaying tactics, but could think of none that wouldn't make her look even more desperate. Abdul pecked her on the cheek and left.

She was alone again, not wanting to remain by herself in the flat. She considered going for a drink at the Serena, but instead went to the Internet café to wear away an hour on an email to David. Perhaps she could convey her sense of relief and liberation after talking with Abdul. Her emotions were changing.

David replied the next day.

TO: Fran
CC:
Subject: TELL ME MORE

francesca u devil. got a man already huh? in a bedouin tent or with a contingent of masai warriors? so who is he? i mean HOW is he . . . a family-sized type of bloke or BIGGER, u know what they say about these guyz . . . i need details and fast!!!!!!!! its all im getting at the mo, second-hand info on the love-life of other folk – im a dry old queen in need of a good seeing-to. if truth be known its been so long now ive forgotten what its like. anyways saw the ex (yaws not mine stoopid) the other day. he wouldn't believe it when i told him you were in zanzi, but

guess where I saw him . . . try fist factory????????? thinks . . .
maybe theres more to him than meets the eye – he said he
woz meeting pals for drinx . . . like yeah? i dont know if u
wanted to hear that but it kinda fits in wiv his personality
dontcha think? im waiting with bated breath for yaw next
instalment – dont hold back on the phyzical stuff, inches
or centimetres its all the same to me. missing you like
crazy and glad my bestest gal-pal is havin fun.
love love love davey XXXXXXXXXXXXXXXXXXXX

He could get it so wrong sometimes, but he invariably
made her laugh. David could pop her pretension bubble
before she knew it was inflating. She closed the Hotmail
page and headed home. The beach-boys on the street were
bugging her. She made a point of being curt with them, but
they wouldn't give up.

'Hey, Mama, maybe I give you something special? I got
good weed, best price. You want?'

They never stopped. Their questions were always asked
with the same smile, that innocent, penetrating, unintelligible
grin. It was like being interrogated by a crazed Buddha. Her
answer was always the same.

'Maybe you help me little? Just few shillings, me not eaten
today. You give me something for food. You know me, sister,
I good man and don't bother you.'

Francesca was rattled. 'The answer's no. I can't feed the
entire island.'

'C'mon, a few *peso* for food, Mama . . .'

'I'm not the bank. I can't help you. I'm sorry.'

Entering the conversation was a mistake she'd made
before; the dope-fiend wouldn't give up. There was something solicitous and dirtily attractive about the man. It was
a perversity that flattered Francesca; she thought that his

85

façade of familiarity somehow marked her out as more local.

The circus attracted others. Francesca panicked. 'Leave me alone, I don't want to know. The answer is no.'

Two more men drifted out of nowhere and looked on.

'Let me go home.'

Their banter wasn't in itself threatening, but Francesca's interpretation of it was. She walked along the alley, pursued by her original assailant who claimed her for his own after shouting down the others. She got to the blue gate and let herself in. He didn't cross the threshold but continued his performance. There were two hundred shillings in change at the bottom of her bag, which she handed over. She felt invaded. Why couldn't he understand he wasn't her responsibility? Was it his demands that left her feeling wretched? It was the guilt of being comparatively wealthy tempered by the sour realisation that she was unable to make any real difference to their lives.

Her frustration was aimed at her antagonist, but she was also cross with herself. She'd capitulated. She felt blackmailed into helping him because his conception of her was as a millionairess. An ordinary middle-class Camden Town existence was far removed from his; she couldn't even try to explain her reality to him. The beach-bums were difficult to figure out. They belonged yet they were dispossessed.

She thought more about the idea. These were people adrift in a country full of extremes, the wealth of the tourist and poverty of the local the most obvious. And in that turmoil they'd spun out of control and sought solace in drugs. The local drugs culture was a mystery to her. Of course she'd taken drugs in the past, cocaine and ecstasy, but her consumption had been purely recreational. She didn't take drugs to forget. Francesca, hypocritically, had never considered alcohol a drug: it was different. She wasn't sure how crack and heroin had come to inform people who (until recently) lived pious lives. Here was a generation divorced from a strong faith and set to abandon religion, or had God simply got bored, lost sight and forgotten them? Nothing is as it seems. The sunny smiles she had seen so many times before became grimaces. Futureless laughs at desperation.

Her phone rang, an unexpected trill. For a moment she wasn't sure what the noise was, then thought that perhaps the ringing belonged to someone else. Her phone hadn't rung in days.

'Hello?'

'Francesca, Lar here. I hope I'm not disturbing you.'

'No, not at all. How are you?'

'Very well, darling, thank you. I was wondering – on the offchance – if you might like to join me for dinner?'

'I'd love to. When?'

'It's very short notice, I know, but how are you fixed for this evening?'

She was delighted at the prospect of dinner with her dowager.

'Would eight thirty suit?'

'That's great, Lar. You'd better give me the directions.'

Francesca reckoned on getting drunk over dinner so left the Jeep at home. She'd find a taxi to take her to Carla's – there was always a group of them at the bottom of Kenyatta Road. Her driver was called Cha Cha Cab Number Seven. His moniker was optimistic: it conjured up an image of a vast Latin-American mini-cab empire. Cha Cha worked by himself in a battered green Mercedes. What should she take for her host? Flowers would be cool, but florists were non-existent. Chocolates, if she could find them, would melt.

She'd go for a bottle. Perhaps they could build their own whisky sours.

Cha Cha took her through Malindi and past the Bwawani Hotel – a monstrous concrete slab of a place built in the seventies. Rumour had it that the disco there was fun at the weekend; she'd not checked it out, though.

'Where are we now, Cha Cha?'

'This is the highway, madam. We head past Mtoni, then maybe five minutes to Malindi Villa.'

It was unlike any highway she'd seen before. The blackness of night and dearth of street-lighting made for a dramatic backdrop. *Dala dala*s and cyclists were extracted from the gloom by the lights of a passing car. With the phantasmagoric vehicles and ethereal riders came dust, giving the landscape an otherworld smokiness. She was travelling in time rather than along a road. The further north they went, the darker it became. Cha Cha turned the car on to a mud track that led into a palm grove. The headlamps illuminated elegant trunks, providing the only clues to the obscure landscape. It was a silent place. The car reached the villa gate, where Francesca was cuffed by an overpowering scent of jasmine. The smell was so strong that she almost buckled.

'Francesca dear, over here, can you see your way?' Carla called from the pitchy darkness. 'You've got to mind your step, bloody trees and bushes everywhere. I should have told you to bring a torch, darling.'

Francesca could just make out the glow from a door. She heard Carla call again and followed the sound. Her way was punctuated by the frantic chirruping of crickets.

'I'm sorry, Francesca, it was silly of me not to tell you how dark it is here. I'm getting forgetful. But you're here now. Come in, darling, let me fix you a drink.'

Francesca was taken by the idle luxury of a red silk sofa

obviously past its prime. The divan wheezed when she sat on it. 'It's a lovely house, Lar.'

'Thank you.'

'Whose is it?'

Carla sat down with two large ice-chunking whiskies. 'It's owned by a company that lets out special holiday properties around the world. They're not cheap, but I don't like hotels. The strange thing is, I knew this place before. I thought I recognised it from the brochure.'

'You knew it when you lived here?'

'Oh, yes, very well.'

Carla excelled at telling stories. She knew what to exaggerate and, more importantly, what to omit.

'Did you miss Zanzibar, Lar?'

'Some things yes, but not really, darling. I left at a turbulent time. The island had just got independence and a month later the revolution started. It wasn't safe and we certainly weren't needed. As I remember, the whole thing happened pretty much overnight.'

'Was there any warning?'

'In retrospect, masses – we just couldn't see it. But you must try to imagine how we were then. We still had *Empire* in us. We were still *Great*. Britannia ruled the waves and you didn't mess around with merrie olde England. I know now that the revolution didn't spring solely from the colonialist and Arab masters, although Britain did much to destabilise the place. It was subtler than that. Its roots were in slavery. A disaffected splinter group from the Africa Sherazi Party was supported by the Chinese – and wham!'

Francesca tried to imagine the sudden change. She found it impossible.

'All told, it was only about a hundred men who started the revolt. They triggered a terrible chain of events. The countryside got it worst – mob killings were rife. Thousands died in the end.' She paused, then added, 'There was terrible cruelty.'

Carla distracted herself with a snag in her nail, but absentmindedly continued her story. 'Strangely, it was the waiting that was worst for me. We were holed up in the house, impotent while it was going on all around us. There was a peculiar kind of terror in our safety, knowing that everything had changed and nothing would be the same again. I remember it as the longest night of my life and, if I'm honest, the unhappiest.' She didn't elaborate on that point.

'There had been riots in 'sixty-one, Francesca, but they were slapped down – for good, as we saw it. That was our arrogance. We were above worrying too much.'

Carla filed her nail, an airily dismissive action that mirrored the attitude of another time.

'And after the revolution, Lar, you simply picked up sticks and went overnight?'

'Virtually.' Her voice was crisp.

'Wasn't that a terrible wrench? Having to leave everyone and everything behind?'

'Darling, I didn't have any option.' She sounded testy. She didn't want to be quizzed on leaving people behind, not now.

Hours had imperceptibly slipped away. Carla's tale of murder and desolation had carried them deep into the night . . .

'What is the time, Francesca?'

It was past midnight, nudging one.

'I'm sorry, I really must go to bed. It's way too late for an old woman to be up talking. Ali will get you a taxi and see you out. I hope you don't mind.'

She kissed Francesca's forehead then vanished abruptly,

leaving the younger woman to hope she'd no␍ her welcome.

Ali sent her on her way home.


## Same Place Before


'I'm going to the Palace of Escape – I mean the Darajani Fort. Do you know it, Mussa?'

'Yes, madam.'

'Well, I'm already late, could you put your foot down?'

Carla had managed to extricate herself from one of John's more boring official events. He was hosting a reception at the house for a delegation of Chinese. She was puzzled, unable to imagine what they wanted there. It wasn't her concern – she had other things to do.

'Don't miss the turning, Mussa, it's hard to find.'

'Very well, madam.'

The Morris echoed in the empty street. There was some-thing reassuring about the sound it made as the gears were changed. For a moment Carla was travelling in the Home Counties; only the heat returned her to Africa.

'So, you dried out then?'

Mussa was quietly studying the road.

'After our wet Muslim picnic, you dried out, Mussa.'

'Yes, madam. But the car was very damp. I hope I haven't damaged the seats.'

'They look fine to me. Smells a little, maybe . . . Give it a good airing tomorrow and no one will be any the wiser. Did you enjoy our swim?'

There had been more than daring in their escapade: during

Ramadan a good Muslim shouldn't bathe in daylight hours, let alone leap into the sea with his female boss. That dalliance was best described as prohibited at the most lenient of times – but was blasphemous during the holy month. Yet those splashy minutes had been a revelation; a wet emancipation that had unintentionally freed a passion inside Mussa. Such intimacy was a problem; now he didn't know how to react to his boss.

'I think I might be in trouble, madam.'

'Why's that, Mussa? Because of our dip? You needn't worry, it's another secret. We share two now.'

She looked relaxed as she checked herself in a small hand-mirror. Her Sobranie tin fell on to the seat, so she tucked a cigarette between her lips. He felt uncomfortable, as if his life were being played with.

'It was a perfect afternoon. I don't think I've enjoyed myself as much in years. I promise you won't get into trouble. OK, buddy?' Carla had reverted to her abysmal impersonation. 'I said "OK buddy?"'

Mussa turned into the lane that went to the Darajani Fort. It was black except for an explosion of stars overhead. 'Yes, I'm OK, madam. How long should I wait for you?'

'I'll be a couple of hours or so. Why don't you pop back home and collect me at, say, ten thirty?'

She made her way through moonless gardens, following voices that floated in heavy scent. 'Darlings! I'm here at long bloody last! I hope you've got a drink waiting for me.'

The Darajani Fort was the place of escape not just for Carla but for its owner too. This was a house without servants, a retreat in which to relax with friends away from the all-seeing eyes of his home in Stone Town. A house for luxurious pleasure.

'Lar, it's good to see you. You're becoming quite a fixture.'

She kissed her host's cheek and was handed a whisky.

Her evenings there were always the same: drunken (but not too much so) and innocent. She'd meet with half a dozen others – all refugees from a starchier world – to gossip about the Africa Bar or the latest affairs that inevitably percolated through the ex-pat community. There were two new faces that evening: Carla was disgruntled to see the German fellow sitting in the corner. What was he doing there? She'd ignore him.

'I've got some fabulous music with me,' she said. 'I picked it up from Patel's today. Shall I put it on?' She placed the LP on the record-player: *Kind of Blue*, the Miles Davis classic. 'Isn't this too wonderful?'

The music was as sultry and moody as the weather. It hung above the Dansette before trickling into the room, hushing most of the talk. Music and whisky made her life bearable. Jazz made it perfect.

'Patel said he'd get me *Sketches of Spain*. Don't know when, though. It's taken the best part of six months to get this. He's promised to get me something new by Ornette Coleman too.'

Carla kicked off her shoes and leaned back on low cushions. She sucked in the sound, her cigarette smoke and drink. It was a momentary escape. The music finished and more drinks were poured. She was introduced to the East German consul, but she cut him dead with English good manners. She was unfaultable, yet rude. She turned her back, preferring to spend time with the wealthy Arab host. Her brusqueness ensured her an enemy, but she didn't care: the island was riddled with rivalries and none ever came to anything. She danced in her stockinged feet with a young woman new to their little scene and made a point of laughing loudly at a private joke. She indicated, cunningly, that it had been at the German's expense. It wasn't, but he didn't know that.

'Another drink, Lar?'

'Make it a small one – I'm feeling a bit tipsy. I should be off soon.'

She lay among the cushions, the smoke from her cigarette wrapped round her like an expensive stole.

A headlamp threw a band of light through the window, briefly illuminating the room and casting long shadows on the wall. The evening's host went to the door.

'Lar? I think your driver is back already. Why not come into town with me later on? I'll send him away.'

Carla sat up, pulling at her skirt to straighten it. 'No, I should go now. I feel a little bit guilty. I think I should pop in to see how Johnno's doing with the Red Brigade.'

Her friends laughed. The consul didn't: he smirked.

She kissed everyone – except the diplomat – on the cheek, making a small promise for a lunch that she'd never keep. There was a right and a wrong way to leave the Palace of Escape; going first and telling tiny lies was part of her ritual.

The lights of the Morris guided Carla back through the gardens. She sidled on to the back seat. 'Thank you, Mussa. Did you get something to eat at home?'

'I waited for you at the end of the lane.'

That flattered her. 'I said you didn't need to.'

'I know, madam.'

The car pulled away and Carla cradled her face in the hand that held her cigarette. She looked into the darkness believing she might see something – there were bound to be ghosts and *shetani* escaped from Stone Town hiding in the trees.

'Did you have a good night, madam?'

'What's that, Mussa?' Carla had slipped into a dream world of *djinn* and spirits.

'This evening. Did you enjoy yourself, madam?'

Carla thought about it. Not really, apart from her music. Everything was too similar – same people, same gossip, same drinks, same same. She wanted a diversion, something to make life interesting. The car bumped off the track, on to the road and headed towards town.

'Mussa, what's the time now?'

'Ten o'clock, madam.'

'Then could you pull over by Mtoni, please? I want to walk along the beach before going home.'

'Is that wise, madam?'

'I don't know if it's wise, but that's what I'm going to do.'

The car nudged in among the palms and the pair walked carefully down the unlit track. Although there was no moon there was a distinctive light, an empty blueness that stretched distance and gave sinister shape to normal things. The palms shushed in disapproval. Nature was conspiring, wishing ill on the two shadows that crept cautiously along the path. A thrill snagged Carla, like the one she'd experienced on the rainy beach. It made her feel sick, yet she welcomed the sensation.

'Let's walk down to the water, Mussa.'

'As you like, madam.'

The night sky was flawless. The Milky Way splashed across the heavens, the trillion stars looking brighter than normal. They sat at the water's edge; only their toes got wet.

'You see that, madam?'

'What?'

'That star right ahead, the bright one.'

Carla looked. There were too many to identify only one.

'Look harder, madam. Follow my arm to the end of my finger.'

Her cheek glanced against his shirtsleeve. She caught her breath, certain that he knew what she was feeling. 'Yes, I can see it now. It looks orange, a bit bigger than the others.'

'That's right, madam. Now you know Mars. Remember it. You'll be able to point it out to others in the future.'

'That's lovely, Mussa. Another secret for us to share.'

Mussa sat beside Carla as he might by a general: he was stiff and correct. Carla let her hand touch his. He flinched and pulled away. The contact wasn't accidental, he knew it.

'Maybe madam should be going home now.'

'No, not just yet, Mussa.'

'I think it should be now, madam. It's getting too late.'

They stood up and walked back through the dark trees.

'Mussa? When we're together like this why don't you call me Lar?'

He didn't respond.

'Only when the two of us are together. It's our fourth secret.'

Mussa started the car and drove back to the Jackson residence. Maybe he'd feel differently when they were safely back home. He didn't know how to feel when isolated with the white woman. His emotions were playing tricks on him.

# CHAPTER 4: LOVE

## A Kiss

The downpour lasted an hour. An extraordinary deluge that had kids *kung-fu* dancing in the soaked streets below. Francesca could see them from her window – they made her feel trapped. She climbed the stairs to her tearoom and looked across town. It was difficult to see far because of the dense sheets of falling water. The clatter was deafening. Raindrops spanked tin roofs like marbles falling on a tray and turned the corrugated iron permanently autumnal; every shade of russet was on the skyline. Magic wasn't long in happening. Out of the thick greyness came the sun, a sudden burst that dissipated the torrent as quickly as it had started. It was her cue.

The twisting alleys to the market were sparkling clean but weighted with humidity. Her clothes stuck to her and she continually wiped at her forehead. The vegetable market was on the other side of town, a criss-cross of humble wooden stalls serried in irregular rows. Rags had been tied between the kiosks. She didn't know if they were a sorry attempt at keeping the customers dry or a marginally more effective sunshade. What Francesca loved about the bazaar were the sounds. Invariably a cockerel would crow

– it always surprised her no matter how many times she heard it. To her mind the bird lived in the market. The idea of it being replaced by another each hour as its predecessor made its sorry way to the pot never occurred to her. There was an abundance of pineapple, mango and papaya – it was their season. Miniature tomato pyramids were precisely stacked on the bare wooden boards of some stalls, as were misshapen cucumbers and ladies' fingers, limes, minuscule aubergines and yellow capsicums. Mounds of sweet potatoes and cabbages, and piles of green bananas spilled from giant crude baskets into the muddy aisles. Red chillies, bunches of mint and anonymous herbs helped decorate the scene.

Smells were a fantastic assault. A small building housed a shambles preparing meat for the market stands. The yells from slaughtermen and the sound of meat cleavers crushing the bones of goats, sheep and cattle preceded a sweet stench like rotting strawberries. Carcasses were draped over concrete altars, the greasy trails of blood washing down small gutters. Past the butchery was the fish market. Whole tuna lay stiffly on the floor, blindly looking skywards. Marble-sized silver-blue eyes stared blankly at infinity. Silvery perch and bright blue parrotfish sat beside large eels with the colouring and pattern of a giraffe. Vast rays were gradually disassembled per transaction, small sharks sold whole, long skinny fish with pointy beaks (as if already skewered on satay sticks) went by the dozen. Flies were everywhere. But even though it was bloody and stank, the market was the best place to buy food. The fish was sublime, only hours old and clear of eye, the fruit and vegetables superb; Francesca didn't try the meat – it was *too* real in there for her taste. Her raffia shopping bags gradually filled up. She purchased a whole tuna, getting the fishmonger to hew it into chunky steaks, then lugged her deconstructed prize homewards to the freezer.

Her phone bleeped. Abdul sent Francesca a text message: '**i come from home an see u.**'

She replied in the same manner: '**Karibu Abdul. Do u want to eat with me? After dark** . . .'

That was affirmative. Francesca cooked up a tuna, tomato and black olive sauce with spaghetti she'd bought earlier. She served it on the platter and they ate upstairs in the tearoom.

'Would you like more beer?'

Francesca sat closer to Abdul: she was feeling tipsily relaxed and affectionate, although nervous at making an advance on him. Abdul responded. He leaned into her and smoked a cigarette. He kissed her. She stroked his head, but he pulled back. 'What's the matter, Abdul?'

'Is nothing.'

'Well, come here, then . . .'

Encouraged, Francesca kissed him once more, but he turned away again. 'What is it, Abdul? You were ready to kiss me a minute ago.'

He looked awkward, embarrassed by the embrace. He blew on to his hands, dispelling imaginary dust.

'I don't get you, Abdul, what is it?'

He said nothing.

'I'm not a mind-reader. What's the problem?'

'Is something I can't do now for religion.'

'Dammit, Abdul, are you saying sex is a no-no if you're fasting?'

He nodded.

She calmed down. 'I'm sorry. It's just that I like you.'

'And me, I like you really, Francesca. Very much.'

It was a result, of sorts. He *liked* her. He *really* liked her. The tricky, slender, haughty man was gradually yielding. But instead of a whirlwind romance, it was courtship. How long had she known him? Three weeks? And now she'd had one kiss. He made her feel coy, she was being wooed. This was unlike the Francesca of Camden Town: where was the pushy, independent urban woman of last month? What was happening to the assertive, tough North London cookie? She had believed she was in control, with her nice car, her own flat, a good job – from which she could take a three-month sabbatical, a full social diary and her dinner parties. But her life was a mess: she'd maxed the credit on her emotions. She was desperate to be courted and Abdul was the man to do it. He departed, leaving her frustrated, bitten by disappointment.

TO: Daveyboy
CC:
Subject: prayers & punishment

Davey – the guy REALLY likes me & i have to say i am smitten by him. Its happened. Well IT hasn't technically happened . . . We havent done the deed yet . . . its a matter of Ramadan you know? Well you wouldn't would you? Since when have you let religion get in your wicked way? Abdul cant have a bonk during the holy month, without upsetting Muhammad. Its all to do with demotion and devotion – he loses Brownie points if he fucks up on the slimming & fornication front and drops down a league to 3rd division. I reckon its all prayers & punishment over here. Have met fab old woman who used to live here donkeys ago. Shes become a gal-pal – i had dinner with her the other nite & we are meeting again tonite. Does she have stories? Have abandoned jeep, i never used it – so much for eastcoast trips etc im a s.town gal . . . you can take a gal from the city but you cant take the town from the gal.

Latest fashion craze here is Bin Laden t-shirts . . . No not really my thing either but de rigueur in some quarters. Strange but i don't feel threatened by it. The Brit Embassy in Dar es Salaam has closed – thats a bit freaky – they said its for regular maintenance but i cant help feeling theyre shit scared about getting bombed . . . Well theres a cheery note to finish on. Snot all doom n gloom here promise! E me soon XXX Fran

## Imperial & Eastern

John Jackson headed up the Zanzibar offices of Imperial & Eastern. The company was established in 1852 as a shipping operation for the enormous ivory trade in the area, but balked at trafficking slaves. Over the decades it mutated into wholesale, before spawning a small banking offshoot. Zanzibar had been their most important East African bureau, but after the 1890s the merchant community had gradually collapsed and the company contracted. The transformation coincided with the island becoming a British protectorate. Now the I & E office fought a losing battle to wrest trade from Dar es Salaam and Mombasa, not that it bothered John that much. Head Office in London left Mr Jackson to run the business without interference; he was a trusted senior partner, 'a safe pair of hands'. John infused his conversation effortlessly with clichés, but even he detested that particular platitude. Although Zanzibar was newly independent it didn't make the slightest difference to the commerce of I & E. The islands were a marginal territory, and the small profits they contributed to the mother company were almost lost in its vast interests. The relationship between office and company mirrored that of atoll and the East African flank.

The Imperial & Eastern offices were situated beside the House of Wonder in a sprawling Arab mansion. The surrounding gardens were John's passion; he'd taken an extra special interest in them. An Englishman with a predilection for topees and very large palms had laid them out thirty years before. John's recent horticultural involvement had converted what was a conventional tropical plot into a botanical innovation, combining both native exotica with herbaceous borders. In his eyes things needed to be pretty; that included preserving indigenous perennials alongside imported umbels and blooms of a more conservative nature. He was attempting the impossible; he wanted to orchestrate nature and master the natural world with five gardeners.

One gardener in particular was a favourite. Iddi was about twenty, of Arab extraction, very slight and very beautiful. Beauty obsessed the older *mazungo*: John needed people, not only gardens, to be attractive. Hence his marriage to Carla. John's admiration for Iddi was covert; he assumed no one else knew. Discretion made it a satisfactory relationship. He had subtly engineered his position at Imperial & Eastern and his posting to the Muslim Zanzibar to nourish his closeted sexuality. Morocco would have been his preference, but the company didn't have offices there.

He noticed Iddi immediately. The young man had started work a year ago, spending his days languidly brushing up leaves, making the job look balletic. John could barely contain his excitement and would find any excuse to bump into the apprentice. 'Tough job, what?'

The boy's broom swished near the older man's feet.

'Like painting the Forth Bridge . . .'

The gardener smiled blankly.

'No sooner have you finished one end than you've got to start again at the other. We don't want you getting blisters, now, do we? Here, let me look.' Large, hairy white hands wrapped around small pale brown ones – he was touching them and his heart pounded. John scrutinised the palms as if prophesying and prayed for a sign. He felt suddenly awkward and stopped the augury.

'They look fine to me, young man. Carry on.'

Iddi turned his hands over and squeezed the older man's fingers. He held on for just a little too long, then laughed. That first evening both John and Iddi were late in returning to their respective homes.

Inside the entrance to Imperial & Eastern there was a small wooden reception area – similar to the ticket office at Guildford railway station. No matter that John had worked there for nearly half a decade, he still felt as if he were headed for the seven forty to Waterloo each morning. The receptionist peered from a little window and directed newcomers accordingly – not everyone was as efficient as Joan. A large central courtyard punctured the tall, elegant white building. Small offices led off from the towering space at ground level and reached deep into the exterior of the place. They were dark, the gloom only broken by scuttering fans and single hanging bulbs. Their greenish, dim light created an ambience belonging to a forties black-and-white movie rather than the more progressive Technicolour times of two decades later. A large teak staircase circled to the first floor, where John had an office suite, and carried on a further storey to where his ex-pat colleagues worked. The Goan wallahs had the ground-floor rooms.

'Good morning, Johnno, how did the drinks go last night?'

'Fine, dear boy, fine. Nothing out of the ordinary. The German chap got a bit squiffy, though.'

'How's Lar? Haven't seen much of her lately.'

'The usual. Spending a lot of time driving around the island and moping off to the Darajani place of a night. She's tickety-boo.'

Conversation with John tended to be on the brief side. He could fillet an exchange with a rumpling of his eyebrows, leaving his colleague in no doubt that the chat was over. For someone who had so much professional socialising to do he was peculiarly private and non-communicative.

'Righto then . . . I'll be getting along, John. I'm going to the Africa later. Fancy a quick one? No? Okey-dokey.'

When John shut himself into his office, his secretary fended off enquiries; she was adept at keeping him in cheerful isolation. He was happy to spend a considerable part of the day working on the *Telegraph* crossword while chewing at the end of his pipe or plotting another development in his garden. Work could be crammed into an hour in the morning and another in the afternoon.

The intercom buzzed. 'Mr Jackson?'

'What is it, Marjorie?'

'Mrs Jackson called to say that she needs to pop out and probably won't be home till nine-ish.'

'Uh-huh. Can you think of another word for "trifling"? F something something V something something something U something.'

'Frivolous?'

'Bang on. What is it with Mrs Jackson, Marjorie?'

'She wants transport.'

She's hopeless, thought John. 'Send her the driver, will you?'

'Yes, sir.'

Carla waited for Mussa in the hall. She wore a graphic floral-print dress and a headscarf, and carried a white patent-leather handbag. She couldn't think why: all she had in it were cigarettes and a lighter. Lolling on a large leather armchair, she started to pout at the mirror opposite.

'Mussa's here, madam.'

'Thank you, Sima. Tell Cook I won't be needing lunch, there's a dear.'

She slipped on to the back seat, her sunglasses down low. She thought they made her look like Audrey Hepburn. 'It's going to be a big trip today, Mussa.'

'Where to, madam?'

'Lar, Mussa. It's Lar when we're together like this. We're going to Grave Island, Chapwani.'

He shifted into gear, the car made a pootling sound.

'When's the end of Ramadan?'

'Tomorrow, Mrs Lar.'

'Tomorrow? Are you planning something special for Eid with your family?'

'I don't have a family.'

The car turned into Main Road.

'My wife died with our first baby.'

'I'm sorry, Mussa. I'm very sorry.'

He stared ahead, as if studying the nearly empty road might evict the painful recollection of a lost love and a lost son.

'Maybe we could celebrate together, Mussa. We'll have our own little party tomorrow night.'

'As you like, Mrs Lar.'

Along from the Sultan's palace, near the dhow tree, there was a tiny stretch of beach. Mussa parked in the tree's shade, and the couple crossed to a small boat at the water's edge. The boatman propelled his silent passengers with the help of a feeble engine; it took half an hour to reach the isolated atoll. They left the pilot mending his nets in intense sunlight that was almost physical. It wouldn't have been a surprise if it had roared.

'I love it here, Mussa. This place has a special loneliness.'

The voyagers crossed a small graveyard crowned with enormous baobab trees. A tumbledown wall fought to keep the sea from eating up the desiccated remains of the necropolis.

'And this is my favourite thing, Mussa. Look here. It's my sailor's tree.'

Graffiti left by visiting mariners was still decipherable on one of the huge trees. *HMS Dragon 1885* had been gouged into the pachydermal baobab, *HMS Hill* was nearly illegible; the names had begun to perish, like all the residents there. The elephantine bark was gradually reclaiming the deep scrawl.

'Some of the people who carved this might have met Stanley or Livingstone. It's like touching history, Mussa.' She ran a finger down a long-forgotten name, stopping for a moment, distracted by her thoughts. 'Even this tree has secrets, Mussa. Did you know that?'

They walked among the scrappy graves, virtually all the resting places of sailors.

'Here, look at this one. "Sacred to the memory of William Mitchell AB, late of *HMS Nym*. Who was killed in cutting out a slave dhow at Zanzibar aged 25 years."'

A much bigger tomb at the far end of the graveyard held someone who, like the authors of the tree's inscriptions, might well have known the great explorers: '"Sacred to the memory of Francis Peters of London Esq. Who died 21 November 1868 aged 31 years."' Carla began to smile as she continued to read the inscription. '"Deeply regretted by all who knew him." Don't you think that's rather droll, Mussa? It sounds as if Mr Peters's friends resented him.' She pulled away a creeper to read the rest of the tablet. '"This monument was erected by the firm of Mssrs Robert Cogan & Company whom he represented on this island for 7 years as a tribute of respect." And that is just too much. An advertisement, for God's sake.'

Carla set off to another grave. 'I think the names are wonderful. "Henry Septimus Griffin" from Epsom, no less. I wonder what made him come here a hundred years ago.'

They walked away from the graveyard along the beach, eventually turning to the middle of the island to look for shade. As they went, the heavy air started to chatter around them. The agitated mutterings of fruit bats got louder as they proceeded. Carla and Mussa neared the mangrove trees, setting a weighty cloud of the animals to flight: they took to the sky, sweeping across the horizon like autumnal starlings in London. Their miniature torsos looked almost human, muscular, strong – obviously the source of any number of magical stories about bats that circulated on the islands, thought Carla. Further on they sat by a saltwater pool, decorated with black-candle mangrove roots. They were quite alone there. Carla let her hand fall on to Mussa's. This time he didn't pull his away.

## Revelation

Her phone bleeped, she'd got a text message: '**i come to yu now.**'

That wasn't such a great idea; Francesca had her evening planned. '**Sorry Abdul, cant see you tonite, im seeing Carla.**'

'**then you want sikuku tomoroo?**'

Francesca sent a text message back asking what he meant. '**tomoro is speshul day for end ramadan**.'

She got it. Eid. '**Yes, Id love to come, tell me where and when**.'

As Francesca entered the Serena she looked back across the road and saw Carla peck a man on his cheek. He walked away and raised his hand slightly to wave; it looked strangely benedictory. Francesca was intrigued. 'So who was that then, Carla?'

'Who?'

'The man you kissed.'

'Someone I've known a very long time, darling. Now, what would you like to drink?' Carla had been too quick with her response, and far too quick to change the subject.

'Come on now, Lar . . . who is he?'

Francesca was conspiratorial. She was desperate to be let into her friend's world.

'It's no one, darling. A whisky sour?'

Carla's feigned indifference was unconvincing. Francesca wanted to know more. She provoked her companion. 'Lar, I believe you're blushing . . .'

The older woman measured her younger companion, seemingly unsure as to whether she should say anything.

Francesca sensed there was more to the story. 'You dark horse, Lar. Now, spill the beans. I'm dying for a gossip.'

Carla ignored the jabber and looked to order drinks.

'I've have thought at your age, Lar, you'd be way beyond caring about stuff like that.'

Francesca was smiling, but the words froze Carla. 'Just because I'm old it doesn't mean I don't *care*, Francesca.' Her voice scattered; she sounded frail, like the total and more of all the years she normally wore so well.

Francesca was embarrassed; she'd not meant to insult her.

'I didn't mean it like that, Lar, I'm sorry.'

'Then what did you mean? Just because you're young, darling, it doesn't mean you have a monopoly on emotion. He is the reason for me coming back.'

Francesca hadn't considered that somebody *old* would have any need for love. She thought that everything softened with age, that passions died down, became far-off memories.

'I left him here four decades ago, and I've loved him for longer than you've been alive.'

There was silence until Francesca ordered the drinks.

'So, there you have it, Francesca. This daft old goat has returned in search of something she once had but discarded. You think I'm an utter fool, don't you?'

'No.'

'Yes, you do. You think I should be sanitised and politely hidden away to sip gin in a retirement home.'

Francesca pursed her lips and felt contrite.

'I'm fed up of being invisible. That's how it feels, you know. I'm ignored in the street and unnoticed in the shops. I often feel quite transparent.'

Carla delved in her bag. Francesca thought she was looking for a hankie and offered her a tissue.

'No, thank you. My pension came as a redundancy notice . . . simply not wanted, dispensable. That's what my adopted son thinks too – I'm not needed. But I don't feel like that, dammit. I don't see myself as being lost to the world. I'm still here. I'm looking for cigarettes, dear, do you have any?'

They lit up and sipped their drinks.

'So you had an affair when you lived here, Carla?'

'You're catching on, darling. Yes, I did.'

Even though there was sarcasm in her voice, Carla looked to one side as if she were checking for eavesdroppers or emissaries. Reassured of her privacy she continued in a calmer vein. 'It wasn't easy, I can assure you. It wasn't the done thing. Of course, romances happened all the time. We're on an island, for God's sake, there isn't much else to do. But us ex-pats tended to keep that type of thing to ourselves. It was segregated loving.'

Carla thought for a moment.

'But a white woman, me, the wife of a respectable business-man, having a black lover? It was unheard-of. Perhaps more so than you realise. You're the first person I've ever told.' Her voice had become barely audible.

'And this is the first you've seen of . . .'

Carla crossed her legs and regained some of her poise. 'His name's Mussa, Francesca. Mr Mussa Abcidi.'

'And is this the first you've seen of him in all this time?'

'Yes.'

'And do you still love him?'

'Yes, I do.'

'And does he love you, Lar?'

The question threw Carla.

'I don't know, Francesca. I really don't know.'

Francesca's fear of getting old transformed with the conversation. She understood her friend's emotions and feelings, and had begun to understand that the vicissitudes of old age weren't necessarily barren. It was the reverse of what she had felt for her mother and her affairs. She discovered hope for her own future.

## Eid with Abdul

Abdul stood at the front door in a garish shirt. It was straight out of the packet; the creases were still visible. His trousers looked new, so did his trainers – they weren't, though, they'd been washed. He was smiling; it was a genuine, goofy expression rather than the enigmatic one to which she'd grown accustomed.

Francesca was wearing an old pair of jeans and a long white cotton shirt.

There was nothing obviously wrong with her body, but she felt inhibited if she showed too much flesh.

'You're all dressed up, Abdul. I feel a bit scruffy beside you.'

'Yes, is what we do for holiday, Francesca. Everyone they have new clothes to make themselves nice to see.'

'Well, you look wonderful. Where are we off to?'

A large field on the edge of town was normally the preserve of football teams and local guys exercising, but that night it was home to a carnival. A transient refugee city made of rags and lit by hundreds of lanterns became the temporary home for hundreds of revellers. Photographic studios made from cardboard and sailcloth had been erected around the perimeter. The interior of one was decorated with the legend 'Happy Chridmas' in plastic letters. Cheap jardinières and gold-coloured tin cups festooned with ancient silk flowers threatened to swamp the sitters inside. Huge fortified dance areas contained enormous sound systems; the noise was cacophonous and spilled from one dance-floor to another.

Francesca and Abdul pushed into the throng and held each other's hands tightly. They were jostled, bodies rubbed against them. The ground was littered with children sitting in clusters, oblivious to the adult crowds trying to pass without trampling them. An entire casino of homemade roulette and blackjack tables served a populace with a hitherto secret need for gambling. Food stands of every description spiced the air. It looked as if the whole of Stone Town had shown up wearing their finest at a crowded, edgy, vibrant fiesta. The town was drunk on the excitement of its inhabitants. Red dust was carried into the air on the shouts of the celebrants and the thump of the discos; its terracotta plumes mingled with smoke from the barbecues and formed a canopy over the proceedings. It was the end of Ramadan, and everyone was determined to enjoy the celebration.

A band arranged itself away from the sound systems; the men wore a uniform of dark blazers and white djellabas and the ladies a motley selection of cocktail dresses. Pastels were the favoured colours. The bandleader introduced their music with what sounded like an official speech. Eventually he arrived at the first number, a traditional song of welcome. A slim girl, wearing a hideous synthetic lilac confection, stood up to sing solo. The bandleader couldn't resist making another comment. 'Small girl, proportional body, optimum voice.' He sounded as if he were appraising the merits of a flyweight boxer rather than the talent of a soprano. The swirling revellers ignored the chorus and pushed forward to the discos.

Francesca and Abdul went into a photographic studio and had a snap taken by a serious man who brandished a disposable camera. It was their first photograph together.

'I bet that's the last we'll see of that two thousand shillings, Abdul.'

'What you mean?'

'We'll never see the photo. How will we get it?'

'*Hamna matatizo*, Francesca. Is no problem.'

The noise got louder, the crowds higher, and Francesca more weary. The dull thud of heat and music ate her energy. She wanted home. 'Let's go, Abdul. This is great, but I need my bed now.'

They fought their way out of the squeeze and found Kenyatta Road, passing a cluster of children in new dresses. The infants wore garish lime-coloured nylon tutus embroidered with sequins and looked as if they'd fallen from the top of a Christmas tree. Francesca found herself both attracted and repulsed by them. She couldn't help her feelings. The crowds on the street careered around the couple as if they were drunk; most weren't – they were naturally high. In ten minutes she and Abdul were home.

'Are you coming in?'

'*Asante*, Francesca.'

The night-watchman's feet dangled from his room under the stairs. He was asleep. She led Abdul upstairs, poured whisky for two – he drowned his with Sprite – and sat up in the tearoom. The whooping street-boys and a blaze of sound reverberated around the streets. After a month of abstinence the Garage Disco was open again, and its muffled music made a break for the rooftops.

'We go to bed now?'

Francesca was pleasantly surprised.

'Francesca, let us go to bed.'

They left their drinks on the roof, and went back inside. Abdul took her by the hand and led her to the bedroom. He switched off the lights.

## Eid with Mussa

'Johnno, Johnno darling, I'm popping out this evening. I thought I'd go to the local Ramadan thing.'

John looked up from digging at his pipe. 'Why on earth would you want to do that, Lar? We've got the palace do to attend.'

'You go, Johnno, you'll enjoy it. Say I'm ill or something. You'll find an excuse.'

'How can I keep saying you're unwell? It looks as if you're avoiding everyone. It's as if you're avoiding me.'

Carla was ready with her shopping bag. She would use it as a device to alter the exchange. 'Have you got me anything for Christmas yet, John?'

'No.'

'Then let me give you a hint. De Silva's has a nice Rolex that would fit the bill. See you later.' Unusually she didn't take the driver on her errand. She was secretly buying an Eid gift for him.

The evening was especially humid; perhaps Muhammad was attempting to sweeten the celebration with syrupy, fragrant air. The Morris was waiting at the front door for her. John had already left for his engagement at the palace and the rest of the household staff, except Sima, had been let off for the night to attend parties.

'Don't look so long in the face! Someone's got to look after the house, Sima. Go to the kitchen and make yourself something special to eat. There are sodas in the refrigerator – help yourself.'

The maid skulked off, unhappy at the prospect of celebrating *sikuku* by herself. Carla picked up a large bag and got into the car.

'Mrs Lar, where are we going?'

'The Palace of Escape.'

Mussa looked disappointed.

'Don't worry, you're coming too. Everyone else will be at the Sultan's bash so the Darajani place is empty. I've been given the keys. It's just for us.'

The Darajani Fort was blacker than usual, its gardens abstract obstacles to navigate. They entered the large main room and found the lights.

'Perhaps you might help me with this, Mussa.' Carla unfolded a checkered travel rug on the floor. She had brought along a picnic and a bottle of wine. 'I know you shouldn't, but this is special. I'm sure God won't mind too much if you have a sip.' She uncorked the Pouilly Fumé. It had begun to warm up even though she'd taken it from the fridge at the last moment, insulating it with a towel. 'Here, a toast: to us!'

The huge room dwarfed the two small smoky figures.

'And this is for you.' Carla handed Mussa a package. Inside was a blazer. 'I guessed at your measurements. The tailor on Portuguese Street will alter it, if need be.'

Mussa put it on and stood up. 'How do I look, Mrs Lar?'

'Very handsome, Mussa, very handsome.'

She got up and tweaked at the cuffs and collar. She stood close to him, near enough to kiss.

\*     \*     \*

TO: Daveyboy
CC:
Subject: gory details

Davey darling i don't know how to say this delicately . . .
But its true what they say! Hes BIG! IT happened last
night! @ the end of ramadan. Abdul took me to a street
party on the far side of town then back to the flat for a
drink and kerpow! We did it. No hanging around. I know
wot youre like daveyboy needing every last detail . . .
Well im gonna be lewd & crude and confide all cos im
desperate to tell someone. (I don't think my dowager will
be quite up to this.) The downside (booooooooooo!) hes
not what you'd call attentive in the loving department . . .
To be honest hes a bit wham bang thank you mam. A bit
stick it in & out turn over & sleep. Soixante-neuf isnt on
the menu . . . But he still expected me to gnaw on the end
of his willy. thinks . . . I'll have to set up an educational
programme and teach him some of the finer things . . . Im
not complaining tho, hes fab. Youd adore him. The old
woman i told u about is a bit of a wild thing herself . . .
She shagged her way round Zanzi 40 years ago . . . I'll
keep you posted on the gossip as i learn more!!!
XXXXXX Fran

TO: Fran
CC:
Subject: OH GOOD GOD IN HEAVEN. HOW FAB

AAAAAAAAAAAAAARRRRGGGHHH! i cant stand it francesca.
u cant leave me hanging on like this (is hanging the right
expression!!!) i need specifics feet or inches. u lucky girl.
what did uncle davey say? as 4 funnilingus u know that

116

makes me squirm . . . poor boy B nice to him & try things
SLOWLY! ive completely dried up so my sex life will now
B led vicariously thru u. KEEP me up 2 date wiv every
development. as for randy old women . . . i don't do OLD.
its young bunnys like u i want to hear about. now 4 the
lowdown on the ex. definitely a closet. saw him strutting
his stuff on gay street last night! praps its something 2 do
with u – u turned him. this can only B a good thing. i cant
wait till u've finished wiv abdul then i can get serviced on
the rebound. u must share and share alike wiv best friends.
i cant wait 4 the next instalment. bin laden t shirts R a
definite fashion no-no. doesnt matter how post ironic u R
about it . . . they don't work.
love love love love love davey

# CHAPTER 5: REALITY

## Rumour

Felix Gomez sat at his usual place in the Africa Bar, swearing at a waiter in Swahili, Hindi and English. The fluent stream sounded poetic, an inconsistent lyrical streak in the bar-owner's curdled nature. The place was crowded with a delegation from the East German and Chinese consulates, and flashy tourists who had stopped by for the evening from a liner moored in the port.

John Jackson was there with a small group of colleagues. He was uncommonly gregarious. 'Another round, chaps?'

'That's decent of you, Johnno, yes, please, G 'n' T for me. Go on, make it a large one.'

'Yes, same here, but only a splash in mine.'

'Unusual to see the comrades in here. What do you suppose they're up to, John?'

'God knows, bloody Reds, always up to something. Probably celebrating another corn quota or the latest directive from Chairman How . . . Do you really care? Felix, drinks, please, chop-chop.'

A parrot sat on a stand in the corner. It was savage; some of its personality had been acquired from its new owner. Felix had bought it on a trip he'd made to London. It screeched: 'Bottoms up.' No one liked the creature.

'Where's Lar this evening, old chap?'

'She's busy, dear boy.'

'We never see her any more, Johnno. You've not locked her away, have you?'

A club-tie chortle chuckled round the table.

'Why should I do a thing like that, Phillip?'

'She's always been the wild card, Johnno. Perhaps it's time for you to rein her in on the QT.'

'Dear boy, Carla has a will of her own. I think me trying to restrain her is very unlikely. Do you think it would meet with the slightest success? I like the quiet life. It's easier to leave her be.'

A cheer went up from the tourists, followed by laughter and clapping. It momentarily distracted John.

'You should keep an eye out, old chap.'

'And what, Phillip, do you mean by that?'

'There's a rumour doing the rounds right now, Johnno, hush-hush stuff and not very nice, I'm afraid. You ought to know it's about Carla.'

The drinks came to the table and the conversation fizzled out as a waiter poured the tonic into hefty measures of gin. He changed an ashtray and returned to the bar.

'What rumour, dear boy?'

'Whisper has it she's having an affair, old chap.'

John clipped a cigar neatly. 'I shouldn't believe everything you hear, Phillip. This place thrives on scandal. Give me a penny each time I'm gossiped about and I'll be quids in. There'd easily be enough to pay for the drinks, even at three bob a shot.'

His attempt to lighten the conversation failed. He knew his wife was different. They weren't close, not that they ever had been: that wasn't part of their marriage. It was a partnership, a jolly good arrangement. His father had said, 'Don't marry for love, marriage is a necessity, Johnny,' and he'd taken him at his word. But she was altered now, more remote, defiant, even. A rumour about Carla wasn't a good thing; he'd got his reputation to consider and his private life to keep covered.

'Might I ask you where you heard this vital piece of news, Phillip?'

His friend frowned.

'Come, come, you can't half tell a story. Who told you this twaddle?'

'The German fellow.'

'And what possible insight does he have on my wife's alleged infidelities?'

'He said she's carrying on with the chap who owns the Darajani Fort. An Arab, for God's sake. I mean, this wouldn't be so bad if it was one of us.'

'I beg your pardon, Phillip?'

'Oh, I didn't mean it like *that*, old chap. I meant at least she wouldn't be mooning around with a wog.'

John downed his drink in one. 'Do me a favour, Phillip, and stamp on this tittle-tattle. It's rubbish and I don't want to hear it again. You can tell the same to that Kraut – bloody Germans. Now, whose round is it?'

'Let's have a bottle of the Widow, barman.'

A champagne cork popped and the tourists sang 'Happy Birthday' to a woman wearing an emerald necklace. The gloom surrounding Felix Gomez lifted with the sound. He didn't much care for singing but champagne corks meant money.

'Let me wish you a very happy birthday too. Go on, enjoy yourselves, you're not going to stint on another bottle, are you?'

Felix collared the man he'd scolded earlier and told him to

fetch Dom Pérignon. 'But they are drinking Veuve Clicquot, Mr Gomez.'

'Tell them we've run out and serve the expensive stuff instead.'

John got up to leave.

'Don't go now, old chap, the place is about to jump.'

'I'm done, Phillip. Now don't forget, knock this tosh on the head for me. Cheerio, chaps.'

John walked back to the house. He sat in the library and poured himself a gin. 'Sima? Sima, is Mrs Jackson here?'

'No, sir.'

'Did she say where she was going?'

'The Darajani Fort, I think.'

Bugger, he thought. Maybe the gossip was right. He checked his watch. Ten thirty. He'd go to de Silva's tomorrow and buy Carla the Rolex; perhaps that might help settle things.

## Money

Abdul and Francesca walked through the vegetable market. They passed an unused pillar-box that had been gagged. It was weathered and neglected, its coat a dull burgundy instead of crimson, as if the original livery had developed a scab. It was a relic, a redundant memento belonging to a time when East African coins and stamps were fixed with an Elizabethan profile. They crossed the road by the *dala dala* stand and carried on down a stretch that housed stalls selling cheap clothes, shoes, household goods and electrical items. They were looking for the man who had taken their photograph the previous night.

'Here, I think he has stall.'

The shop sold children's clothes. Miniature trousers tied with tiny belts and colourful little shirts crowded the place. Francesca felt uncomfortable in an emporium devoted to kids. The place threatened to suffocate her.

'We there.'

'You go in, Abdul. If you don't mind, I need the air out here.'

He didn't understand her excuse and walked inside. She waited on the kerb, inspecting the shop opposite, hoping her sudden fascination with ironmongery would in some way negate the contents of the place behind her. The starchy man who had taken the picture stood behind a pile of peachy knickers; he'd got a stack of snaps in front of him, but located theirs quickly and handed it to Abdul.

'C'mon, then, Abdul, let's have a look.'

He opened the envelope on the street and passed the contents to his lover. The image was badly composed, the sitters only just in frame. Francesca looked faintly surprised in it, as if she'd never had her photo taken before. Abdul wore a resolute expression that was aimed not towards the camera lens but at the doorway. He was looking blindly into a lateral infinity. She was disappointed with the result: she'd been hoping for a camp, tacky picture she could send to David. She glanced at it again and wondered if cropping would salvage it. She was disturbed. The figures in the picture didn't look like them at all: it was spectral, an X-ray. Abdul was keen to see the result but she didn't hand it to him straight away: she looked at the snap again. The image was unnerving and ominous. She worried that Abdul might interpret it in the same way. He pulled the photograph from her, and seemed pleased with it.

'Would you like to keep it?' she asked.

'Why you not want?'

'You keep it, a souvenir of our special night.' She was happy he'd taken it from her.

Abdul put the snapshot back into the envelope and closed it carefully: he was safekeeping an amulet. He patted his chest pocket, as if the gentle taps would guard the picture, then blew into his hands.

'Francesca, I want that you can help me.'

'Of course, what is it?'

'Maybe you can give me little money?'

She hadn't anticipated the question. It threw her momentarily.

'Yes. How much do you want to borrow?'

'Forty thousand.'

Francesca didn't like to carry much cash on her; she had to go back to the flat for it. The amount was a surprise. 'Why so much, Abdul?'

'I have many problem, I think you good to help me.'

She was flattered he had felt able to ask; it couldn't be easy being a Muslim man asking a Christian woman for help. At the same time it troubled her.

'C'mon, then, let's go back and sort it out.' Her cheery voice covered her concern; it was not unlike the constant smiles to which she'd become inured.

After she had given him the money Abdul kissed her cheek. 'I speak you later, Francesca.'

'OK, whatever. I'll be here.'

His steps grew faint on the stairs. It had been like paying off a hooker rather than lending a friend – a lover – money. She called Carla. 'Lar, could we meet for a drink this evening?'

'That would be nice. At our usual, darling?'

Carla arrived at the Serena wearing a local *kanga* as a shawl. She looked effortless and stylish. Francesca felt inept and plain.

'Did you enjoy the end of Ramadan, Francesca?'

'I had a wild time, it was great. And you?'

'I'm far too old for that type of thing, darling. It was quite enough listening to the noise on the streets. What did you do?'

'I went to a big party . . . A friend took me.' Francesca wanted to tell Carla about her friendship with Abdul, but couldn't find the right opening. 'It's not so easy living here, is it, Lar? I mean culturally.' She lit a cigarette. 'Y'know, it's not that I've got a problem with the people, Lar. I suppose I'm just different. I find it difficult to explain.'

Her expression led Carla to guess there was an ulterior subject. 'Francesca darling, what on earth are you talking about?'

'I think I'm having an affair.'

'Darling, don't you *know* if you are?'

Francesca's conversation was clumsy; she sensed it mirrored her physical appearance. 'Yes, I do know, but it's gone odd on me.'

'Darling, you're five thousand miles from home in a foreign country, what do you expect?' Carla was motherly, concerned yet realistic. 'Now, tell me, what makes your affair odd?'

Francesca told the old woman of her courtship, Ramadan and the money. It was the forty thousand shillings that bothered her. 'I feel like I've paid for sex, Lar. It's the Puritan in me, I feel . . . tacky.'

'Francesca, this is a poor country. You haven't been paying for sex, you're helping a friend who has less than you. Don't get high-minded about it. You have to look at life here through different eyes. You can't bring your Camden Town standards to Zanzibar.'

'But how do I know he's true and not just after money?'

'I can't answer that, darling. Use your instinct, find out for yourself – but, above all, calm down. Now, where are our drinks?'

Francesca nodded as the waiter placed a whisky in front of her. 'How did you conduct your affair, Lar? Was it the same then?'

Carla deliberated, unsure what to say. It wasn't that she wanted to keep the secret – quite the opposite, in fact. The novelty of being able to confide in someone after so many years of silence jarred her. 'I don't know. No, nothing is as it seems, Francesca. My romance was hidden . . . taboo. It was unbearable.' She fumbled with her cigarette packet, an inconsistent, ungainly movement in an elegant woman.

'Why, Lar? Why unbearable?'

'Let us leave it for now.'

Francesca couldn't give up the conversation. 'Was it the revolution, Lar?'

'That was part of it.'

Francesca remained silent, allowing Carla to quarry her past. She moved the ashtray like a chess piece before speaking.

'I had a terrible miscarriage, Francesca.'

'Here?'

'No, back home. We'd been evacuated, and I was newly pregnant. No one knew. At twelve weeks I lost my baby and had a hysterectomy. It was the only time I was pregnant.'

'I'm sorry, Lar.'

'John never knew. Well, he knew I'd lost a child that wasn't his. He thought the Darajani fellow was responsible.

He didn't know Mussa was the father – he wasn't deemed an option. Mussa was merely the driver. You know, I don't think John ever looked at him all the time he worked for us. A local judge, a Goan man I believe, once said to me, "The English have a subtle racism." There was nothing subtle about it. Believe me.'

They lit cigarettes. A tear swelled in Carla's eye and she made an excuse about the smoke stinging as she swept it away. She inhaled deeply to try to anchor herself as far away from emotion as possible. 'I have told you too much, Francesca, and I don't know why.'

Carla's voice and manner were unwavering: her stiff British breeding and rope of pearls chained her to a show of restraint. She glanced involuntarily downwards, a nervous jump of her eyes that failed to disguise her unhappiness. Francesca shuffled in her chair.

'It's something we share, Carla. I tried for a child, but never conceived. It's inexplicable, and one of the biggest regrets of my life.'

The older woman softened and touched Francesca's arm lightly. It was an attempt to stopper emotion. She opened her mouth, but nothing came out. She couldn't speak about their shared inability to have children. It had always hurt her and was as raw now as ever before. She coughed. 'We adopted in the end because John was keen to have a family. It was another part of his disguise.' Carla snorted at her revelation, her clinical observation. 'It's a terrible admission, but my whole life has been about deceit. Seventy-four long years of pretence.' Her lips tightened; she didn't quite bite them. 'I need a very stiff drink, Francesca, and I need it now. Waiter, *tafadhali* . . . More whiskies, please.'

The two women drank heavily.

\*     \*     \*

TO: Fran
CC:
Subject: I reckon it sounds like value for money

francesca baby don't get yer nick nacks twisted. who hasnt
paid for a shag? its not like its never happened before . . .
with you maybe but not with this girl. & 40 grand is only
30 squid – sounds like bargain basement 2 me. praps
yer old gal-pal is rite . . . look @ it as help rather than as
payment. u girlies R so fuckin complicated sometimes . . .
miserable if u'r not getting it & fed up when you do. can
men do anything rite?????! dont answer that . . . i already
know!!!!!!! keep it up girl – i bet u end up marrying in2 his
tribe – ill have 2 wear purrrr-dur for the occasion. do u
think a long black frock wiv matching mask will suit me?
kinda like the idea of all that eye-flashing from behind a
yashmak – i think id make a good muslim wifey. enjoy
Fran – @ least u'r snot here in the rain. by the way – is that
story about a dog-size rat true? gross.
love love love love
love davey.

## Mussa Now

Mussa Abeidi's flat was on the boundary of the old town.
Although built in 1948 it had an antiquity and history that
seemed greater – much of Stone Town looks as if it might
be a thousand years old, but it's mostly nineteenth century.
A small courtyard at the back of the building was home to the
ancient Morris. On the first floor, a flaking green door opened

into the first of two small rooms, one for sleeping and one for living. An ancient two-ring Baby Belling sat in a corner of the living room, with a pot and two plates. The second plate was an optimistic addition, an unanswered prayer for company; it was never used. Nine other tenants in the building shared the simple bathroom. There was a small cheap cupboard in his bedroom; it usually contained his suit and tie. A yellowed letter with an English address was pinned on an ochre wall, above it were two monochrome pictures of women, one black and one white. Mrs Abeidi and Mrs Jackson. It was a shrine. Both the photos were faded and curled, and taken in happier times. It was strange having one of these lost women come back into his life. His solitary existence had told him they were both dead. Now the white *shetani* was back on the island, but she wasn't haunting him: her alien presence felt like a song, something happy.

At ten Mussa was still in bed, lying like a corpse on top of the sheets. The air was leaden and humid. Sweat ran from his face down his neck. He'd try to save his energy for the five minutes before rising; he still didn't feel well.

Sleep caught him again; he didn't wake until after twelve. He bathed in a bucket and shaved his thin grey beard, wanting to look his best for his visit to Carla Jackson. He touched both photographs – a small devotional gesture that, over the years, had eroded the corners of both images – left the room and started the bronchial car.

'Mussa, I thought you were coming earlier.'

'I'm sorry, Mrs Jackson, I had errands to run before finding you. I'm not too late, am I?' He had told another of his honourable fibs.

'You're here now, that's what counts. Come outside with me to the garden. Let's shelter under the palms.'

Older and old walked slowly together in the powerful heat.

'We'll lie like a couple of cats out of the sun. What do you think, Mussa?'

Ali placed cushions outside for them. Shade from the tree protected the elderly companions. What small breeze there was vanished, and drowsiness took hold of them both. Carla fell asleep propped against Mussa.

She woke to find him toying with a stick in the dirt. She had not been close like this to a man in years, not since she'd left Zanzibar. There had been several affairs since then, although they were no more than heartless, desperate attempts at reliving a lost passion. Intimacy was something she'd not felt in four decades and it was a lovely feeling to wake beside him now; she'd thought it might never happen again.

'Did you dream, Mrs Jackson?'

'I can't tell you. My dreams run away as quickly as they appear, taking the stories with them. Did you, Mussa?'

'I dreamed of us when we were young.'

A sour-sweet residue of the past lingered for them both.

'I think of us like that all the time. There's not a day gone by that I haven't remembered. I still love you, Mussa.'

Silence. Carla pushed back her hair and blinked: she felt as if she'd betrayed a secret. Her words hung in the air.

Mussa seemed hesitant before speaking, perhaps cautious of treading a dangerous path. 'How can that be, Mrs Jackson? Look at us. We have both changed so much . . .'

Tiredness and olden days redefined the couple, old age rendering them both curiously genderless. He *was* male and she female, yet the geography of their faces and the shape of their bodies converged somewhere in a neuter middle ground. Time had modulated their youthful beauty into a different perfection. But that was irrelevant; they were still both passionate.

'I love you. That's never changed, Mussa.'

He didn't respond.

'I feel bound to you like no other man. You were the father of my child . . .'

He looked shocked – alarmed at information that was too momentous, giddy from the revelation. Carla knew she was unable to talk about her lost baby without crying, but added, 'He died early on in the pregnancy. I'm so sorry.'

A tear streaked her cheek; his eyes remained dry. Mussa had lost two sons and a wife, but now, at the end of his life, he'd regained a lover. Allah could play strange tricks.

She reached over in a small dance-like motion, stroked his face and kissed him. They had both faded. Beneath his clothing she felt his bony arms; he'd transformed from the strong young man of forty years ago into a skeletal old one. A vaguely familiar jacket disguised his emaciation.

## More Money

Francesca sat in the flat doing damage to the whisky bottle as Fatima cleaned around her. It was too hot to move. 'Fatima, why don't you go now?'

The cleaner hadn't understood. Francesca spoke her moronic lingo and accompanied it with a mime. She resolved once more in her tipsiness to learn Swahili. Fatima left her employer delving in the freezer for more ice. Francesca decided to lie out on the roof with her booze and a new book by Cormac McCarthy. She had surprised herself with the amount she read: books lasted no time in Stone Town. She'd try to slow down, or she'd have to reread everything she'd brought with her. Lethargy hung in the hot air.

The electronic couplet from her phone could mean only one thing: '**i come you house at home yes**.'

It was the first she'd heard from Abdul in two days. She was pissed off because, after taking the money, he'd vanished but relieved that he was chasing her now. She sent a text message back: '**Karibu – im drinking on the roof come & find me**!'

Loneliness ate at her again. She wouldn't turn him away.

It was dark when he arrived.

'Hello, stranger, where've you been, then?'

'I have problem but it gone now.' He sat beside her on the high bench, poured himself a whisky and Coke and took a cigarette.

That annoyed her: what was wrong with asking first? She didn't mention it for fear of losing control and rowing again. 'It's good to see you. Are you hungry?'

Abdul shook his head.

'What's the problem, then?'

'It nothing you understand.' He was curt and broody and crunched the joints in his hands.

The rapid clicking of his knuckles irritated Francesca. 'Well, cheer up, you're with me now.' Her need for his company superseded his bad humour. Even so, she wanted to brighten his ominous influence. 'Shall we go out? Let's go to Sweet Eazy for a drink.'

He was indifferent.

'I'm going anyway. Will you join me or not?'

Abdul was hard work. Perhaps she was better off going by herself. He got up and followed.

'Abdul, what's up? I can't take the gloom-monger bit.'

'Is problem of money.'

She didn't want to hear this. 'Come on with you. Let's talk about it over a drink.'

Sweet Eazy had once been a prosperous merchant's house. Elegant curved doorways, cool white walls and continually wafting ceiling fans hinted at past wealth. It was quiet. They sat at the heavy wooden bar with icy beers.

'OK, Abdul, tell me all about it. What's happening?'

He surprised Francesca with his reply. 'Maybe I get business. Special for cutting up hair. I make money like that.'

A hairdressing salon seemed a peculiar solution to his problems. 'Don't you need to know how to cut hair?'

'I do that. Maybe you give me money to start?'

'Abdul, I don't think I can. What would it cost?'

'Two millions.'

'Don't be foolish. I don't have that type of money, I'm sorry.'

He peered at his drink: he was dreaming.

'That's nearly two thousand pounds. Can't you do anything else?'

'Is bad for me and everyone.'

'I know it is.'

'How you know? You know nothing of Zanzibar life.'

'Abdul, I try to understand. I'm not blind, I know there are problems.'

He gazed at her petulantly from above his glass – becoming a caustic man with a lager-coloured trunk. He put down his beer.

'I can't save the island, Abdul. If I can help *you* in any way I'll try. That's all I can do.'

She ordered more beer hoping it might lessen the charge in the atmosphere. It didn't. There was silence for just a little too long. Francesca threw an idea over the bar to Abdul. 'I've been thinking of taking a trip, getting away for a few days. What do you think?'

'That it must be good for you.' He sounded morose.

'Would you like to come too?'

He didn't react – he was trancelike.

'I was thinking of going to Lake Victoria. Go on, come along. What do you say?' Her efforts at cajoling the man weren't working. This was the first time she'd given any thought to travelling to the mainland interior. Lake Victoria was only a name, but she hoped it might also be the catalyst to lighten her leaden lover.

'I say it good for you, but me no.'

'Abdul, I don't get it.'

'Is too much for money.'

'Well, to hell with you, I'm going anyway.' She was overreacting again, and calmed down to find herself committed to a trip that had been originally no more than an idle thought. 'I'd like to have the company . . . It'll be my treat, Abdul.'

He gazed into the table as he would a mirror; Francesca couldn't see any reflection.

'Please, Abdul, it would mean a lot to me.'

He wiped the film of beer off his lips with the back of his hand. 'That OK. I come with you for safari. When we go?' His depression had inexplicably shifted.

'You mean it? That's great, Abdul. Let's check it out together and figure on how we'll get there.'

Zanzibar is riddled with stories; making sense of them is the trick. When Francesca asked for information about the train one tourist told her, 'God, what a shit-awful plan! Nobody takes the train. Why don't you fly?'

She asked around. Emerson, from the hotel, was rather taken by the notion, provided she travelled first-class in her own compartment. Then she was told a black tale of mythic proportion regarding the last time he'd made the same trip.

It involved a train crash, six dead, thwarted rescue, a night in the bush surrounded by beastly noises, murderous poachers taking pity and giving him a lift, finding a hotel in nowhere, being robbed, a terrible car accident, losing his phone and discovering his best friend had died on his eventual return. It was all so gloriously OTT and *African* that she resolved to get the first train out of Dar es Salaam to Mwanza, the main port on Lake Victoria.

TO: Daveyboy
CC:
Subject: I'm taking a trip

Davey darling, im nipping off out of Zanzibar and headed inland for a few days. Im goin to Mwanza with Abdul. You know, for all my worries & misgivings about him im pretty hooked. Hes a doll . . . I cant help it! Thinks . . . im falling for him. Hes complex and vulnerable & even tho we have differences i just know that we're so right for each other. I can guess what youre thinking – but i don't think its actually love, just a deep friendship. Ok get off my case davey-boy! Heres the info you really want: hes become dynamite in the sack. Thats right DYNA-FUCKING-MITE! Satisfied now? Hope your current lack of carnal pleasure has resolved itself cos you aint getting your paws on Abdul . . . You know i love you!
xxxxxxxxxfranxxxxxxxxxxxxxx

It would take two full days and forty-five thousand shillings each to reach Mwanza. They had a cabin with bunks in first-class, prison-issue green sheets and an attentive guard who'd fetch chicken and cold beer from the dining car. Apartment C, coach 1161. The berth was an institutional

135

brown, long, skinny, and with a small hand-basin in the corner that didn't work. Boarding four thirty p.m., train off at five.

Abdul was anxious. 'I have chain and sleep on top bed. I can kill bandits.'

'Where are you planning on going, Abdul? Apache country? It's not the Wild West.'

'I told about problem on train. We maybe attack by robber.'

'Abdul, I've travelled on trains all over the world, we'll be fine.'

He was unconvinced. 'This not like other place, Francesca.' He positioned himself on the top bunk.

'Put the chain away and come down here. Relax, Abdul.'

He confessed to never having been on a train before.

Francesca found that hard to believe. 'Never, Abdul? Ever? Then stop this silliness. We'll not be killed in our beds. Enjoy the ride, come and look out of the window with me.'

Sundown in Dar es Salaam was a bruised blue. The day's dust hung in the air but everything else sagged to the ground in the oppressive heat. A giant engine heaved the enormous bulk of the train through the shanty suburbs and into the night. The occasional shriek of wheel on rail was like the banshee squeal of some spectral carnivore. Abdul locked the compartment door and the two of them screwed like crazy by the window with the lights off.

An African dawn. Francesca looked into the vast landscape. It was milky, cold, prehistoric. The train clattered through a wilderness of baobab trees and far-away blue mountains. It was astonishing. Abdul was still asleep on the top bunk; he gripped the chain in both hands and murmured dreamy

words of defiance. They stopped at innumerable small stations; by nine they had arrived at Dodoma. The station was a
swirl of boys carrying huge placards with entire shops pinned
to them. Watches, jewellery, toys, radios, combs, sunglasses,
hats and dolls. It was the latter that made them look like
enormous voodoo pinboards. Piles of shoes and mountains
of plastic beakers, fried food and fruit lined the platform. The
train drew away from the temporary commerce of the station
into a massive plain littered with colossal stones, boulders
stacked by giants.

By lunchtime they were in Salanda. There were way too
many food stalls for one train. Chicken carcasses boiled in
cauldrons of oil and mounds of chips and kebabs spilled
off trestles. Through the bustle of the temporary market
came music. Thirty yards away there were four musicians,
a man and three women. The man sawed a simple bow at
an instrument made from string and a gourd. The women
played drums made from discarded plastic containers and
they all sang. The man shook a tinkling leg – it had bells
attached. It was yawping, discordant, rhythmic and melodic;
music spiced with dreams. More noise, the sale of nuts and
cold water; everything happened around the train.

Francesca tried to buy fruit and saw the musicians pass.
One of the women looked up: her eyes were dead and grey
and had fallen inside her skull. Each of the four held on
to the other as they carefully picked their way to another
carriage. The blind band played again. This time she could
hear melancholy.

The train lurched, the couplings clanked and the wagons
moved on. The travellers did little other than gaze from the
window and sip warm beer. A fan nattered ineffectually
overhead; the open window provided no breeze as they
melted their way through Palaeolithic scenery. Time lingered;

a day is a week, a yard a mile, a yard a mile, a yard a mile. After a day and two nights, the train pulled into Mwanza at nine a.m.

'I haven't a clue where we'll stay, Abdul. Did you remember to pick up my guidebook?'

The answer was no.

'We'll have to shop around, then.'

A taxi took them to the Tilapia Hotel and, rather than look further, they stayed put.

'This is too camp for words, Davey would love it.' Francesca stood in the Hepburn Suite aboard the *African Queen* houseboat. 'And the view . . .' A door led to a balcony that looked across the lake. An impressive sight, it was inconceivable that a fresh-water stretch could be so massive. 'It's a sea, not a lake. God, it's beautiful . . .'

Abdul beckoned her to come indoors. He wasn't interested in the landscape. He drew the curtains, switched off the lights and pulled her on to the bed, clinging to his delirious lover. They didn't surface until sixish, starving hungry.

Abdul reacquired his swagger; his impenetrable nervousness had vanished with the trip. Now he was cocksure, attentive, promiscuous with his kissing. Francesca loved the attention of her slender, difficult man. She loved his blackness, loved his masculinity. That was an awful lot of love she was thinking about. Surely she couldn't be falling that much for him?

Drinks first – it didn't matter how hungry they were. An eccentric mix of people populated the Tilapia Hotel. Francesca speculated that she and Abdul were the only tourists there. Otherwise, an unlikely infestation of Jesuits and Sisters of Mercy, a smattering of UN officials and their counterparts from WHO formed small groups at Reception and in the dining room. Mwanza is refugee country. But it was the guys at the far end of the bar who were the strange ones. They were South African cowboys, all of them guzzling Johnnie Walker Black Label.

When Abdul went to the gents', one of the group approached Francesca.

'Hello, ma name's Roy.' He put out his hand to her. He'd drunk as much as anyone else, but hid the fact behind tiny, deep-set, impenetrable eyes. An unreal thatch many shades darker than the colour sprouting at his temples sat on top of his head. 'Whatya doin' here?'

'I'm on holiday with my boyfriend. And you?'

'Business – diamonds, gold, that type of thing. Let me buy you a drink.'

'You're not listening. I'm with my boyfriend – no, thank you.'

He took his wig and poison back to his buddies. She was pleased Abdul had missed the exchange yet conscious of having referred to him as her boyfriend. The truth was that she was besotted with her lover; a realisation that both delighted and, abruptly, hit her. It was the emotion she'd hankered after for so long, that dreamy, heady sickness. She felt perfect, and with that knowledge, beautiful now. At long last Francesca knew what romance was, and what everyone else experienced when they fell in love, but she couldn't see Abdul obsessing over her. To her mind his compulsion was evidence of a love that, in some way, belonged on a higher level. His attention gave her a sense of power, of being needed, of being adored.

Francesca's mobile rang.

'Carla here. I haven't seen much of you lately. Is everything OK?'

'Fine, no problems. Sorry I didn't tell you but I'm away for a few days. Can I call when I get back?'

'Of course, darling. But just quickly, what are you doing for Christmas? If you're footloose I'd like you to come over for dinner.'

'Carla, that's very kind. I'd love to join you.'

'I hope you don't go in for that continental thing on Christmas Eve. I'm a bit of a stickler for the day. Make it about eight, darling. 'Bye for now, enjoy yourself.'

TO: Daveyboy
CC:
Subject: safari

Dearest Davey boy – have i had a weird few days. Went to Lake Victoria with the man – still vvvvv sexy . . . But i don't want you getting all jealous so i wont give you any more details except that hes ADORABLE! There is something addictive about him. Hes enigmatic – with a kind of lonely beauty. Im getting a bit too lyrical aren't i? But thats how i feel. I bet you'd think he was a moody fucker – its like its his very Africanness that is coming out. Ok enough already . . .

We went to the strangest island nature reserve. I don't know about you but i always thought nature reserves would be a million sq miles of bush & stuff but not this one! Not much bigger than a semi's backgarden – more wildlife tho . . . I nearly got devoured cos bloody Abdul – who knows it all (not) – led me into the nesting grounds for all the crocodiles. I was then nearly impaled by an impala . . . snipped at by snakes and eaten by a fish eagle . . . If that wasnt enuff i got chased by a bloody wildebeest. Its like a zoo without cages or Windsor Safari Park without the car . . . Stayed in campiest hotel . . . try the African Queen . . . a bit more you praps. Did three

nites there & flew home – couldnt face the tropical
trans-siberian slow train back. The plane is something else,
a 12-seater and very rickety. Ran vvvvv low on cash cos i
thought itd be safer to leave the wonga @ home – I was
down to pennies in Dar es Salaam – and desperate cos
stupid bloody me took my ATM card instead of my Amex.
I was desperado for a hole in the wall but nobody seemed
to know what i meant. I discovered civilisation @ Standard
Charter Bank thank fuck. I have NEVER been so happy to
find a cashpoint.

Wot you doin for Chrissy? My dowager has invited
me for xmas dinner & im really looking forward to it.
E me soon xxxxxxxxxxxxxxxxxxxxxxxxxxxxxxxxxxxxxx
xxxxxxxxxxxxxxxxxxxxxxxxxxxxxxxxxxxxxxxxxxxxxxxfran.
Happy xmas, miss you
PS . . . as a matter of amused interest whats the pervert
ex up to?
PPS . . . nearly forgot – yes its true about the rats – the size
of a jack russell.

# Christmas 63

'Lar darling, Happy Christmas.' John handed Carla a small
parcel wrapped in pink crêpe paper and tied with a green
ribbon.

Inside was the Rolex she'd seen in de Silva's. 'Johnno, you
shouldn't have. It's so expensive. But thank you, darling, it's
wonderful.'

Carla buckled up the watch and stood admiring it at the end
of her crooked arm. 'I love it. I really do. Here, darling, a little

gift from me. Happy Christmas.' She produced a large box from behind a ludicrous palm press-ganged into Christmas tree service. It looked eccentric under a weight of tinsel, silver baubles and angels.

Carla's gift was heavy. 'Goodness, Lar, what is it?'

'Open it and find out.'

John stared at the wrapping, trying to guess at the contents. 'It weighs enough. It's not a case of whisky, darling?'

'No.'

'A typewriter?'

'Why on earth should I buy you a typewriter?'

He finished unwrapping the package; there was a cardboard box to dispense with before he could get to what was inside.

'Lar! How perfectly super. A tape-recorder. Where on earth did you get hold of this? Nairobi? We've got to try it out straight away. Get Sima and some of the others in, we'll sing a couple of carols.'

'I've got you three spare reels as well, darling. They record an hour on each spool.'

'Lar, this is grand. It really is.'

John was genuinely pleased: it was the first time Carla had given him anything he actually wanted. Both gifts were excessive; he was trying to woo Carla with a watch, and she was attempting to absolve herself of guilt with a reel-to-reel.

'Come on, Lar, hurry up and get the staff in. I'll see if I can get this contraption rigged up. What time's lunch, darling?'

'Do we have to, Johnno? I mean it's so bloody hot I was thinking of taking a drive today. Why don't we have a supper instead?'

The festive excitement soured.

'Lar, I hardly ever see you as it is. This is Christmas Day, for God's sake. Can't we be together for a spot of lunch?'

'Why don't we eat later?'

The atmosphere thickened.

'No, Lar, we bloody well won't. It's Christmas Day and the least you can bloody do is spend it with me. I'm your husband.'

'Johnno, stop getting so worked up. What's this all about?'

'You bloody well know, Lar. Start behaving like a Christian.'

She was paralysed.

'You might try to look as if you're married to me and not some damn wog. Have a little respect, even if it's only for yourself.'

She was terrified. What did he know? 'I'm not sure what you're picking at, John. Would you like to explain yourself?'

'News spreads, Lar. Don't think I haven't been told.'

Sickness enveloped her: it was the dread of hearing him speak Mussa's name.

'I know you're carrying on with the Darajani fellow, as does everyone else on the island. Pack it in before it gets out of hand. You're staying here for lunch, that's final.'

'It's not true, John.'

At that moment panic flustered her. The denial was instinctive rather than considered and her speedy response lent weight to the accusation. John was quite sure he had the truth.

'I'm sorry, John, I really am.'

Now Carla wanted to laugh: the irony was perfect. The gossips on the island had got the wrong scent. She decided not to refute the accusation again and attempted to look disconsolate. Relief and elation powered inside her. She wanted to sing. 'I'll fetch the staff, John. Lunch will be at two . . . I'm sorry. You've got to believe me.'

Their marriage was a business, a brisk arrangement, a

dynastic union. So long as neither was too open about their mutual indiscretions their 'understanding' remained satisfactory. That was the lie of their existence: nothing was fine, she was tainted by his unhappiness. John's sexuality was an untalked-of component in their association, which Carla coyly thought of as his 'little hobby'. It seemed that repression was their only chance of liberation. John rigged up the tape-recorder and Carla clacked from the room.

Sima, the cook, two of the gardeners, including Iddi, Mussa and three of the guards arranged themselves in an uneasy formation by the Christmas palm. Carla sat in front of the assembled throng in dutiful-wife mode. She looked only at one person. John was going to conduct and record simultaneously. 'After three, everyone, nice and loud . . . "Good King Wenceslas looked out . . ."'

The noise was dismal. 'No, no, no. Stop, stop!' John flicked a switch on the machine. 'Now that was terrible, everyone. Don't you know the words?'

The choir murmured a reply that was neither yes nor no.

'Come on, now, let's put some effort into this. From the beginning again. One, two, three . . .'

The same raggedy din ensued. John stopped the rendition.

'Johnno, darling, I think you'll find that particular good king doesn't figure much around here. Why don't you drop it, sing something everyone knows?'

He was ruffled. He'd wanted a traditional Christmas morning. Sima suggested a number by Cliff Richard that met with mixed approval from the chorus. John had no option other than to go along with the majority, but it wasn't what he intended. He played with his new toy as the staff rasped a reticent version of what was a normally rousing number: 'Summer Holiday'.

Sima did best: she was the only one present who knew all the words.

John checked the sound levels on a dial.

Carla watched every breath Mussa took, resentful that she couldn't be with him that afternoon yet thankful their affair was still secret. 'I think that's enough, Johnno. We've got to let Cook get back to work or there'll be no lunch. I'm going to take the car for twenty minutes. I need to drop off a gift to the doctor's little boy.'

'Can't you let the driver do that?'

'It won't be the same, Johnno. Ramil is such a sweet little chap. I won't be long.'

'Just make sure you're not, then we'll have time to go to the Africa for a glass of champagne before lunch.'

'Tee-tee, John.'

Mussa trailed behind his boss as she walked quickly to the car. 'We have to be nippy, Mussa. Drive me to the doctor's. I won't go in.'

A gift was deposited with the servant who answered the door, and Carla dashed back to the waiting vehicle. The boy appeared. 'Ramil! I'm sorry I can't stay and open it with you. I'm being a Mummy Christmas today and I've got other presents to hand out. Happy Christmas, darling! 'Bye.'

The car was already moving as Carla shouted the greeting. She leaned forward from the back seat and clicked her handbag open. 'We can't meet this afternoon, Mussa. I'm staying at home.'

He nodded.

She delved into the white patent bag on her lap. 'I have to. I'm sorry, Mussa. Here, a gift for you.' She handed him a tiny package. He opened the card first and her photograph fell out. She'd inscribed it on the back: 'Darling Moose, wishing you the happiest seasonal greetings, my fondest love X.'

'Mrs Lar, I like that new name. Thank you.'

'Well, open the parcel Moose, go on.'

A small gift box from Ranti de Silva & Sons was inside the outer wrapping. It sprang open to reveal a gold charm. 'What is this, Mrs Lar?'

'It's you. Well, actually it's a reindeer. It was the nearest thing I could find to a moose. No one will know the difference, Mussa. I have one myself, see?' A gold bracelet rubbed against her new watch. There were several charms on it including the antlered beast. 'You could attach it to a key-ring or something. Don't look depressed, Moose. I can't help this afternoon. I have to be with my husband. It's not as if Christmas is your thing anyway. Can you drive me back now? I mustn't be late.'

She felt guilty, accountable to both her lover and her husband; Mussa would have to give way.


## Christmas Now


'Happy Christmas, darling. I've missed you these last few days.'

'Happy Christmas, Lar. It's great to be back. Here, I've a little something for you.'

'How kind, you shouldn't have.'

They immediately opened the bottle, overwhelming the Glenmorangie with ice.

'How was your trip, Francesca?'

'Fantastic, just wonderful. I took my friend Abdul, we had a great time. I think I've fallen in love.'

'Darling . . .'

'I know, I know, but I think I have. It was one hell of an experience for him too. He'd never flown before and didn't look out of the window until we'd been up for thirty minutes. He loved it in the end.'

'And?'

'And what, Lar?'

'Is he in love with you?'

'I think he might be, but he's impossible to read.'

Francesca's phone beeped. She'd got a message from Abdul: '**me think of u u call my after**.'

Carla didn't comment on the noise, but Francesca sensed it annoyed her. The two women walked to a small table laid with linen, heavy cutlery and crystal.

'Carla, this is superb. I'd forgotten how good a table can look.'

'Red or white?'

They opted for a bottle of Nuits St Georges.

'Have you brought a cellar with you?'

'It's my little extravagance, darling. I can't be without a good bottle for too long.'

The phone beeped again: '**why not u call**.'

Francesca was embarrassed by the disturbance and switched it off.

Ali carried in the starter, a carpaccio of tuna.

'You've not said anything about Mussa, Carla.'

Carla nibbled at the fish, but left the majority on her plate – it was how she ate all her food. 'He's fine, Francesca . . . This silly old fool is still in love. Can you imagine it? Cupid's arrow has struck again. It seems Eros has been quite busy of late.' She pushed at the fish with her fork, making ripples in the flesh. 'But it's secret, darling, isn't that rum? My affair is still hidden away. You're still the only person who knows.'

'So what happens next, Lar?'

'That could well be the question you ask yourself too. Nothing can be rushed at my age. Strange, isn't it? Those who really do need to be quick can't be, and those with all the time in the world run helter-skelter into everything. I think that's what I miss most about youth. I wish I could fire along like you instead of creeping.'

They lit cigarettes as Ali cleared the first-course plates; Francesca had eaten all of hers.

'Isn't it wonderful that you feel like this? I hope Abdul and I will still be as smitten when we're your age.'

Carla was preoccupied. 'What I really miss is time. I know I don't have much any more. It's running out on me, darling. I'm scared of dying.'

'Carla, don't be silly. You're in the rudest good health of anyone I know. I'd say talk of popping your clogs is a bit premature.'

'You don't understand. I don't *want* to die. I can't bear the idea of leaving everyone behind. I love life far too much. It's unreal sitting on the edge. I know it will happen, but I'm not ready for it. I can't bear the finality. I'm foolish, I know, but it scares me. Nothing prepares you for it.'

There wasn't anything the younger woman could say.

'I don't want to be *you*, darling, if that's what you're thinking. I want to be me at your age. I want to have another go, try to right some of my wrongs.' Carla laughed at her whimsy; it wasn't bitterness so much as inevitability that amused her.

Francesca remained silent. A spindle of her subconscious hankered after Carla's life for herself.

'This is too depressing. The last thing you want to hear is an old woman bleating on about death. This is Christmas Day, for goodness' sakes. I *am* silly – I'm sorry for this nonsense.'

Francesca was pleased with her friend's honesty – it brought them closer to each other. 'Carla, it isn't depressing, really. I have no idea what it's like, but don't torment yourself with regret.'

'I said enough of talk like that, darling. I'd intended to have a jolly good time with the guinea-fowl, wine and, most of all, you. I don't want to drone. But I do want to hear about your romance.'

After dinner Francesca got a cab and headed home. She switched on her phone, ready to call Abdul. It made a succession of bleeps: he'd sent her a dozen text messages. She loved that. She called him straight back.

TO: Fran
CC:
Subject: WHAT ARE YOU LIKE?????

FRANCESCA! FRANCESCA! FRANCESCA! wot in gods name R u thinking of? Its all v well nipping orf 2 the colonies 4 a few months but who sed anything about falling in love?????????? u'r sposed 2 b recovering from a failed romance not courting a new 1! what R u girlies like? i guess itll b a visa 4 the UK next . . . dont tell me u havent already thought about it – i know u 222222 well. hed bedda b worth it. u might like 2 know that the animal life in this part of the world is pretty wild 2 . . . yep ive been laid but unlike u mine wos just a shag & not a very good 1 @ that. @ least i know i can still do it.

crimbo wiv the parents . . . again. they keep on about

how it mite b their last. FOR FFFFFFFFUCKS SAKE ...
friggggggggggggggging pensioners. cant say im envious of
u lording it up wiv lady thing of twing ... cant understand
y u'r not in the sack with the sexy abdul ... darlin u gotta
go 4 it. have a fab time wotever u do. happy new year fran
& i miss u 2
love love love love love love love love love love love love
love love love love love love love love love davey.

# CHAPTER 6: NEW YEAR

## This is God

The food stalls in Forodhani Gardens were closed. No food, no trestles, not many people. Only the cigarette booth remained open.

'Where is everyone, Abdul?'

'A problem with sickness.'

'What?' Francesca tried to imagine a disease that could affect a food market. She supposed it might be salmonella.

'What problem?'

'Government they shut Forodhani and places where people go to meet because of disease.'

'Yes, Abdul, but what disease?'

'*Ki pindu pindu.* How you call it? Cholera.'

'But that's terrible! Is it here?'

'Is come, yes.'

The spectre of pestilence was a bitter dream. This was Zanzibar, an island of holidays and high-days; naïvely, the worst disease she had thought she might catch in the tropics was malaria.

'So what do we do about it, Abdul?'

'A meaning?'

'How should we protect ourselves?'

'Is nothing for us. This is God, Francesca.'

'It might well be God, but it is also you and me.'

'I know. But is God's way.'

They walked through the road tunnel that swept under an impressive building by the side of the fort. Francesca had written to David in one of her emails that it would make a wonderful house. When she discovered it was an orphanage and a home for the blind she had gone off the idea.

'Is there any precaution I should take, Abdul?'

He showed little interest in her and blew silently into the palms of his hands.

'What is it with you, Abdul? Why don't you care?'

'Is what I tell you.'

'Jesus, Abdul, cut the God stuff. There must be drugs I can take. Should I be on antibiotics?'

'Francesca, you don't listen me. Me, I not afraid of disease, of what God he does is right. This disease is right that we should suffer.'

'Cholera, Abdul, is the result of poor sanitation and polluted water. You're not telling me God is a plumber in his spare time?'

Was he smiling or frowning? His protean expressions invisibly returned. 'You don't know about such thing, Francesca. You must not speak.'

'Don't tell me whether I can or cannot speak. That really pisses me off.' Her voice rose and she tried to calm down a little by taking a measured breath. 'All I was trying to say is that the spread of cholera in this instance is more likely to be man's work rather than God's.'

There was something brutal in his eyes. She'd not seen anything like it in anyone before. He made her nervous.

'What you know about God? I tell you God is here for us. He save the people and take to heaven. You have no God in your head.'

'Abdul, I don't need the Sunday-school lecture, thank you. You're not listening to me. At this moment I'm not remotely interested in your or anyone else's God. All I want to do is make sure I'm safe from sickness. Is that difficult to understand?'

The boy at the Internet café waved to Francesca, a cheery, nothing's-wrong-with-the-day gesture.

'This, this is all God, Francesca. He look after us.' Abdul pointed around them and jabbed at the air.

'And, Abdul, this is where we part company. I've had enough of this for now. I'll call you later.'

She left him on the street and entered the café.

TO: Daveyboy
CC:
Subject: bad news

Daveyboy, hope the yuletide thing wasnt too dire. Bad news this end . . . Seems cholera has broken out. It makes me kinda nervous – much more so than the Taliban babes flaunting their t-shirts. Abdul is pissing me off with his god-slot crap. I mean how can anyone believe that its god who has done this – hasnt he ever heard of sanitation? Its like living in the middle fucking ages. Everything thats bad or anything thats good is because of Allah or the Almighty. Theres a desperate kind of irresponsibility here – i mean wots so bloody wrong with at least trying to help yourself? Its like its gods sole frigging duty to nursemaid everyone . . . Im beginning to think that Zanzibar is rooted in fatalism. Theres a resignation in people that i have never

seen before, a belief in an omnipresent and all-powerful deity that overrides rationality. And its bloody infuriating, its like they are denying their own freedom. Sorry about the whinge – maybe its island fever
xxxxxxxxfranxxxxxxxxx

Francesca decided her first stop should be the chemist near the market: the pharmacist would be able to direct her to a doctor. She was sent to a surgery on Vuga Road. A small, flower-filled garden surrounded the low white building. She could see it was too late, that it had already closed for the day. At the far side of the garden a man sat beneath a tree, peering into the fast-falling night. Francesca walked up to him.

'You want help, madam?'

'What time does the surgery open tomorrow?'

'You can come at eight.'

'Thank you.'

Francesca hesitated, hoping she might see someone still working inside.

'Is it emergency, madam?'

'I hoped to catch someone tonight. There's nowhere else I can go to, is there?'

'Maybe a hospital can help. There's one near here.'

'I don't think so. I'll come back in the morning. Thank you, *asante sana*.'

Her phone beeped.

'**wy you bad to me**.'

Abdul could wait: she didn't want to see him right now. She put the mobile back into her pocket and walked towards the road. The man pushed the gate open for her and her phone beeped again.

'**i no undrstod your**.'

She switched it off.

154

'Are you tourist, madam? You can ask at your hotel for a doctor.'

'It's OK, I'll come back.'

The man was of Indian origin. His tiny, delicate features were eroded like his clothes. There was something feminine about him – it was the way he stood, it was in his movement. A battered charisma floated beneath his scrappy exterior. He captivated her.

'Do you work here?'

'Yes, madam, I'm the guard.'

It seemed unlikely: how could such a refined man have such a masculine occupation? She didn't believe him.

'Yes, I have been the guard here for many years. This was once my father's surgery.'

'It was?'

'Oh, yes, but he's been dead a very long time now, madam.'

'I'm sorry, and now you look after his old business?' Francesca couldn't connect today's rags with yesterday's middle-class pedigree.

'It's not his business any more. None of this. It was all lost when he died. It's ironic that I'm here to look after his ghost, don't you think? I've become his keeper.'

They sat together on the low wall that surrounded the clinic. A large bough of bougainvillaea crowned them.

'My name's Francesca.'

'A pleasure to meet you, Francesca. I am Ramil.'

'Did you live here as a little boy?'

'Oh, yes, we had that side of the building and my father's clinic was here at the front.' Ramil gazed at the past. 'My mother spent all her time in the fabric shops. She drove Papa crazy. Always something new in the house.' He smiled as he painted his picture, a small comfort for what had been. 'It was very different then, madam.'

'My name's Francesca, Ramil.'

'Francesca, yes. It was all different. A pity I couldn't be a child for ever. What do you think?'

He laughed at his observation.

Francesca remained expressionless. 'How did everything change?'

'I'm not really sure, it just happened, Francesca. My father got into trouble with some men. It was an accident, I'm told. I do believe that. But I was small, a little boy, and I don't remember. Some things are best forgotten, don't you think? But he was killed . . .' He trailed off.

'I'm sorry, Ramil.'

Francesca offered him a cigarette, and they both lit up.

'Maybe childhood is blessed with magic. What do you think, Francesca? Don't you think growing up and losing those years is tragic?'

'No, I don't think so.' She didn't want to pick over her own miserable infancy.

'Maybe you're right, Francesca, but I was lucky then . . .' A story of turtles and fishes and a marble pond in a glamorous bar decorated a snapshot of a long-ago world. Francesca was entranced.


## A New Flat


'Moose, we have to be careful. Mr Jackson knows something is going on.'

Mussa looked alarmed.

'Not between us. He accused me of seeing someone else. I've told him it's over and he believes me.'

'So what do we do, Mrs Lar?'

'We need to be extremely discreet. I've found a flat to rent. We'll meet there in future.'

Mussa was unconvinced by their folly. Maybe he'd been right: perhaps she was playing with him – pulling him into a trap.

'I'd no idea how difficult it is to find a place. Zanzibar is full up. But I found a flat off Main Road. I've told Mr Jackson that I'm using it as an office.'

'That's impossible, Mrs Lar. It's too close to your home.'

'It was the only one I could get, Moose. You mustn't worry.'

Carla gave him the address: it was near the junction of where Main Road dissected Portuguese Street. 'I will be there this afternoon. I'm going to tell John's office I've sent you on an errand. Meet me there later.' She got out of the car with a bagful of items for the new flat. 'Moose, we must never, ever be seen entering the building at the same time. Please be careful.'

Mussa drove back to the Jackson residence. He sensed his passion might be informed by powerful magic. It was eating him. Maybe he should break the workings of the spell by not showing up.

The apartment was large – two double bedrooms, a big living room and a rooftop terrace; Carla would use the interior, the tearoom was too public. She furnished it simply with unwanted pieces from her home; there was a Zanzibari bed in the larger of the two bedrooms.

'What do you need a bed for, Lar? I thought it was an office.'

'Johnno, an afternoon nap is the same in an office as it is anywhere else. I'd have thought if anyone could testify to that it would be you.'

'I was only asking.'

The anticipation of Mussa's first visit was too much. Carla busied herself with hanging curtains, making the bed, anything to provide a distraction. He knocked. She opened the door as if admitting a fugitive. He slid in, unable to rid himself of the witchcraft.

TO: Daveyboy
CC:
Subject: Stone Town News

Davey darling – sorry if i sounded like a depressive in my last despatch – i spose i was feeling a bit low. Anyways . . . have now patched things up wiv Abdul but not until he sent me 30 text messages THIRTY I ASK YOU & all in the space of 3 hours . . . Nothing like being popular what? He came over last night & screwed me rotten – sorry that was coarse but i knew you wanted to know. He stayed over . . . now thats a FIRST! Then we woke up to another terrible row . . . Abdul suddenly freaked out about the money i spent when we went away. He kept saying it was his and that i have taken it from him. He got so angry ranting about how i had spent HIS money – that it took two hours for me to persuade him that wot i spent was my business. I still don't think he gets it – i know he still thinks it was rightfully his.

The cholera epidemic is a bore – the discos (yep there are 2 of them! this place doesnt really do disco if truth be known) are closed by the cops @ the mo to try & help contain the outbreak. Theyd send folks home if they could. Patchy reports about how bad it is – some say its nothing to worry about but i heard yesterday that 60 are already dead. Its worst in the bush . . . though it is creeping into town. Mustnt shake hands wiv folk – but MUST wash veggys and cook everything 2 a crisp. Fuck . . . the last thing i want is to shit myself to death.

Its weird but the longer im here the LESS i see of people . . . Ive noticed that just about everyone is missing something – a toe – a leg – an arm – their teeth – a finger – their sight – an ear. Theyre like ancient living sculpture – everyone has had a bit knocked off . . .

What are you doing for new year? Provided i havent caught the plague im thinking of having a dinner @ my place . . . Praps ill invite the dowager.
Keep the e-sss comin
xxxxxxxxxxxxxxxxxxxxxxfranxxxxxxxxxxxxxxxxxxxxxxxxxx
PS. i feel like a bride when i go to bed, not cos of Abdul but cos of the mozzie nets. Ive got a huge one that looks like a wedding dress & takes up half the room.


## Juju


Reluctantly Francesca gave up on the idea of vaccination as a way of protecting herself against cholera. Carla had reassured and calmed her down, explaining that she'd be injected with the very thing she was trying to avoid and that the jab wasn't recommended. It was pointless overreacting: all she needed was to be vigilant and scrupulous in her cleanliness. The unknown, that's all, had freaked her out. Abdul said the first case had been reported in the Mombassa district; his mother had known the dead woman.

'I'm sorry, Abdul. Maybe it's best if you stay with me a while. Could you do that?'

'I not know.'

Her invitation was not wholly altruistic: this was an opportunity to get closer to her lover.

'You'd be safer here. Stay for a few days till it blows over. Or at least think about it. Do you fancy a drink?'

Large whiskies were poured and they climbed the steep stairs to the tearoom. The sun blazed but the shaded terrace was cool. Francesca brought the CD-player up with them; Damon Albarn did his gorillary thing.

'There have been people here, Francesca. Bad people.'

'What do you mean, Abdul?'

'Very bad man has been here to hurt you.'

'You're not still bleating on about that Pompom chap, are you? No buggeries have taken place up here, I can assure you.'

Abdul stood, scrutinising a bench. 'It here is proof, Francesca. Is not Popo Bawa, but someone put curse on you.'

'For Christ's sake, Abdul, what is it?' Francesca wandered over to inspect the proof. The decapitated head of a chicken, its eyes tightly closed as if asleep, lay on a cushion. 'Oh, yuk. Throw it away, chuck it over there.'

He didn't move, his expression blacker than usual.

'Well, if you won't, I will. Get out my way.'

She picked up the cushion and lobbed the bodyless fowl over the edge. It clunked down the corrugated iron and whizzed off the edge to the courtyard below.

'I tell you, man wants to put curse.'

'Abdul, it's not a man, it's a feathered rat who's done this. It's that vile crow. It constantly brings crap up here. The chicken head is his filthy lunch.'

He considered the birds, both dead and alive. 'I think it bad man. You should be careful.'

160

'Relax, Abdul, it's not black magic. Come here and sit down, you loon.'

The superstitious one anxiously gulped from his drink, and the non-believer happily slurped at hers. Abdul was fretting, he seemed convinced that someone had cursed Francesca. Maybe a *djinn* had taken the shape of a crow and come here to work his bad magic.

He looked twitchy; he was upset.

'Sometime *shetani* they come to me and speak,' he said quietly, without looking at her. Francesca put her arm round him. 'The spirit they come in night. He grey and with fur and he climbs on my back . . .'

She felt privileged: she was being let into the secrecy of the place.

'And sometime they say too much and they hurt me.'

The intimacy of the revelation was as confidential as her admission of childlessness – except that his was part of the culture, geography, history of Zanzibar. The mystery of *juju* and local mythology was something she knew little of, but here was a man telling her about magic for real. His story entranced her.

'Is because of my mama I have this. She give it to me.'

Abdul believed his mother had made a pact with the spirit world to help her conceive. The deal was that she could have a child, but the offspring, Abdul, would belong to them. That is why he was visited during the night. He showed her a skinny belt made of bound cloth containing special verses and shells: it helped to protect him. 'They speak to me, Francesca, and I can't get them quiet sometime. It a pain when they shout loud. And sometime he so heavy I can't breathe in my sleep. Do you have *shetani*? In London?'

'No, Abdul – at least, not quite like that. There are ghosts – well, some people believe there are.'

'Spirit is important here. You have respect to them.'

Her sensitive man reeled her in with his account of the occult. She believed him implicitly.

'It's New Year's Eve tomorrow night. I think I'll have a dinner party, Abdul.'

He was still obsessing about the chicken's head and his story of the *shetani*, biting his lip and looking as if he were in prayer. He blew into his hands.

'I'm going to ask Carla and her friend Mussa for dinner. Would you like to come too?'

He awoke from the reverie and agreed cautiously.

'And think about my offer, Abdul. Stay here if it helps.'

'Francesca? Maybe you help with money.'

'How much do you need?'

'Ten thousand.'

She tried not to let the request rile her, and surrendered to his need instead of her misgivings.

## Happy New Year

Rather than driving, older and old sat in the back of a taxi.

'I'm glad you're coming with me, Moose. Don't feel nervous about meeting Francesca, she's a lovely girl.'

Mussa was uncomfortable at the prospect of dinner.

'Her flat is off Kenyatta Road. She'll be standing on the street to meet us – she doesn't know her address, I ask you.'

Carla's small-talk didn't make it any easier for Mussa.

'Lar, maybe I should go home.'

She missed a beat and felt momentarily winded. 'You called me Lar.'

He said nothing, only looking at his friend. He was nearly invisible in the dark, apart from the reflection in his spectacles.

'Mussa, is it finally OK now?' Surreptitiously she took and held Mussa's hand – she didn't want the taxi-driver to witness the moment. 'Don't worry about tonight. Francesca will be there with her friend, a young man called Abdul. I'm sure you'll get along splendidly.'

Carla's words were not a comfort: Mussa dreaded the meal. Their relationship was a secret so entrenched that the idea of coming into the open was agonising. He was afraid of forty years of suppression being lifted by two strangers. He never dined in company: how should he behave?

'Look at you, Moose. Please relax, this isn't supposed to be an ordeal. You're making me nervous too.'

The car passed the deserted Forodhani Gardens and headed through the tunnel to the bottom of Kenyatta Road.

'My God. This isn't it, is it?'

'Yes, Lar.'

'You mean Main Road is now Kenyatta?'

It was dark: the only source of light came from a small tourist gift stall. A cheery boy ragged his customers into parting company with two thousand shillings for a cheap bead necklace. He shouted after them, 'Remember me, I'm Simba, Simba the lion,' then laughed instead of roaring. Carla spotted Francesca standing in the street a little further up. The car stopped for the dowager and her escort.

'Lar,' Francesca pecked her cheek, 'and Mr Mussa. I'm very pleased to meet you.'

Mussa shook her hand.

'*Karibuni*, both of you. My flat's round the corner. I'm so dizzy, Lar, I've been here two months and I still don't know my door number. I hope you think my cooking's better than my homing skills.'

The trio entered an alleyway. Carla walked close to Mussa; they didn't touch.

'It's right here, but it's difficult to describe how to get to.'

They walked through the blue gates into the courtyard.

'Mind the step now. I hope you've both got stamina because we've got the stairs to get up.'

At the bottom of the flight Carla took hold of Mussa's hand.

'Come on, folks, this is the hard bit, but it's worth it. I've got wine chilling and the whisky's waiting. Abdul's upstairs. He's really looking forward to meeting you both.'

'Are you on the top floor, Francesca?'

'Yep, all the way, Lar.'

The older couple remained on the first step.

'Francesca, I had an office here. It must be the same flat.'

'You're kidding me, Carla, you had my place! Well, come on, hurry up, I can't wait to hear what it was like then.'

# New Year 1963

'Lar, darling, aren't you ready yet?'

'Just one tick, Johnno. I'm trying to fix this necklace. Give me a hand, will you? I can't get the bloody clasp done up.'

Carla sat in front of a large dressing-table; a whisky and soda fizzed to one side and a Sobranie burned in an ashtray on the other. 'Thanks. A quick dab of perfume and I'm done.' She applied the Chanel No. 5 devoutly.

'It looks like you're crossing yourself when you put your smellies on, Lar.'

She scented her wrists too: she didn't normally do that.

'Can't you hurry, Lar? The driver's waiting. We're already late.'

Instead of the Morris, Mussa stood by a ridiculously glamorous convertible. It was a big American auto, wholly unsuitable for use on the island's tracks. It only ever made the trip between Shangani and the Sultan's palace. John had bought it from a friend who needed the money; he hated the vehicle, only suffering it as an act of charity. It was more suited to the white mink of a Hollywood film première than the cream linen suits at a New Year's Eve party in Zanzibar.

Carla sat on the back seat with her husband; the roof was down and she felt the childish urge to wave at everyone they passed in the street. It was nearly uncontrollable.

John disturbed her juvenile fantasy. 'If the Darajani fellow is there I'd be grateful if you gave him a wide berth, Carla. I don't want a scene tonight.'

'I've told you a hundred times already, John, that is history. Can we please have done with the subject?'

She knew Mussa had heard the exchange: even the back of his head looked tense.

New Year at the palace was as big as Eid. The Sultan threw lavish parties. Braziers burned fiercely at the entrance, and a guard of honour – decorated with feathered turbans, ceremonial daggers and straps – stood by the gates. A brightly coloured Persian carpet, scattered with the ubiquitous rose petals, stretched from the door to the street. Carla thought they'd been dipped in something: there was a distinct whiff of Worth rather than roses hanging in the air.

'Right, driver, I think pick-up at one should do the trick. There's a good fellow. Come on, Lar, you're pouting. Smile, please. We're supposed to be enjoying ourselves.'

The palace hallway was crowded with four fat, flashy chandeliers, beneath which were gargantuan urns holding a spectacular array of imported flowers. John was momentarily seduced by an unfamiliar pink floret, and quite forgot where he was. Another display of fiefdom awaited their arrival: ten servants dressed in tatty imperial French costume stood at the foot of the stairs.

'It's not quite Versailles, is it?'

Carla's catty remark awoke him from his floral dreaming. 'Don't be snotty, Lar, it doesn't suit you. Now, come along.'

Two portraits glowered from a wall towards the impressive staircase. A diffident duke and duchess (immortalised by a cack-handed artist) were more forbidding than welcoming. The stairs led up to formal rooms on the first floor; the main party was here.

'Lar, Johnno! Good to see you both looking so well. Long time, Lar. What have you been up to?' Phillip had cornered the Jacksons. He was overbearing, a bit squiffy, an overgrown schoolboy who'd been sent to the tropics by a parent with connections. 'You've been quite the vanishing type, Lar. I haven't seen you at the Africa for ages. Gomez is here somewhere, miserable little wog. You look nice – oh, the Christmas prezzie?' Phillip focused on her necklace. 'Seems a bit much, Johnno. A diamond necklace? You're not trying to butter her up, now?'

'It's the watch, actually, Phillip. Now, before you completely hog us, my husband and I should mingle.'

Rage consumed John: he couldn't let a subordinate allude to his marital problem publicly. He hissed at his wife to lead the way. She threw back her voice, like a ventriloquist talking through a puppet: 'I bet it was that little creep who did the stirring. Am I right, John?'

He didn't reply. His attempt at affability was betrayed by a hideous smile.

The Sultan sat at the far end of the room. The managing director of Imperial & Eastern and his wife paid their respects. 'Your Highness, a super do, really jolly good indeed. Isn't it, Carla?'

'Yes, darling, a wonderful spread. So nice to see everyone here, Your Highness.'

Husband and wife were both masters of pretence. Champagne was poured for the guests in crystal flutes; the Sultan and his entourage sipped mint tea. Servants slid round the room dispensing quantities of liquor and fiddly canapés. Carla's shoes were nipping at her heels.

The German chap made his way over to the Jacksons. 'We haven't seen much of you at Darajani, Mrs Jackson. Have you been away?' His question was pointed and delivered with the smug satisfaction of a man indulging in a discreet revenge. The rumour of Carla's affair had permeated the entire ex-pat community, the Consul had made sure of that. The Sultan was probably well versed in the fiction too. Carla laughed.

'For God's sake, Lar, what is it now?'

Her laugh got louder, and John more irritable.

'Can you please pipe down, Lar? I don't see what's so hilarious.'

Carla left John and the German and went to a private chamber at the back of the building, where the Sultana held court. It was an exotic room, full of women – Carla was the only ex-pat. She didn't like the Sultana, a grand, sour, bloated woman who gorged herself on pomegranate seeds and sweetmeats. Carla did the formalities: it was the only way of controlling her mettlesome urge to laugh.

She returned, chastened, to John, dignitaries, businessmen and bores.

At midnight rockets blasted and a scatty display of Catherine wheels and roman candles lit the gardens. It was the only bearable moment in the whole tedious evening.

'I think that might be our cue. Can't we go now, John?'

'It wouldn't look good, Lar.'

'I don't think I can stand another minute – my face is exhausted from smiling. Why don't I slip away? I'll see you at the house later.'

John could see the Darajani chap deep in conversation with the German. He was reassured that they both looked set to stay. 'Go on, then. I'll be another hour. Will you be up when I get back?'

'Yes, darling. We'll see 'sixty-four in together later.'

The House of Wonder was decorated with an endless supply of fairy-lights, which gave Harrods a run for its money. She crossed the brightly lit road and found the convertible parked by the Forodhani Gardens.

'Moose, let's leave quickly.'

'Where is Mr Jackson?'

'Don't worry about him. He's staying at the palace. We've got half an hour.'

Mussa parked the car at the main house in an attempt to camouflage the tryst. Carla went to the new flat first, leaving her shoes in the back of the car and walking through the streets and up the stairs in her stockinged feet. Mussa arrived a few minutes later, unable to resist the intensity of the magic or his need to see her. They went to bed and finally consummated their affair.

Carla arrived home minutes before John. She sat in the library slugging at a whisky.

'Do you have one for me, Lar?'

She poured him a drink, trembling slightly as she handed it over.

'Are you OK, Lar?'

'Mmm?'

'I said, are you OK?'

'Yes, fine, darling. Perhaps a little tired. Was it fun in the end?' It had been a rhetorical question, and she found it difficult to concentrate on his answer.

'There was talk of a local problem. Some chap said he thought trouble was brewing.'

'Like what?'

'I don't know. It'll blow over, these things normally do. Something to do with the East Germans or the Chinese.'

He sat close to her; his presence made her claustrophobic. He patted her knee; it made her feel like a pet. She knew what he was thinking. They had made love in the past but it was always an unmitigated failure, crowned with remorse. John felt obliged to honour all of their wedding vows; she did not. He also felt the need for children: they were a necessity, a prerequisite of normality, an essential addition to their lives. He clung to the desperate notion that the currency of family would imbue him with respectability. Progeny would ensure public acceptance of a man with a secret.

'Time for bed, old girl. Will you hop in with me tonight?'

She froze.

'Come on, Lar.'

The idea repelled her.

'I can't, John, I'm sorry. Maybe I'm sickening for something. Not tonight.'

They went to their separate bedrooms. John took a book with him.

# New Year Now

'Carla, Mussa, this is Abdul.'

Abdul greeted them like an *escari*, a night-watchman. He was stiff with procedure, awkwardly shaking hands with the old couple. Mussa was even more ceremonious.

'Let me get you a drink, Lar. What would you like, Mussa? I hope you don't mind the music.'

The hypnotic rhythm of a chill-out groove swam throughout the room.

'Do you have something a bit jazzier, Francesca? Maybe Sinatra? I don't suppose you listen to that type of thing normally.'

'It's in there somewhere. Abdul, can you see to that? Look in the CDs. I'll pour the whiskies, and juice for you, Mussa.'

Older and old stood in the living room looking around as Francesca attempted anxiously to organise her guests.

'Francesca darling, the place hasn't changed a jot. It's exactly the same. Oh, the stairs to the terrace – I'd quite forgotten them. They're a bugger, if I remember rightly.'

'You're right, Lar. Coming down is hardest, especially if I've had a drink. Shall we take these up?'

The older couple went first, sedate, yet holding firmly to the banister. They crouched on the small landing before climbing to the deck above. Francesca and Abdul stomped up behind.

'What a view, Francesca. I'd forgotten how lovely it is. Look, Mussa, that's my old house over there.'

The Serena was visible over the rooftops. He looked hard into the night, seeing more than a converted house or a swish hotel. He could feel the town's breath. The draught distracted him from his thoughts.

'How long were you here, Carla?'

'Not long at all. I took a lease on the place and next thing I was off because of the uprising.'

Francesca was frustrated. She wanted to hear a Shangani story. Subconsciously she wanted to mirror her friend, akin to Carla wanting to be young again like Francesca. But learning now of Carla's link with the apartment made that fantasy deliberate. Jealousy of her older friend's life choked her: Francesca wanted to be Carla.

The older woman sensed disappointment. 'It was a very special place, Francesca. This little flat saw so much in such a little time.'

'Why did you need it when you had the other house?'

Carla looked to Mussa: he didn't notice, he was still reading history. 'I needed a separate office. The main house was big, but it was filled with people, servants. I needed a spot where I could work without disturbance.'

Abdul performed an autopsy on the conversation, dissecting each word, trying to unravel the mystery behind the old *mazungo* woman and her companion. He couldn't fathom any significance.

Francesca thought it time for dinner. 'OK, everyone, I'm starving. Let's go down and eat.'

The table was laid with tinny cutlery bought from the market; it was impossible to get good quality stuff. Francesca hated the cheap glasses too: they had a tacky flower motif printed around the edge. None of it was as stylish as the display she'd been treated to at Christmas. Her food was good, though, bouillabaisse followed by a shellfish thermidor. The older couple ate a tiny amount; she and Abdul wolfed the meal down.

'Did you know this flat too, Mussa?' She was eager to include her other guest as he'd not spoken. Mussa looked up from the food and concentrated on Carla, saying nothing. Carla stroked his knee under the table: it was a secret reassurance, a prompt.

'Yes, I knew this house. I came here with Mrs Lar.'

He didn't elaborate. The two women had no idea that he was paralysed by the threat of disclosure in front of the other man, a local, a Zanzibari.

Francesca and Abdul cleared the table. Carla wanted to revisit a previous scene. 'Would you mind terribly if we had a peek round, Francesca, for old time's sake?'

'Not at all, go ahead. We'll be a few minutes with the washing-up.'

Carla and Mussa walked into the dimly lit hallway to the larger of the two bedrooms. The Zanzibari bed was gone, and so were the drapes, but the sense of the place was intact. They stood at the foot of Francesca's bed in semi-darkness. Mussa touched Carla's back. 'I was happy then,' he whispered.

'Yes, me too, Moose. Happier than I've ever been. I shouldn't have left, should I?'

'No . . . Never.' He pulled Carla towards him. The tiny shadow of a movement echoed a passion of four decades earlier.

'All that time ago, you said it would be terrible not to have a secret, so you gave me a hidden beach and said it would be our first. You needn't have. There was already the beginnings of one I couldn't tell you about . . . Mrs . . . Lar.'

At that moment she understood Mussa was still in love with her. Nothing and everything was changed.

\* \* \*

'Hey, folks, I've got something special. I saved it from my duty-free.' Francesca brandished a bottle of champagne.

'Is it time for the countdown yet? Abdul, you're the man with the watch. How long have we got?'

'Is near six.'

'You mean twelve, you silly sod. Here, let me see, blimey! Five, four, three, two, one . . .'

The champagne cork flew, and the laboriousness of earlier vanished with the dying year. Mussa, Abdul and Carla were relieved of something old: the New Year's effervescence rinsed away their trouble.

'Cheers, everyone.' Francesca kissed Abdul; he spilt his drink in the middle of the embrace. Carla and Mussa appeared to toast their hosts with bubbly and soda, but their drink wasn't to the young couple: it was to themselves.

'Francesca darling, we really should be getting home now. Thank you, and thank you, Abdul. It was a lovely meal. Are you ready, Mussa?' Carla was already ushering him towards the door.

'It was our pleasure having you both, wasn't it, Abdul? Happy New Year again. Let's see you to a cab.'

The street was littered with people looking for a party, but there was none. A worried town council had banned large groups from gathering in a bid to fight the cholera epidemic, although it didn't dampen optimistic carousing.

A small pale man stood swaying on the street corner. He strained to stay steady and conceal his drunkenness, but gave himself away with a mumbled singsong of incoherent prayers. As the small dinner party approached he stared at them blindly, refocusing like a camera zoom. He blinked, trying to shake out his inebriation.

'*Habari.*'

Francesca recognised him. '*Nzuri*, Ramil. Happy New Year.'

He shook her hand and held on for too long; perhaps it helped steady him. He stared at his feet.

'Ramil, don't you think you should go home? I think the beer's got the better of you.'

Ramil shook his head as if to say no, but stumbled off up the road. He was headed in the right direction. Carla didn't take any notice; he was just another drunk. She didn't realise her little spy with a bleeding finger had grown up to be a sad guardian of another time. Cha Cha Cab Number Seven took his passengers to their homes.

Francesca and Abdul returned to the flat. She thought about clearing away the empty bottles and glasses, but changed her mind. 'C'mon, Abdul, I can think of something else we should be doing.' She led him to the bedroom and they both fell on to the bed.

'Francesca, I love you.'

His words threw and delighted her. 'And . . . I love you . . . too.' That phrase had been mentally rehearsed countless times, but now she came to say it she faltered. It didn't really matter that she'd fluffed her big line. She'd said it – *he*'d said it. 'I love you.'

He pulled her down on top of him, holding her tightly. 'I want nature, Francesca. It better like that.'

They had rough, savage, violent sex. It was a painful and passionate result of drunkenness and the sudden euphoria she experienced at his affection. He penetrated her without a condom. She didn't care: unconsciously they had set about re-enacting an event that had occurred in the same room nearly forty years before. But there was a difference: in 1964 there had been tenderness.

\*      \*      \*

TO: Fran
CC:
Subject: I'm worried about you

happy new year franny baby – how woz yaws????? but
more 2 the point wots happenin about cholera. r u sure u
should b there? am vvvvvv worried about u. y not bugger
orf 2 the mainland . . . anything 2 get away from the
disease. let me know thats wot uve done . . . PLEASE!!!!!!!!!
& wot of abdul??? i mean how weird is texting u like
that. is the boy obsessive????? y doesnt he use the fucking
phone like an adult – have u told him only 12 year olds
send endless fricking messages?????? if i were u id let
him coooooooooool orf – there must b another shag in
town! u mist a blinding nite in blighty. vvv much coke
& xtra large hangover 2day. cant stay in front of screen
any longer . . . have 2 get hair of dog . . . am gagging 4 a
bloody mary.
love love love love love davey
ps ive seen that fella again

Francesca felt rough too. In retrospect, she realised she had
done the majority of the drinking last night. Carla had
tempered her consumption because of Mussa, and Abdul
never drank much. She felt sick. The email didn't make
her feel any better. David's concern was sweet, but she
wasn't about to run away from Zanzibar or dump Abdul
for another model – that was more David's style. She'd
fallen in love, not just with a man and his life but with the
place. Zanzibar had captivated her with its magic; she was
intoxicated by the island and it was only now that David
had questioned her presence there that she understood this.
Zanzibar was inside her. But something else gnawed at her

too. Unprotected sex. She wouldn't tell David about that. He'd kill her. She could have kicked herself. Why had she done it?

TO: Daveyboy
CC:
Subject: Relax baby, I'm fine

Davey boy – i have only just got my act together – i had stinky nite too. Im as hungover as ive ever been. Dont worry about cholera . . . im being vv good about keeping everything clean. Have the man staying with @ the mo. Maybe i painted too bleak a picture because hes not that much of a nutter! No drugs this end – dont want wots available – mainly scag & crack. Not your cuppa either . . . i know!

The best thing ever this morning . . . a STRAIGHT rainbow! Have u ever seen such a thing? It just hung in a long line in the clouds. Helped lift the nausea momentarily. I will think of u when i go home to puke . . . like rite now!

xxxxxxxxxxfranxxxxxxxxxx

Abdul was still lying in bed. He had agreed to stay with Francesca for a few days until the cholera epidemic died down. The irony of this was that she suddenly felt trapped: the idea of him staying was better than the reality. She was being a contrary, hung-over bitch, she knew it.

The cleaner thumped at the door.

'Fatima, Happy New Year! I not need you today. Don't worry about the washing. You come tomorrow? *Kwaheri*.'

Francesca couldn't kick the clunky pronunciation. She politely shooed Fatima away, to ensure Abdul remained hidden in bed. She wanted her private life to stay that way.

## Full Circle

'Mussa, I hope the New Year dinner wasn't too much for you.'

'No, Lar, it was very enjoyable.'

He was lying. They sat on the porch, familiar, intimate, reunited. The fear of what she might find on her return had been exorcised. Mussa was here and he felt the same as she did. Their affair was still effectual, but now they'd made it complete. The circle was full, the magic of the islands ensured that they were both there to close it. The right decision had been made: it hadn't been the idle ramblings of an old woman desperate to recapture a dangerous past after all.

'Are you OK, Moose?'

'I'm old. There's nothing wrong with me except old age.'

Carla wasn't sure. 'A rest would do you good, Moose. Why don't you use my room?'

He would sleep on her bed, a concept that had once been impossible. The significance of it now eluded them both. He lay on the sheets and drifted. Carla came up to see him; he was sound asleep. She undid her dress and climbed carefully in beside him, anxious that he might wake. She hugged herself into his back and felt his every breath.

Mussa awoke in the early evening – he'd slept all afternoon – and was surprised to find her next to him; he was even more so to see she was wearing her petticoat.

'Moose, you're awake? I thought I'd lost you . . .' She got

off the bed. 'I've been thinking . . .' Unusually, she grasped for the right thing to say. 'Why don't you stay here, with me? Here, in this house, just the two of us. I want you to.' Desperation clouded her words.

'That's impossible. It will make a terrible scandal, Lar.'

'And why should we care about that, Moose? Let people think what they want.' She had reassured herself with the flightiness of her answer. 'We're old enough to be the grandparents of scandal. Please, stay with me.'

The old man hesitated. 'What good would it possibly do? We'll get hurt again, and then you'll leave me.'

Carla couldn't easily reply. His life was in Zanzibar and hers elsewhere. 'Mussa, please don't look for problems, not now. I feel deep in my heart we'll be fine, believe me.' She had skirted the issue, she knew it, but she didn't want to destroy the happiness that was gradually returning. 'I promise you, Moose, it won't be a repeat of then. It could never be like that. Stay. Stay here with me.'

He took her hand. She had somehow managed to recapture the emotions of a young woman, simultaneously corrupting him with her enthusiasm. He wanted to make love to her. 'How can we make this possible, Lar? Do you have the magic for that? I know I don't.'

She wouldn't lose him again. It was time to right one of her wrongs, and she prayed that her promise wouldn't prove empty.

# CHAPTER 7: A VOCATION

## Charity Work 1964

Carla's life was structured around shopping and avoiding certain other expatriates. If she wasn't doing that she had her charitable vocation to see to. Carla had spent the last two years fund-raising for a project that was attempting to eradicate malaria on the islands. The venture had done rather well: it was reckoned that within the year there would be no more mosquitoes. A strategy of spraying had been a great success: some districts on the island were already free of the insects. She drew up a plan to invite some of the people she normally sidestepped to a moneymaking garden party. She'd get Charlotte from the Anglican church to help. She was good at things like that.

The church had a poignancy of its own. It was built towards the end of the nineteenth century on top of the old slave market. It was said that the black marble disc in front of the altar marked the spot where the slave-post had stood. Carla believed it. The building generated sadness. The exterior was Moorish, but that didn't disguise its alien presence. Inside, it was more Chippenham than tropical. Brass plaques celebrated those who'd been despatched in the name of imperial antics and First World War heroics. It *was* England.

A stained-glass window, in honour of Stanley and the other explorers, had a few cracks; she thought they needed seeing to before they got worse, and for all the cleaning rosters that were drawn up, the place was defiantly dusty. Carla inspected the pews and tut-tutted as she walked down the aisle.

'Charlotte. Yoo-hoo.'

The vestry door opened and a small woman with white hair and a stiff gingham dress emerged. Charlotte blinked pop-out eyes – as if she'd been deep in hibernation rather than pottering in a church. She clutched fifty pale blue airmail envelopes.

'Charlie, be an absolute brick and give me a hand with a charity do I'm throwing soon.'

Charlotte sensed this was an order rather than a request.

'I need to invite all *your* lot. The Babbington-Clawses and the Edwardses. Are the Scott-Hardens around at the moment?'

Charlotte tried to ascertain exactly what might be involved. She was a nervous, troubled woman, a bit twitchy. Carla had never really looked at her before: the tiny, anxious movements of Charlotte's hands surprised her. 'It's nothing more than a spot of typing. Be a darling and include the details with the next parish newsletter.'

Carla could see Charlotte was about to place the current issue in the pigeonholes at the back of the church. 'But, Mrs Jackson, you've just missed it. I've got it here.' She ogled her airmail bundle.

'I'm sure you'd be able to include a little note from me too. It won't take long to add. Here it is.' Carla handed the timid woman a folded piece of paper. 'You're such a good egg, Charlie, where would we be without you? Pop over to the house an hour before kick-off on the day and we'll have a little drink together. My thank-you for your hard work.'

Carla turned to go. 'Oh, one last thing, Charlie: please tell the Bishop the Stanley window is in need of some attention. Cheerio.'

Carla didn't worship at the cathedral but John did, and his largesse gave her *carte blanche* to behave as if she were its sole benefactor. Charlotte scurried back to the vestry and began to tap at the typewriter. If she was lucky she'd get it done by five.

When Carla stepped from the Morris she noticed something curious about the town; a strange energy hung in the air that she couldn't readily identify. Before she went into the house she whispered to Mussa, 'Meet me in the flat at six thirty. Please don't be late.' Then she clicked into the hallway. A package from England was waiting for her. 'Hoorah! At long last! The gollies.'

She nipped into the kitchen to find Sima and Cook. 'I thought you might like one of these each. You can have the drummer, Cook, and Sima, I think you should have the guitarist.' She gave an enamelled pin to each of them. They were Robertson's Jam golliwog badges; each character played a musical instrument. Carla had saved up vouchers from the jars and sent them off months ago. She thought the staff would like the gifts.

'Cook, I have a do to attend with Mr Jackson tonight. Could we have a late dinner this evening? Something light, I'll only be peckish. I should think ten will do the trick.'

Cook vaguely noted her request. It was unlike Hammid to be anything other than attentive, but Carla thought he looked conspiratorial.

\* \* \*

## Charity Now

Francesca was feeling great, so much more confident now that she was in love. It was a sensation that gave her impetus, it was a cue to do something, be more outgoing, to live a bit. She met a woman who worked for VSO in the old post office. A lot of voluntary work was being carried out on the island and Francesca hoped she could attach herself to it. It wasn't as simple as she'd imagined: her skills in music publishing weren't easily placed in a developing country. Until now, her days had consisted of rootling in the market, sunning herself on the roof, reading any number of books – she'd just finished Ackroyd's fabulous London biography – and drinking. She needed something to do before tropical *ennui* set in. It was mentioned that a women's co-operative in the south of the island might do with some help. It would be her humanitarian calling.

A French woman organised the project. She was diminutive, avian and warbled Swahili with a thick Parisian accent. Her English was incomprehensible – God only knew if the local women ever understood a word she said.

'We basket-make in colours. Not weaving to traditional pattern, it's better for to have design, yes?'

Francesca nodded agreement, although she had only a vague idea as to what with.

'The people are only in development and we have house for sixty. With your *specialité* we find homes for *productivité*, no?'

'You want me to market the baskets?'

'*Exactement*, I think we sell to good stores in Londres, Paris – what if New York?'

'I certainly have friends who work in those cities. I'll see what I can do.'

The idea was grand but the reality of providing merchandise to expensive boutiques was improbable. Nevertheless, Francesca was up to the challenge. The women's group was a good thing, even if its leader was eccentrically filled with outlandish optimism.

'You come and see us work. It will good for you be.'

'Yes, of course it will.' Francesca wasn't wholly certain of how the plan would work, but she was enthusiastic – half the battle, surely? They agreed to visit the collective the next day.

Francesca hoped her example would inspire Abdul. It might provide just the motivation he needed – get him proactive, encourage him to go out and look for work. Her possessed relationship with him was fuelled entirely by sex, alcohol and her money – even she realised it needed more than that if it was to survive. She found Abdul in the flat and told him her news.

'What you do is fresh, but me I need business.'

'I know, Abdul, but it'd be easier if you actually got out and tried a bit harder, don't you see that?'

'Where to try, Francesca? All business gone with Osama.'

'There must be something you can do. Think about it.'

He flicked through the stations on the radio. One frequency sounded especially serious. As he listened he rubbed at his temples; it was the weary caress of someone suffering from a terrible migraine.

'Do you have a headache, Abdul?'

'Me? No.'

The dirge from the radio continued.

'What's that all about, Abdul?'

'It's report of the dead.'

Francesca stiffened. 'The cholera epidemic?'

'Maybe, but here we die of everything.'

'Is it a news broadcast?'

'It like telephone. If you mama she die, then radio tell everyone about her dead. It for all people.'

'But is it about cholera, Abdul?'

'Most of people die with accident like car or magic.'

She didn't want to hear about *juju*: she wanted to know that she'd be disease-free at the women's collective.

'*Hamna matatizo*. Is no problem, Francesca. Not for you.'

Reluctantly she left Abdul listening to the sombre broadcast.

TO: Daveyboy
CC:
Subject: my canonisation – I'm a saint

Daveeeeey – ive turned into the Mother Teresa of Zanzibar. Thought it best to do something saintly round here (the tan is perfect . . . but theres only so much roasting a sun-whore can do). Im now working wiv a co-op of basket-weaving women (i know that sounds way remedial, but it isn't – honest . . .) & a mad French bird whos organising it all. I think shes a sadist her handshake is lethal – my hand still v bruised after agreeing to help her – the excitement was too much – she gripped my mitt with such ferocious strength i thought my eyes would pop. Went today to see it all. Wow! All the women gather under a tree and weave the most amazing stuff – i always thought it was done by machine. It takes ages to make

one basket & they sell them for pennies. The lady of the
lamp (Frenchy – not me) wants to sell them abroad – she's
thinking dead posh shops. Any chance with some help on
this? Whaddabout you? You must have some poofy pals
who work in fancy gaffs? Will try & get j-pegs over to you
next week. Can you feel the angelic glow come off me?

Abdul is still staying with me. Great for early morning
shags but dopey by night-time. He has no stamina! Hope
practice will make perfect. Cholera not mentioned much –
i think its disappearing. Thank fuck. Cant stay on line all
day – my vocation is calling . . .

xxxxxxxxxxxxxxxxfranxxxxxxxxxxxxxxxx
PS no more news about your fling?

# Surprise

Carla got to the flat at six, having been insufferable all afternoon. She'd been snappy, unable to concentrate; the heat
was unbearably invasive. The idea of meeting up secretly
with Mussa before seeing John had been all-consuming.
She sank on to a chair upholstered in vinyl; it used to sit
in John's office. Remaining calm was impossible so she
smoked nervously, tapping her ash into a seashell. The
Rolex said six thirty. Where was the sound of his feet? He
mustn't be late. She fixed herself a warm whisky, making a
mental note that a refrigerator was needed. The squeals of
kids playing on the streets echoed up and the call to prayer
kissed the town. Light another cigarette; quarter to. Where
the hell was he? She paced the room and felt idiotically
melodramatic with a drink in one hand and a cigarette in

the other. She was the expectant father waiting for the phone call from the hospital – a boy! Still no footsteps on the stairs. She started to worry. Perhaps something had happened? The minutes passed sluggishly. She didn't want to sit in the tearoom upstairs in case she missed his tap at the door. The heat was filthy. Seven thirty. She couldn't wait much longer; she had to meet John at the Africa. At ten to eight she left, battered by a lost opportunity and the fear of something terrible.

The Africa Bar was busy. John had secretly arranged a surprise party for their wedding anniversary. Carla had purposefully forgotten the date years ago and had wondered why he'd been so adamant about her attending the Africa with him tonight. It made sense now, as did Cook's suspicious behaviour. There was a resounding chorus of 'Surprise!' as she walked in. It was more of a shock. The Scott-Hardens came up to greet her first. She had no prospect of escape – it was too public, too terrible.

'Congratulations, Lar. Here, we thought you might like this.'

A Lalique crystal crab was presented to her; she couldn't help but feel it was for years of dutiful service. The monstrous invertebrate threatened her with its pincers. The Babbington-Clawses were also homing in fast.

Carla pushed through the congratulatory crowd and found her husband. 'Johnno, what a surprise.' She couldn't think of anything else to say.

'Shall we get the party girl a drink, then?'

His jovial welcome irked her. She felt nauseous and swallowed hard. Her throat tightened. 'I can't believe you've done this. How could you, John? You know how I hate this kind of thing.' She smiled at another guest: it materialised as a pout. She suspected that John had seriously thought the party might help their stagnant union. 'Why don't you do something useful, Johnno? Perhaps you'd like to look after this.' She pushed the glass crab towards him. 'It's your matching pair.'

Carla immediately traded her glass of champagne for a whisky sour, and another, and another. Felix Gomez watched from his stool, omnipresent and sly. He knew more about Zanzibar than anyone. He was detached, sober and hungry, ready to snack on the misdemeanours of others.

A cake was brought in. 'Here's to the happy couple, everyone. Seven glorious years. Raise your glasses now!'

Cheering, laughing masks surrounded them. Theirs was merely an illusion of togetherness.

'A knife, anyone? Where's the knife?'

Phillip trotted around the room, trying fatuously to locate a blade with which to cut the cake. 'There's got to be one somewhere. Gomez? Gomez? Call this a restaurant, do you?'

'It's a bar, Phillip, I call it a bar.'

Felix's face remained static as he spoke. He left his seat and knocked the parrot stand on his way out. A minute later he'd returned with a knife.

'Who's got a camera? Come on now, own up, one of you must. Couldn't possibly miss a moment like this, now could we?'

Phillip's role as master of ceremonies was an agonising failure. Mrs Babbington-Claws came to the rescue. She spoke quietly: 'Big smiles now as you cut the cake. One, two . . .' Her voice sounded tender.

The flash popped and froze the drawn, resigned expressions of two people who'd never loved each other. The party cheered, the cake was cut.

'Speech! Speech! Chop-chop. Let's hear it from the horse's mouth, Johnno . . .'

'Thank you, Phillip, that's quite enough for now.' John used his superiority to rein in the drunken buffoon.

It was too late: calls for a speech were coming from other quarters.

'Let's be having it, Johnno! Speech!'

'Don't be bashful, come on, man!'

John stood reluctantly behind the gateau and the crystal crustacean and nodded for silence. It would be another discourse like any other. He had to get through it. 'Thank you, thank you all for coming along tonight and for being such good liars.'

'Anything for a free snifter, old boy.'

'Phillip! I said enough.' He had finally silenced the fool, although the rest of the party had perceived his aside as a jocular ribbing.

'Thank you, Felix, for hosting this evening.'

Felix bowed in acknowledgement.

Carla stood rigidly, trying to anticipate her husband's words.

'It's been a thoroughly lovely evening, so nice to be with one's friends, but best of all it's wonderful to be with my wife.' He glanced at Carla. 'We've been married now for seven lovely years, and I can tell you all that Marilyn is wrong. There's no itching in this marriage.'

The party laughed politely.

'Our relationship is based on a bedrock of trust. We're a true partnership and we couldn't be closer. And, as a token of my love, I'd like to present you, my darling, with this.'

He hoped his speech would scotch the rumour-mongers once and for all. He fished into an inside pocket and removed his cigarettes.

'Cheapskate!'

'Hang on a minute, chaps. I know the blessed thing's in here somewhere. Ah, *eureka*. Carla, darling, a token of my affection.' He handed her a small box.

The unreality of the evening was condensed into this public gesture. In Carla's eyes, it was a retirement do. Sum total of seven years with John: one glass crab and a trinket from de Silva's. She opened the box and found an eternity ring inside; the diamonds looked too big – it was ostentatious. She knew John hadn't chosen it; it wasn't his style. He'd probably called the jeweller and asked him to select something; the man knew her ring-size. 'Johnno. It's . . . very sparkly.' She left the ring in its box.

'Well, darling?' John glared at her, then at the ring.

She hesitated to put it on; it developed a greater significance.

'Does it fit, Lar?' He was losing patience: Carla shouldn't snub him, not now, not in front of everybody. 'Darling?'

The sweet, simple compliment became a threat; it was strange that such a lovely word could sound so venomous. The way he enunciated those two syllables seemed almost silent: they were a menace, like a snake. Carla shoved the ring on, John sighed audibly, the room clapped.

Mussa was waiting to pick up the revellers. It was gone two a.m. Carla climbed into the back of the flashy auto, desperate to touch the back of his neck or slap him for standing her up – a potent mix of tenderness and violence. She wanted to speak, but couldn't because John was beside her.

'Back to the house then, old boy.'

Carla scratched at the seat in frustration.

'Well, what did you think? It wasn't that bad, Lar, was it?'

She had nothing to say.

'Well, was it, for God's sake?' John's voice rose. 'What more do you want me to do, Carla? What is it with you? What do you bloody expect of me, woman?'

'I'm sorry, John. Not now.'

'Not now? *Not now?* Then bloody well when?'

'This can wait until we're in the house. Thank you.' She was taken aback by his anger. He could normally be counted on to suppress his emotion. Why the sudden change? He shared the same anger as Stone Town.

John and Carla waited for Sima to answer the front door.

'Dammit, I left the crab in the car. Hang on, John, I'll just be a tick.' She ran to the garage before he could speak. 'What happened, Mussa? Where the hell were you?'

Mussa was still sitting in the driver's seat. He turned to look at her. 'I could say the same, Mrs Lar. I came to the flat at six thirty, I waited at the door for an hour, then had to go to the Africa to pick up Mr Jackson . . . and you.'

'I was at the flat. I was waiting.'

'No, you weren't. You were at the party.'

Mutual hurt flavoured the conversation.

'I was at the flat, Moose.' Carla felt tearful. 'I left at nearly eight o'clock. I had to find John at that stupid bloody party, I couldn't wait any longer.'

The confusion revealed itself; they had waited according to two clocks. Standard and Swahili time. Mussa had been at the flat six hours after Carla. It was no one's fault. Carla wanted to bite his cheek. She went back to the front door; John and Sima were waiting for her.

\*     \*     \*

190

TO: Daveyboy
CC:
Subject: down at the first fence

Davey, you can put any ideas of me having my own saints
day out of your mind. My career as saviour of the island
has been short-lived: i don't have the correct visa. Even
charity/voluntary work requires the right permit so i told
Frenchy that id try & help when i was back in London, so
dont stop looking for shops. It'd be v stupid to try & risk
it as immigration here are shits. @ least that's wot ive been
told, they specialise in asking for large amounts of money
for imaginative documents if you follow my drift. I was told
of one guy who spent a month trying to avoid paying $1000
for a new permit even though the visa he had was legit. I
can do without that kind of hassle. Corruption isnt the norm
for tourists, but it is if youre here for a while. The police and
co get paid around 30,000 shillings a month – thats about
£25 – so you can imagine they are susceptible to a little extra
financial help. Its like that for a lot of people. The shitty thing
is that if the money went to government in the first place
then they actually might have cash in the coffers to pay their
staff with. Impasse all round.

Abdul is still with. We're getting into a real domestic
bliss thing. I like him being here. The more i think about
his situation the more i realise theres nothing he can
do so im happy to help look after him. We're quite the
married couple, going to the market each day together, me
doing the cooking, drinks on the roof. He gets a bit weird
with my cleaner, Fatima. I dont know what it is, jealousy
maybe, but theres a definite undercurrent.

Now, the MOST important news. Living in a developing
country really means only one thing . . . LOSING WEIGHT.

I am ecstatic, the one pair of jeans i brought with me is
actually loose around my bum. How good is that? I feel
like the me that was aged 16 and two sizes smaller. Maybe
a new career in modelling awaits? Cant wait for you to see
the super slimline me . . .
hope youre well xxxxxxxxxxxfran


## An Afternoon Before in Shangani


'And how are you today?'

John sat at the breakfast table looking at the bundle of
*Daily Telegraph*s that had arrived that morning. They were
two months out of date. He didn't look at his wife. 'Fine,
thank you, Carla.'

Sima stood by a large sideboard: she was trying awkwardly
to lever a slice of pineapple on to a plate with a spoon and
fork, silver-service style.

'For goodness' sake, give it to me and stop fooling around,
you silly girl.' Carla's sharp tone made both John and Sima
look up. 'I'm sorry, Sima. Please, give that to me, I'll do it.
Thank you.' Carla took the plate and sat opposite John. She
wasn't hungry, but made the motions of eating.

John had eaten well; he started each day with a large
cooked breakfast, no matter how hot it got. 'I think your
performance last night was cruel, Carla. I threw that party
for you, I thought it might help.'

Quite what, John couldn't bring himself to say. Any refer-
ence to their problems was always camouflaged. He dreaded
where the conversation might end. Implicitly Carla encouraged the silence.

'Let's forget about it, shall we? And please, John, never do anything like that again, ever.'

The atmosphere was artificial: fake civility consumed them. Maybe she had strayed too far out of her depth. She was dangerously near to something that might prove final, yet felt unable to help herself. Her feelings for Mussa were overpowering. She was in love for the first time in her life and desperate to hide this from John. 'I'm going to spend the afternoon in my new office,' she said. 'I'll see you back here for a drink at about seven.'

'It's Sunday, Lar. Why on earth should you be working today?'

She had lost count of the days and needed to make up an excuse quickly. 'I've got my charity do to work on. It's not long until the big day.'

John did not question her further. It would be better for them both if she slipped away quietly and calmed down.

'I'll need to use the driver,' she added. 'I have letters to deliver. You won't need him today, will you, Johnno?' She endeavoured to sound disinterested as she made her request. John started on a crossword.

'No, you take him, Lar. I might do some work on my planting and have a day in the sun with the gardeners.' He'd look for some help from Iddi and make his own diversion.

Carla took it as read that he would indulge in his 'little hobby': it made her desires for the afternoon that much easier.

She walked to the flat and found Mussa waiting on the landing. She kissed his lips nervously. It was dangerous to do that in public, even though she knew no one could see them on the stairs. The risk was the thrill. They slipped inside, went straight to the bedroom and spent the entire afternoon ensconced in the Zanzibari bed. Carla adored lying in his arms.

'Mrs Lar?'

Carla moved her head from its sleepy position on his chest.

'Mrs Lar . . .' He said no more.

Carla dug her fingers into his waist, trying to catch the moment for ever.

# CHAPTER 8: EXPLOSION

## Small Change

Abdul's role within the relationship grew. He enjoyed wielding the wallet, a charade in which Francesca was happy to indulge him. It gave him a sense of being the provider and her of being looked after. It was a deluded, symbiotic union, into which both of them bought unquestioningly. It was part of the spell the island cast. A normally sassy woman had embraced a lotus-eating fantasy, and a usually practical young man had acquired illusions of another life somewhere far away where money was given free from machines in walls and never a problem.

'Francesca, you take me London with you?'

'It won't be easy, Abdul, but I'll try.'

She started to dread a time without her lover. The fear had sneaked into her recently and become an invidious constant.

'Let me ask at the British consulate. I have to find out how to do it. Don't worry, Abdul, I'm not going to lose you.'

He gripped her, strafing her face with a rapid succession of tiny kisses.

'Abdul, you nutter, let me go . . .' She was laughing and pulled back expecting to see a foolish, comic smile, but he

195

looked pained. He blew into his hands. She'd got used to this habit now.

'Me I go to market then for special food. We have *sikuku* for London tonight. You have more money?'

She was pleased that the idea of celebration had pulled him from his mercurial gloom. 'Isn't there any left, Abdul? I gave you fifty thousand the other day.'

Abdul had taken to shopping on a lavish scale: he liked his friends to see him with notes instead of small change. 'Me, I spend money yesterday on food and the wine.'

She could hardly argue with him; their consumption of alcohol was large and the fridge and freezer were always full. She gave him more cash.

On the rare occasions that Francesca went shopping by herself, or anywhere else for that matter, Abdul constantly paged her. It wasn't unusual for her to receive twenty messages in a couple of hours. They were inevitably along the same lines: where are you? What are you doing? Are you coming home? Are you OK? When are you back? They were puerile, but became part of their relationship. Abdul's presence was constant. She hadn't told David about the continuing text-messaging; she knew he wouldn't under-stand its significance. She did: in her eyes the silly beeps and banal correspondence emanating from her phone came to represent the strength of their relationship. It was an affirmation of how close they were; a constant reminder of how much she and Abdul cared for each other. But it was never the same if Abdul went out and left her at home. She imagined this was because he found it difficult to page her if he was walking along the street or doing the shopping. Anyone would, wouldn't they?

Abdul left the flat with another fifty thousand shillings and without his lover; Francesca busied herself sending emails.

She was at the Internet café for an hour and had been sitting at home for a further two. Abdul wasn't back, and she was annoyed. His phone was switched off. She felt unable to leave in case he should return. That was irrational; he had his own set of keys so why the hell didn't she go out? She worried that maybe something had happened. That was an excuse, though: her concern was that he might be with someone else. The more she thought about it, the angrier and more convinced of his duplicity she became. It was a poison that consumed her. The whisky bottle took a battering.

A while later Abdul blew in, clutching several big shopping bags, most of which carried food and wine. Another contained clothing. Her conversation was forced; his was relaxed – he'd had a busy afternoon buying for the household. He went to the kitchen to deposit his purchases. 'You want drink with me, Francesca?'

'I've already got one,' she snapped.

'Maybe you cook for me later.'

She tried to look indifferent, but couldn't help saying, 'I don't feel like it, do it yourself.'

Abdul got a beer and tried to kiss her but she pulled away.

'What is it the matter with you?'

'Nothing.' She tried to look busy by thumbing through an old magazine, a pointless exercise as she'd read every word in it. She was a lousy actress.

'You have problem? Me, I think you are not happy, Francesca.'

'You're bloody well right.'

She walked from the room and he followed her. 'What make you angry, Francesca? I not know.'

'You taking all bloody afternoon, if you must know. I've been stuck here waiting for you.'

The concept of waiting wasn't of great importance to Abdul; he'd spent all his life waiting for something or someone and a few hours on a Wednesday afternoon were no different. 'But me I been shopping for *sikuku*.'

'Yes, I can see.' She exploded: 'Bloody clothes shopping! What is it with you? You're spending my fucking money like it's nothing.' Her rage was fuelled by the whisky. 'I've been waiting in all this bloody time so you can go out and buy yourself a sodding new shirt with my bloody money. You've really upset me, Abdul. I thought we had more trust than that.' She held up the bag with the clothing and shook it like it might rattle.

'That isn't for me, Francesca.'

'Oh, so now you're doing a spot of shopping for someone else? How kind. Don't tell me, it's your sister who needs a new blouse, or your cousin, or your mama. It's always someone, isn't it?'

'No, me I buy you present.'

Silence. She clammed up. This was terrible. How could she have been so stupid? Of course he loved her. He'd spent his time attempting to buy her a gift and she had turned into a harridan. Why did her mind play such terrible tricks? What could she do? He had bought her something special to wear for his celebration, nothing more than that.

Abdul took the carrier bag from her and opened it to reveal a red nylon dress and a bead necklace hung with a silver dolphin pendant.

'Abdul, I'm sorry. That's lovely. It was so stupid of me to say those things. The dress is beautiful.' She put on the necklace with a little help from Abdul, and went to change into the dress. It was a clingy garment, the type of thing she would never normally wear. The fabric, the style and the shape were horrible, but she adored his intention. 'Don't I look good?' It wasn't a convincing show. 'It's beautiful, Abdul, really it is, thank you.' She hoped he would forgive her outburst, that he would understand her passion for him, but he was preoccupied with another package. 'What have you got there?' She sounded a little too interested in his business, almost manic.

'Me I get new phone.'

'You've got what?'

'This Ericsson, very good.'

The brief exultation in the ugly red dress disappeared. She sounded hollow. 'And what else have you bought?'

Abdul looked offended. 'This I buy with my money.'

He tapped at the box with his fingertips, a staccato, rapid, annoying noise.

'Your money, Abdul? Your bloody money? Where did you get it from?' She was beginning to shout.

'Money me I saved.'

'You mean it's my money that you've saved.' Anger effortlessly embraced her. She blossomed with rage. 'So what else have you bought with my money? Go on, tell me.'

'Why your money, Francesca? Me and you we are same.'

'The same? No, we're not. This is cash that I've worked for, not some fucking charity handout.'

'You say we are together.' He shook his head as he spoke, to all intents contradicting himself.

'Yes, we are, Abdul.'

'Then we share together all things.'

'That's just where you're wrong. I can't believe you did that. You don't run around spending someone else's money.'

Francesca left the room, furious with herself and more so with him. Subconsciously she knew that she'd facilitated Abdul's careless spending. He had betrayed her selfish expectations of him. The light and heat in the bedroom seemed brutal and exposing: she felt ugly. Her anger increased. Disaffection drove her back to the other room where she found Abdul reclining on the sofa.

'And you can move your bloody arse, Abdul! Stop lolling around and fucking do something.'

He didn't move.

She was starting to yell: 'I said do something! If you want to spend money, piss off and find a job, won't you?' Tears poured down her face. She was a red, sore, messy woman howling for what she saw as faithlessness. Abdul went to touch her. 'Take your hands away! I don't want to speak to you! Get out of here – get out of my flat!'

'What you speak to me like that?' He rubbed his face, then swiped at his shoulder as if brushing away an invisible insect with the sudden movement.

'Haven't I made myself clear, Abdul? I said piss off.'

He swept out of the building and she collapsed on her bed, sobbing.

Abdul raged at the situation: the crazy *mazungo* witch was trying to destroy him. How could she take him in and throw him out in such a humiliating way? He keyed into his phone and sent her the first of forty-seven messages. Unhappiness pushed his obsession over the edge. She had to know how he felt: she had to see his misery.

An hour later she'd turned off her phone and was as drunk as she'd ever been, the whisky bottle empty beside her. She was sick for another hour. The city ate at her. She felt butchered, disassembled, fingered by depression and rotten with despair. Voices rose from outside; someone knocked on a far-away door. All the sounds laughed at her and relished her unhappiness. She fell asleep.

Francesca slept through to the following morning. On waking, the stench from the bathroom made her feel like vomiting again. Her head thumped; her wretchedness gnawed at her. She mopped up the evidence of yesterday's violence; the toilet was splattered with a film of regurgitated whisky and gastric acid. It was an alcoholic testimony to despair. A cold shower helped alleviate the nausea; she inhaled the mist of water thrown up around her. The water tank drained, and half an hour later she was still sitting, disconsolate, under the dripping faucet. She made coffee and smoked three Marlboros in quick succession, then went to find a cab.

'My darling girl, what a surprise. Are you OK?'

Francesca told her story to Carla.

'Wasn't that a bit abrupt? Francesca, you're so headstrong. You must calm down.' Carla took and held her hand. 'You're being irrational. You're not able to see the differences between your lives. Abdul is a young man who's been on as much of a roller-coaster as you have. You must understand, Francesca, he's not a bad person. Poor, yes, but that's hardly criminal. He hasn't set out to be cruel to you.'

Francesca felt her fingers being squeezed.

'The money thing is a problem, I agree, but I'm sure Abdul isn't malicious. Explain your feelings about this to him, or how could he understand? He's never had any money of his own.'

The younger woman was sobbing again.

'Come here, soldier, let's be having you . . .' Carla cradled her. The older woman was smaller than Francesca, yet she appeared bigger, stronger, more mother than friend. Fragile fingers combed the matted head that lay crying in her lap.

'I feel so miserable, Mum.'

'Sweetheart, I'm Lar,' she whispered and held her with a strength and devotion that Francesca had never felt before.

\*     \*     \*

Francesca took a moment before she punched in the last digit of his telephone number. Queasiness racked her. She wanted his phone to be engaged or switched off, but a strange voice answered.

'Can I speak with Abdul, please?'

'This not Abdul.'

'I know, can I speak with him?'

'He no here.'

'Are you a friend? Could you take a message?'

'This not his phone any more, sister. My phone now, he have one new. *Kwaheri.*'

As she hung up, the call to prayer went out. It sounded like an orchestra tuning: the local muezzin was joined by a hundred other voices in beautiful discord.

TO: Daveyboy
CC:
Subject: Abdul's gone

Davey boy, im as miserable as sin. Ive had a terrible row with Abdul & thrown him out. He got so he was freaking me with a constant drain on my resources. He bought a new phone with my money, i got drunk and exploded, you know how i get when im on one, now Abdul knows it too. I flew right off the handle. Ive tried to find him and patch things up but hes sold his old phone to some stranger and i cant get through to him. I miss you so much, i wish you were here.

Carla has been lovely, i cant begin to tell you how special she is. We have known each other for little more than two months and i feel as if ive known her forever. She is such a support, so caring, shes someone i never want to let go of. She should have been my mother, i

love her. Im going out now to try and find Abdul, he must be around the town somewhere. I cant believe that im getting more heartache here than i did at home. It feels like it must be me, im flawed, is it that i cant love anyone? I'll e you soon to let you know how ive got on. Hope youre well
I love you, Fran x


At night, Stone Town becomes a city of cats. They are invisible during the day, only decorating the streets with their subfusc presence when the last great belch of redness has sunk safely below the horizon. From behind each door and every bin comes the mewling of secret residents. The brutish creatures, with scars and saggy eyes, mange and nervous disorders creep into the comparative safety of darkness and dance silently by.

Francesca shared the alleys with the feline usurpers, the animals looking as aimless as their human companion. Abdul was nowhere to be seen.



# Return


The cholera epidemic dissolved. It vanished as mysteriously as it had arrived but no one other than Francesca seemed to notice. The food stalls in the Forodhani Gardens had reopened and the two discos were operating again. There was a tacit understanding that the danger had gone, but nothing was said. There were no announcements in the local papers, not that Francesca seriously expected any. Cholera was hidden yet omnipresent – none of the tourists had a clue as to what might be dripping below the surface. Disease was part of the deceit of the island, like the endless smiles that demonstrated one thing but meant another – another secret behind another mask.

Francesca was strangely calm. She was miserable because she couldn't contact Abdul, yet she didn't have the frantic, tense panic that had recently consumed her. Everything seemed that extra bit slower and mindless. It was because of the heat: it comforted her, deadening the hurt. She had experienced a vast range of emotion in such a short time and now her energy was spent. The sense of nothingness was an anticlimax; normality and routine picked at her. She was empty, insulated and numb, as if her spirit was sleeping. Francesca's inertia made her visible only to certain people. The beach-bums looked through her but the crone who sold sweets, sodas and household goods from a doorway on Gizenga Street never failed to say hello.

'Hey, Mama Two Thousand, you not been here a while.' The shopkeeper joked that Francesca always spent two thousand shillings; it had become her name. 'You not want nothing today?'

Francesca entered the gloomy, poorly stocked store. She looked at the shelves. There was nothing she needed, but she picked up a tin of sweetcorn, a bottle of cooking oil and a glittery red toothbrush. She fumbled to pay the woman. 'Actually, can I have a cold soda, too? Do you mind if I drink it here?'

She was given a small wooden box on which to sit and drink the Sprite. It was just inside the counter, so she could watch other customers lean in from outside to make their purchases. A young man dressed in rags bought two cigarettes and cadged a light. He saw Francesca hiding. 'Mama, you buy me soda too?' He puffed at his Sportsman and blew out the smoke through a gaping gargoyle of a grin. The shopkeeper shooed him away.

'Why is he happy?'

'What you mean, Mama Two Thousand?'

'What has he got to be happy about? What does a smile like that mean?'

The shopkeeper nodded and smiled too. It was as if Francesca had eventually rumbled the big, ongoing joke that the island had been playing since her arrival. 'We call that smile "cow-shit", Mama.'

Francesca didn't see the connection.

'Let me explain. When you see cow-shit after it been in the sun it look hard. But when you step on it, it wet inside. That what the smile is like: on the outside is happy, but inside there is hate.'

Gradually the island developed another complexion.

Her phone beeped.

**'why yu bad? wot u expect me do? fuk for money**?'

The message took her aback. The phone beeped again.

**'how yu tret me is bad**.'

And again.

**'yu think yu money is so speshul wot bout me**?'

An overwhelming sense of relief splashed down on her after she had received the messages, even though they were hostile. They represented the passion in their relationship: they proved to her that Abdul was still in love. She mentally thanked God for his new number and the chance to communicate again, although she'd wait until later before calling. Maybe by then he would have cooled down. Three beeps from the phone helped lift her despondency.

\*　　\*　　\*

She sat up in the tearoom, dangling her legs over one of the high benches, toying with her phone. When would be a good time to call Abdul? She hit the 'call' button, then pressed 'end' before there was time for a connection. She did the same thing again, anxious to speak, yet nervous of making contact. Having his new number was like owning a small bit of him: it meant they would still be together. Convinced that their need for each other was equal, she reassured herself once more and made the call.

'Hello, Abdul? We should talk.'

'You want that we should speak?'

'I think that would be nice, don't you? I'm at home, why don't you come and see me?'

'I come your house later, then.'

The brief conversation hadn't been quite as awful as she'd anticipated. Abdul sounded withdrawn, but after their terrible row who wouldn't? Francesca blamed herself for the hiatus: she had been drunk, possessive, argumentative, ignorant. She had been drunk often recently. Carla was right: she had misunderstood the world she was visiting and that was the problem. When he came to her flat later she would make up for her impetuous behaviour, try to understand him better, play for a truce. Things would be good again. An alcoholic wouldn't think any other way.

She knew the sound of his feet on the stairs – that stomp could only be his – and was standing at the door as he walked up the final flight.

'You look well, Abdul.'

'And you . . .' Abdul touched Francesca's face with the back of his fingers; it felt intensely personal and affectionate.

'Come in, won't you?'

He looked around the living room as if he'd been away for months, even years, instead of two days.

'Would you like a soda, Abdul?' She felt vaguely ridiculous, formal, even, and wasn't quite sure what else to say. 'Let's have a beer – you'd prefer that, wouldn't you?'

She went to fetch the drinks without waiting for his response. She came back into the room and he patted for her to sit beside him on the sofa, like the woman wearing the green uniform had at the harbourside café. They'd not yet drunk from the bottles before they started to kiss. The reconciliation happened swiftly. Abdul's hurt was dissipated by three beers and a seduction. They fucked wildly in bed; his penetration would expel the recent anger and diffuse their impasse. Their sweat soaked the sheets.

Abdul got up to wash – he always did after sex. On his return, he found Francesca sound asleep. He climbed back on to the bed and sat watching her in the dark. A complicated dream forced her to move slightly, stretch out, murmur and flex. Abdul remained awake and impassive, staring straight through her in a secret trance. This was the time that Popo Bawa might come. He decided not to sleep – not so that he could guard the room from a creature that was half man and half bat but to resist the whisperings of his own demon.

Nothing was the same now. Abdul had moved back into Francesca's flat, and this was where she thought she wanted him: her obsession and greed for the man dictated that they be together. But his presence was disquieting and their romance soured. Francesca was unable to escape from its poisonous bond. Gradually she was sucked dry, subject to mistrust of her own feelings and apprehension of his. Abdul exacerbated the situation with what she understood to be his control and domination of her. Capitulation rendered her unable to go anywhere without his supervision. Ironically she'd created her own incarceration.


TO: Fran
CC:
Subject: COME HOME

franny, wot has got in2 u??????????? u r worrying me sick. this guy sounds like hes ill. i mean cant u see it? he is overwhelming u, i can read it in your e-mails. please speak with your dowager, speak with anyone – but get good advice. mine is get the hell away from abdul & do it now. hes DANGEROUS. i have half a mind to come out there & bring u home myself. wot was it u said about going to chill? & wot type of break is this? it sounds like fucking hell 2 me. u have to do something about it otherwise you'll find abdul does it 4 u . . . please e me soon & tell me you've got shot of him. i love you
daveyx

David was right: this wasn't a relationship, it was misery. She'd seek out Carla and take her advice.

# CHAPTER 9: RESOLUTION

## Malindi Villa

Mussa considered Carla's offer: it wouldn't be easy for him to move into her home. These situations didn't happen to old Zanzibari men: they were the preserve of another generation and another nation. But unlike Carla's fear of invisibility, the transparency he had acquired with age was a cloak he could use to his own advantage. No one would see him. He could move into the Malindi Villa like a shadow, on the condition that his presence was that of a visiting friend – there had to be propriety and dignity in front of Ali and the other houseboy. He wouldn't share a room with her. Just being together was the pleasure, the magic. It was the same for them both.

Carla and Mussa sat in the heavily scented shade of a frangipani tree, both whispers of what they had been. Should any stranger observe the intimacy between older and old they might assume it was a familiarity gained over many years of companionship instead of separation. The rekindled love affair had acquired comfort and conviction, an assurance that belied the newness of their understanding.

It was why their love was perfect; it was still *new* after four decades.

Carla expelled any reservations. 'It wasn't too late after all, was it, Moose?'

'It feels like a dream.'

She swatted at a fly; an idle, half-hearted gesture.

'Maybe it's a spell, Lar. Why else would two old fools still be chasing each other?'

'It isn't a spell. It's real. At long last we're making up for all that unhappiness, Moose.'

Carla's urgency to find love was as desperate as Francesca's, a similarity neither woman would see. The difference was Carla's conviction: it was true, even though she had no idea how she would proceed now that she was reunited with Mussa. That doubt wouldn't destroy the moment. The judicious, questing woman was reconstructing a beautiful fantasy in which Mussa would wittingly partake.

'It's paradoxical that we've found a future together at such a late date, don't you think?'

Mussa's thoughts had slipped elsewhere; he was fighting runaway daydreams. He could see his dead wife and the young Mrs Jackson. He tried to imagine two dead children, one from each woman. He didn't reply.

Carla made noises about lunch and whether they should eat in or out. Mussa had no opinion: it was a decision he could not make. A net was cast around the old man, the same webbing that caught and frustrated Abdul – a mesh based on power. Both Carla and Francesca were aware of the clout wielded by their comparative wealth. Although they didn't consciously flex their purses, control was the unintentional result. The difference between Abdul and Mussa was that the former felt he had something to prove. Mussa had lived his long, poor life with dignity; he was too old now to care much for the prizes of materialism. He would let Carla make whatever decision she needed; it would be all the same to him.

'Bibi Carla, Mrs Jackson, you have a visitor.'

Francesca walked past Ali to sit with the couple. How could they exist so effortlessly in apparent harmony? The assumption of happiness made her resentful. She lit the first of many cigarettes.

'Are you OK, darling?'

'No, Lar, I'm not. I'm having a terrible time with Abdul. He's suffocating me. I've managed to get away from him this afternoon because he's gone to visit his mother.'

There was a wildness about Francesca that seemed to change the temperature of the room.

'I apologised for our row, I've tried to make things better, but he's sucking me dry, Lar.'

Mussa coughed. The sound asked whether his presence was needed. He stood up and left the two women alone, saying he was tired and needed to sleep.

'It's not only a financial thing. He's bleeding me dry of myself. I feel trapped by his anger and bitterness. I think I've destroyed him in a funny sort of way.'

Francesca was partly right; she had inadvertently liberated a madness that had always skulked within Abdul. She was the trigger, a touch-paper to his incendiary needs. Perceived lavishness warped his reasoning. But she hadn't reckoned on the desperation she'd woken in herself.

'Lar, he's becoming impossible. Look . . .'

She switched on her mobile telephone. It searched for a frequency, then started to beep rapidly. Carla wasn't wholly sure of the significance, until Francesca explained that each beep was a text message. She wiped the messages without reading them. As she did so the phone beeped again. He was sending text after text into the ether. She felt besieged by technology, harassed by her lover.

'Oh, my goodness, Francesca. This isn't rational behaviour. Do you know what the messages say?'

'They're too upsetting. I won't read them any more. He talked of killing me, killing himself. He says I destroy every-thing.'

Carla hugged her, the same loving embrace she'd given Francesca before.

'I feel so vulnerable, Lar. He might hurt me.'

'Now, stop this nonsense immediately. He won't do any-thing of the sort. I'll not have talk like that, Francesca. This is nothing more than passionate tomfoolery, upsetting silliness, believe me. You mustn't worry. We'll soon sort you out.'

Francesca wasn't so sure. 'He has keys to my flat. I don't feel safe at home any more.'

'Then we'll change the locks. Let's approach this sensibly without adding to the excitement. You need to take control of this, my darling.'

Carla's protective influence was calming; her motherly instinct reassured Francesca.

'You don't think it'll make things worse?'

'Francesca darling, it couldn't *be* much worse between the two of you. I can see a man who is obsessed and a woman who feels defenceless. We're changing your locks.'

Carla called for Ali and asked him to take Francesca to a hardware store in town. This business would be resolved that afternoon.

She dreaded finding Abdul in the flat and felt only vaguely safe in the company of the locksmith and Ali. It was a race against Abdul's return and the tension was overwhelming. The man changing the locks couldn't work fast enough for her. Abdul might just walk in. Each time she heard the downstairs gate open her heart stopped. It was imaginary; no one was coming into the courtyard. He completed the work and handed her a scrap of paper with the total scrawled in an almost illegible hand: forty thousand shillings to change the locks on the front and courtyard doors. Francesca noted that it was exactly the amount she had given Abdul when he first started to ask for money. There was something wry about the equation.

Ali and the workman left her in the echoing apartment that now made noises she'd not heard before. A door slammed and she jumped. It was the wind, there was nothing sinister about it. Like there was nothing menacing about the taps, ticks and knocks of the place: they were the pulse of the building, a rhythm that was ever-present but which she now interpreted as alien. Maybe she'd never listened to them before. Her phone was still switched off. She'd fix herself a drink, stick a CD on and hide in the tearoom of her dreams.

Solitude didn't last long. The knocking started as a continuous rap, an almost mechanical sound. At first Francesca thought it was someone hammering in a nearby house. The noise got louder, more frantic. She remained silent, not wanting to breathe. His fists crashed on the door to the courtyard and he started to shout her name over and over. It was a plaintive, tragic sound. She couldn't block out the noise. Sudden silence.

Francesca only left the tearoom when she was quite sure Abdul had gone. She sat in her living room stoking herself with whisky and cigarettes, becoming strangely sober. The muezzin called, signalling that the sky had lost the sun. She hardly heard the incantation. In the darkness she'd try to make herself into a spirit, a spectral someone in the corner of the room. Soon the firefly sitting at the end of her cigarette was the only thing visible. It got too dark; she imagined vanishing like a *shetani* into the gloom, and switched on the light. The steady rap, rap, rap started again. Maybe Abdul had been downstairs all the time. The noise developed into a ceaseless thumping, as if he might pound the door down. He was calling her name. It didn't sound like a name: the shouts were akin to battle cries. Woeful shrieks from the losing army. She couldn't stand it.

She went downstairs and talked from behind the bolted gate. 'Abdul, please, you've got to stop this.'

Her voice silenced the despair clattering on the other side.

'You must go home, please. Go home. It's best you leave me right now.'

There was compassion in her voice, which startled her. She imagined she'd be shouting, but softness came out. 'Please, calm down. Go home and sleep. Let me telephone you in the morning.'

Abdul remained silent. Perhaps her empathy had surprised him as it had her.

'Can you hear me? Go home and rest.'

'I love, why you try to kill me?'

His few words were a valediction. She heard his steps fade into the tight alleyways of the brooding hot town.

There was a peculiar lightness in her now. It was a relief to have spoken gently to Abdul. Her distress and unhappiness were ebbing away, and she could breathe again. The flat still sounded peculiar, its noises changed. She turned her phone back on, and the final salvo of Abdul's lunacy caught up with her. Instead of being frightening, the text messages were pitiable. She didn't read them all, preferring to delete the last of the electronic blips.

The phone rang. For a moment she thought Abdul might be charging back in.

'Francesca darling, how are you getting on?'

'It's OK, thank you, Lar. Abdul banged on the gate this afternoon and again this evening, but I told him to leave.' Francesca attempted to sound calm.

'Do you think that talking with him is a good idea? Maybe it's best to give him a wide berth for a while. Let him cool off, darling.'

'I had to speak to him. I couldn't leave him shouting into the night. He understood me, Lar. He's gone now.'

'And you're sure you're OK?'

'Yes. Don't worry. I'll be fine.' Her words were transparent, her attempt at masking them with confidence a miserable failure.

'That settles it, young lady. You're coming to stay with me tonight.'

'I'm fine, Lar.'

'Francesca, you are coming to stay and that's the end of it. You don't think that I've lived all these years not to understand when a friend needs help, do you? You're coming to me. We'll have a secret time together – I'll make whisky sours and we'll behave like teenagers. It's about time we were irresponsible together. You're not going to deny my old bones this small pleasure, are you?'

Francesca was laughing. 'I'd love to behave like a teenager with you. Thank you, Lar. I'll be with you soon.'

# Revolution

The continuous tapping turned into thumping.

'Lar, Carla, wake up, damn you.' John was knocking at her bedroom door: he sounded frantic.

'What in God's name is happening, Johnno? What time is it?' It was nearly four a.m.

'Hell and a half has broken out, Lar. Can't you hear it?'

Carla listened groggily and heard the crack of a rifle. Then she heard the rattle of machine-guns. A car screeched round the corner and left its echo in the street.

'The *escari*'s locked the doors, Carla. You should come to the other side of the house. Keep away from the windows.'

Carla was still hazy with sleeping pills: although she'd heard the gunfire it hadn't registered as such. 'Can't this wait until the morning, John?'

'Get out of bed, Carla. I mean it.'

She followed her husband into the library and was surprised to see the staff gathered there – except those who lived out. Mussa was absent.

'There's a serious problem, Lar. I think it's a revolt.'

'Johnno, we've only just had an election. Are you sure it's not just nonsense?' She spoke on a yawn, her drowsy speech slurred.

The staff sat silently, other than Sima who started to cry. Carla looked at the girl, then into the faces of the others. Whatever was happening it was grave. Lorries trundled down the road, men were shouting, the gunfire came nearer.

'For God's sake, John, get on the bloody phone this instant and find out what's going on.'

'Don't you think I've tried? The lines are down.'

'What about the cable and wireless people?'

'I've looked, but there's an armed guard of sorts out there. The chaps inside have been bundled into lorries. I think it's the ZNP.'

'Well, we've got to do something. Get an *escari* to nip over to the palace. They'll know what's happening.'

'Don't be so bloody stupid, woman. No one is going to leave this house tonight.'

The dull thump of a mortar reverberated around the small streets. The shouts sounded more like screams. The machine-gun fire was continuous now.

The panic of outside invaded the room.

'They will kill me, madam, help me.'

'Sima, don't be silly. I'm sure there's a perfectly rational explanation. It'll have blown over in the morning.'

The cool English rhetoric didn't console the terrified girl.

Carla snapped at the maid: 'For God's sake, Sima, pull yourself together and calm down.'

John looked as concerned as those around him, but Carla still didn't grasp the danger. Sleep and an unbreakable belief in herself and what she represented clouded the clutter of reality. 'You're all behaving ridiculously. The government will have this sorted in a trice. That's probably their gunfire we can hear now. Quieten down, the lot of you. That goes for you, too, John. Try to set an example.'

Her stuffiness was ignored. The alarm was real, gradually turning into terror. A window at the front of the house shattered.

'Right, then, that does it. They can't get away with this.' Carla got up from her chair as if to go to the front door and reprimand the transgressor.

'Where the hell do you think you're going, woman?'

The string of nervousness strangling the others in the room suddenly ensnared Carla. She sat down again; her heart was beating rapidly.

'Where's Mussa?' She swallowed a wave of fear and tried to keep steady.

John looked puzzled: why should she worry for the chauffeur above anyone else on their staff? 'I'm sure he's fine, Carla.'

'Is he safe?'

'Carla, how on earth should I know? He'll be at home keeping well away from trouble, if he has any sense.'

John knew that her response was jarred by fear, an irrational retort to the astonishing event that was unfurling outside. Many such uncharacteristic flashes had zipped through his mind.

'We must find him, John.'

'We'll do no such thing. I insist that everyone stays exactly where they are. Come here, Lar . . .' John put out his arm to her, a genuine, if awkward movement. Sima started to whimper. Her tiny sobs helped magnify the terror that Carla was suffering. She clutched the girl and tried to soothe her – it was a crack at reassuring herself too. The sounds from outside were disconcerting – both deafening and silent; it was impossible to tell what was happening from the noise alone. Eventually Sima fell asleep on Carla's lap, her thin breath acting as a counterpoint to the horror beyond – she wasn't much more than a child. She was still bound in Carla's arms as the sun gradually poured into the room. It would be the only moment of coolness before the full strength of January sunlight took hold of the day. No one other than the child slept – although the stillness of those present gave the illusion of deep sleep.

\*     \*     \*

## Malindi Villa or Darajani Fort?

Francesca hailed a cab and took nothing with her but the glittery toothbrush and an enormous sense of relief to Malindi Villa. Riding away from Stone Town in the taxi was a release; the malevolence and distress of earlier fell away from her like the nasty red nylon dress Abdul had given her. It slipped from her body. The moon was full, so she could see her way through the exotic tangle of fragrant garden. Carla and Mussa were waiting for her at the door.

'*Karibu*, Francesca, welcome. We thought it about time we revisited our distant past, didn't we, Moose? Yours might not be quite so far away as ours, but we'll let you join in anyway.'

Francesca hugged her friends.

'I've sent the boys home for the night. I thought it might be fun for us to stay up late listening to Tony Bennett and Matt Monro.'

Malindi Villa flexed: it re-formed to the old ways of the Darajani Fort, except Carla was its mistress now.

'I've got potato and cassava chips for us to snack on, and I've already poured whisky for you and me. Could you fetch the glasses, Francesca? There's a good girl.' The careless crispness of Carla's voice was uniquely expatriate, from another time.

'We're going to tell silly stories and secrets and sprawl out on the carpet together. I think I might try to smoke my cigarettes as if I've never had one before. I want everything to be new again.'

Carla's contagious, hacking laugh reverberated up from

her belly, infecting the air around her. The potency of her amusement astonished them, reducing her friends to giggles. It was the catalyst, the vehicle on which to escape the present, a conduit to all their pasts. They were in search of a shared innocence from different ages.

'You're too silly, Lar.'

'Don't call me silly. I'm a very wise old woman, aren't I, Moose?'

He was shaking instead of laughing aloud; a tear careered joyfully down his cheek.

'You'd both better give me a hand with building a nest in the middle of the floor. That's what youngsters do, isn't it? They make dens out of cushions so they can hide from the world.'

Francesca thought back to her first day in Zanzibar. 'Adults do that as well, Lar.' She remembered wanting to hide from the world in the perfect blue stone bath.

The wind took up with the trees and started to whisper; a branch tapped at the window.

'Why don't we turn the lights out and use candles, Lar?'

'Moose, what a thoroughly excellent idea. Of course that's what teenagers would do.'

Francesca gathered up cigarettes, the crisps and the glasses of whisky for their indoor picnic. She carried them to the den on a teak tray with a complicated brass inlay. Three novice teenagers sat in the dark. A candle burned between them, lighting up faces far removed from pubescent years, hormones and spots.

'I don't think we'll play the music too loud. That's not very adolescent, I know, but Moose and I won't be able to talk above the din. Now, what are we going to tell? Ghost stories or secrets?'

Francesca found herself dumbstruck. She felt momentarily

hopeless; the twig tapping at the window distracted her. It sounded like Abdul.

'Which of you will tell me a secret?'

Mussa started to speak: 'There was a time, a long time ago, when a young woman was shown something in the sky. It was a gift that she was told to share with others. But I know she didn't.' The old man rearranged himself for comfort and, before recommencing his story, asked for a cigarette.

'A cigarette, Moose? Really?' Carla was taken aback.

'Lar, I really can smoke like it's my first time. I would very much like to try one, please.' He held the Silk Cut right at the end of his fingers; they shook slightly as he was given a light. He brought the smoke into his mouth and blew it straight back out. 'How do I look, Lar?'

'About fourteen, Moose. Stay that way for ever, won't you?'

'I'm getting distracted. The secret . . .'

The wind seemed to go on for ever, and the tapping took on a monotonous regularity.

'Many years ago, a beautiful woman was taken to a hidden beach. If my mind serves me well it would be nearly forty years back. We were beautiful then, weren't we, Lar?'

'Moose, I suspect you might be telling a story that Francesca already knows something about.'

Mussa raised his eyebrows and looked quizzically at Carla from behind his spectacles: had she forgotten one of their secrets? The three of them snuggled together as he continued his tale.

'There was a special beach of white coral sand and palms. No one had been there before, except these two. Sometimes at night it became another world, stretched out and blue. Even the palms changed colour. One night, the couple sat at the water's edge. The young man was in love with the woman, but he hadn't told her so. He couldn't then.'

'Were they a local couple, Mussa?'

'Oh, yes, Francesca, they lived here on the island.'

Wind rattled the doors. It was an eerie breeze: it didn't feel big enough to make a noise.

'He knew she loved him, but she didn't know he loved her. As the night unrolled, a canopy of stars shone down on them. The stars haven't been as bright since – not, that is, until tonight. But there was one special one; an orange light that was extra bright. The man gave it to his lover as a gift, on condition she showed it to another. Did you ever show that star to anyone, Lar? Our star?'

Carla ceased being a teenager: she was tearful. 'No, I didn't.' She sounded contrite, chewed up, as if she had betrayed her lover.

'Well, don't you think it might be the right time now? Can you remember what our star looked like?'

'Can I? Of course I can. That tiny orange speck was the thing that kept me sane over the years, and when it vanished from my sky in the north I knew it had gone back to you in the south. Mars was my messenger.'

'Then let's show Francesca our little planet. Perhaps she will pass on our secret to someone else and keep the chain alive.'

The trio walked slowly to one of the large doors that led outside. The sky was perfect, densely packed, constellated with zodiacs. They walked into the dark, the moon having run off to another department taking the wind with her. Carla lit the way with the candle. It was silent and warm, the heat insulated the world against sound. The indistinct figures walked towards the edge of a coral-rag cliff and sat tight together. A little scrub grew up the sides of the sharp precipice; the rock was uncomfortable to sit on. Not even the busy gardens of the Malindi Villa could get a hold on the prehistoric mantle.

'So, Lar, can you find Mars?'

She looked deep into the sky. The Milky Way was encrusted across the skyline, but she found the planet effortlessly. She had been telling the truth: Mars was hers. 'It's there . . .'

Francesca peered into the firmament.

'Can you see it, darling? That star right ahead, the bright one?'

There were too many to identify only one.

'Look harder, Francesca. Follow my arm to the end of my finger.'

Carla had her right arm around Francesca's shoulder, her left pointed to a spot in infinity. She looked Sagittarian, as if she were an archer carrying an imaginary bow. Francesca strained to catch sight of it.

'Is that it? The orange one? Is that your star?'

Mussa nodded. 'It's all of ours, now.'

The silent silhouettes sat looking into space, satisfied that the secret had a new messenger. It was capricious, indulgent, a romantic nonsense that all three enjoyed. A sense of quietness settled on them: they were intoxicated by the celestial charm. Then, for that moment, everything was perfect. Their well-being was an unexpected, meditative, comforting sensation. Francesca had never experienced anything quite like it before.

The rushing noise from out of the dense garden changed the reverie. It was absurd. The perfection of the night mutated and the action played itself out as a slow-motion film. Bewilderment crossed Mussa's face as he stood up to confront the stranger. Carla's head turned and she looked upwards. The candle blew out and the night flooded back in. Francesca put her hands to her ears and shut her eyes tight. All she could hear were words falling as hard as rain smacking a tin rooftop.

'Why.

'You.

'Try.

'Kill.

'Me?'

A swirl of confusing dark shapes shuffled on the cliff edge. It was difficult to distinguish what was happening to the abstract bundle. There was pushing and thrashing.

'What you do here? Where are you, Francesca?'

Abdul had found them in their hideaway fantasy.

'Leave us alone, Abdul. Get the hell away from me.'

Mussa struggled to hold back the younger man. Francesca got to her feet and tried to help. She imagined an inner strength would come from somewhere: people find hidden power in times of huge stress – like the woman who had lifted a car from the ground to release her trapped son. But her arms were weak. For a moment she was seventy-four years old and just standing was an effort. She was witness to a bizarre dance of manners. Abdul was easily strong enough to flatten his frail opponent, yet he postured, inflating his chest like a seal without striking him. It was a masquerade, a complicated charade of bluff.

'Why you hurt me?'

Francesca's reply was barely audible: 'Abdul, you're hurting yourself and everyone else. Leave us alone, for God's sake.'

Carla joined Francesca in a sorry attempt to support Mussa. The old man was a feeble barrier: rather than trying to hit out at the intruder, he had moulded his body in an effort to obstruct him. Mussa lurched to the side, propping himself on his knees, panting as, unexpectedly, Abdul skipped backwards.

Francesca was convinced her invocation of God had in some way touched Abdul because he'd gone as quickly as he'd arrived. There was silence, apart from Mussa's deep, ruptured breathing.

## Afterwards

Carla sat dazed on a sofa; a Sobranie had burned itself out in an ashtray. She had a glass of whisky; she'd drunk a lot through the night, but she was sober. There was a stranger in the room. A man wearing a uniform and a hat spoke to her. She wasn't listening.

'Mrs Jackson?'

She lit up again and took a gulp from the nearly empty glass.

'We've met before. Frank Millichip from the British Consulate. We'll have you off the island in no time. You'll be perfectly safe, provided you follow instructions.'

Her mind was elsewhere. She wanted to make sense of the situation.

'Why have you come to see us? Where are the police? Why aren't they doing anything?'

'They were the first to be attacked, Mrs Jackson. They were overrun and their weapons taken. The same happened at the Mtoni barracks.'

She reached for her lighter as she inhaled from her cigarette, and realised it was already lit.

'It's a serious situation. Reports suggest some of the fighting has died down in the township, although there's still gunfire.'

What should she say? What questions do you ask in this situation?

'Are many dead, Mr Millichip?'

That sounded so dry.

'I don't know. Accounts vary dramatically.'

Carla rubbed her wrist, then played with an ornament on her charm bracelet. It was the reindeer she'd bought for herself. She pushed the gold bauble hard into the soft skin of her arm. If she didn't feel pain, she might believe this wasn't happening. Millichip coughed: he was watching her experiment. She let the bracelet drop loose; the legs on the reindeer were bent.

Carla spoke, but her voice wavered: she sounded vague and confused, almost elderly. 'I need to trace my staff. That's right, isn't it, John? I couldn't possibly leave the island until I know where everyone is.'

Mr Jackson sat opposite his wife. He was silent. She turned to Mr Millichip. 'You can help me with this, can't you?'

'Are they British citizens? . . . They're not. Then I'm afraid there's nothing I can do. I certainly won't be able to track anyone down until this nasty state of affairs is tidied up.'

Carla's voice rose: 'Then who can look for me?'

'It's not safe to go out on the streets, Mrs Jackson. I can't be held responsible for you if you don't remain here. I'll give you more news as and when I get it, but until we can evacuate I must insist you remain put.'

No one understood her agony. It was the not knowing, that dreadful, terrifying void. It was overwhelming. Where was Mussa? She went to bed and eventually fell into a deep, exhausted sleep.

That evening Frank Millichip returned to the Jackson house. The fighting had escalated in the countryside; it was all but done in Stone Town other than sporadic bursts of gunfire. Looting had occurred on Main Road and Portuguese Street. Ranti de Silva's shop had been broken into and all his stock was gone. Carla started to shake.

'Frank, would you be able to contact our doctor, please?' John's request was ridiculous, but Carla needed sedation.

'It's not possible. I'm afraid Dr Fernandez was one of the first casualties. He was trying to flee with his family and got caught near the hospital.'

Carla vomited. Her face was ashen. 'Fernandez, with his family?' she wailed. 'And his little boy, Ramil, is he dead too?'

The consul looked embarrassed by her emotion. 'As far as I know, Mrs Jackson, his family are safe.'

There was no other news: the Jackson house was to remain in a desolate limbo.

# Afterwards

'Will he be OK? Please say he'll be fine.'

The old woman sat dazed on the red silk sofa. A Silk Cut, unsmoked, burned to the filter in the ashtray, the long trunk of grey ash already cold. Maybe her words were a prayer, or perhaps she was speaking to herself. Mussa lay with his head on her lap, his breathing still erratic. Francesca came back into the room with tea.

'Mussa? Mussa, would you like a cup?'

The old man stirred, as if he were being woken from the deepest sleep.

227

'If you can, Mussa, I think you should drink a little of this.' Francesca knelt down beside him, holding a cup of strong, sugary tea; she was a mother feeding her child.

Carla put her hand on Francesca's shoulder. 'Let me do that, Francesca. Come along, old fellow. We'll soon have you shipshape, Moose.' Her cheery words were more to reassure herself than her patient. 'You were so brave, my darling. You saved Francesca and me. What a performance. Now, let's be having you, soldier . . .' She tried gently to move Mussa.

'It's fine, Lar. I can sit up. I've not lost my arms.' Mussa struggled upright, his breathing even more laboured. His papery skin was drawn across his face forming into fragile pleated fans that wrinkled out from beneath his glasses. He blinked slowly.

'Lar, do you think I should call a doctor?'

Mussa looked incredulous. 'A doctor, for me?' He caught his breath – his body seemed to shrink. 'I don't need a doctor . . .'

Carla's look said otherwise: she was imploring, beseeching the world to help, but she wouldn't let Mussa see her concern. 'That's not such a bad idea, Francesca.'

'No, Lar, I don't need to see one.'

'He could see to us all. I know I wouldn't mind a little something after what we've been through. That was way too much excitement for one evening, Moose. Go ahead, Francesca, call one. It'll do none of us any harm.'

The younger woman left the room and searched in her bag for her phone and address book. Eventually she spoke to a man who said he would come out to see them, but he was unfamiliar with the house.

'Take the Mtoni road, Dr Hussein, past the oil depot for another mile or so. I'll wait for you at the corner on the left-hand side. I'll carry a torch . . . Thank you.' Any anxiety about encountering Abdul was overridden by the urgency. Even if she did, she was sure he wouldn't do anything other than berate her and wail. She took her mobile phone with her anyway.

The tea was forgotten, untouched and tepid. Carla knocked over the cup and swore. She made to rise, to clear up the mess before it soaked into the rug, but sank back beside Mussa, ignoring the mishap. In only twenty minutes the figure on the sofa had grown even smaller. He was a doll, a crumpled marionette with cut strings. Carla kissed his hand. 'Francesca won't be too long now. She's gone to show the doctor where we are.'

Mussa sighed. 'I don't need a doctor, Lar . . . I know I don't.'

She encouraged him with a smile. He looked uncomfortable and she put another cushion behind his head. He gasped as she did so, alarming her. 'Did I hurt you, Moose?'

'I ache all over, Lar. It's my age. I'm old and I'm tired. That's allowed, isn't it?' He attempted to laugh, but the only sound to emerge was a rattle.

When he closed his eyes, something more than sleep would begin to claim him. The feeling of heaviness was soothing; it rolled in and enveloped him. In this new darkness, his hands felt like warm marble. They were huge, completely out of proportion with his body, belonging to a colossus, not a man. He thought that if he were young they would be easily big enough for him to pick up the sofa that he lay on. But he was old, and the weights on his arms were ready to drag him down. He could feel them pulling him lower. His mind began to wander; he had a lot of life to think back on.

'Lar, it was you who gave me secrets.'

'What do you mean?'

He took his time before speaking; his breath was thin. 'For the last forty or so years my secrets were the only things I had that were truly mine.'

Carla held his hand tightly. She looked able to keep him in this world purely by the strength of her grip.

'Look, I still have a piece of one here.'

The old man pulled his hand slowly and shakily from Carla's and put it into a pocket. He took out a key, on the end of which hung a battered gold charm. A beast with antlers.

'Oh, Moose . . .'

Carla choked, then sobbed. It was impulsive and she felt foolish. She had a handkerchief tucked up her sleeve just as she'd always done since she was eight. As she dabbed at her eyes, she saw the amulet drop to the floor. She stooped to retrieve it and noticed his hand was limp. 'Moose . . . Moose, darling, wake up, it's me, Lar. Moose, please, please, wake up . . .'

Her whisperings made no difference. He was gone.

'Moose, don't go now, you can't. The doctor will come . . . You can't leave me, darling. Please wake up . . . please . . .' Carla slumped beside him, shaking with silent tears.

A loud bang echoed across the garden.

Francesca looked into every car that went past, hoping to recognise the doctor, which was impossible since she'd not met him before. Her eagerness for him to arrive stretched the time she waited into a spell. Her mind was racing, filling with images of Abdul, Mussa and Carla, Mars, teenage picnics and secrets. *Whumph*. The dull thud of a mortar mauled the air. It diverted her attention.

*Whumph*. *Whumph*. The bass notes of other bombs followed, chased by the streaks of tracer bullets burning into the night sky. The prattle of a machine-gun joined the percussion. She looked around her, half expecting to see tanks rolling down the road. A *dala dala* whisked past, seemingly oblivious to the guttural hacking of ammunition. The noises were so alien, yet instantly recognisable. Instead of filling her with fear their echo jangled and played in her head, not making sense. Another bomb detonated; its sound tore across the land, louder than thunder.

A car's lights flashed. 'Francesca? Hello?'

She looked into the dark interior. All she could see was a hand on the steering-wheel. 'Dr Hussein?'

'Yes, Francesca. Please, get in.'

She sat on the front seat, entranced by the artillery but happy for sanctuary in the car.

'Dr Hussein, what's happening? It's gunfire, isn't it? They aren't fireworks, I know they're not.'

'Don't be alarmed. It's the army. They're celebrating Revolution Day. It's a tradition here. You needn't worry.' He smiled benignly. 'Now, which way do we go?'

They parked the car by the gate. Dr Hussein picked his way carefully to the villa, following Francesca and her dim torch. 'What a beautiful smell. Frangipani. It's one of my favourite scents.'

Francesca didn't notice his comment: all she could see was an open door and a tiny figure sunk on the floor clutching her head. She knew that Mussa was dead.

Carla had a glass at her side: she'd poured herself a drink. She knew there were other people in the room, but didn't know whom and wasn't listening to them anyway.

'Mrs Jackson? Mrs Jackson?'

She lit another Silk Cut and took a gulp from the nearly empty glass. The nest of cushions was pushed to one side.

The teenage years, all gone. That was final. 'Who are you? Where are the police? Why aren't they here?'

'Mrs Jackson, we don't need the police. I'm Dr Hussein.'

She was rubbing her left wrist and suddenly looked down at it. She had expected to see something other than her watch. 'Is my driver safe?' she asked.

The doctor was puzzled.

Carla had heard the bombs and knew the fight was starting – the revolution had begun. Where was everyone? The room was familiar but it wasn't home. She tried to remember what to do: she should tell everyone something. 'Keep away from the windows, that's it. Come to the back of the house. I need my staff. I need to know everyone is safe, don't I? I'm not taking the boat away from here until I know they're safe.'

Carla felt a woman's arms fall round her shoulders. Where was John? Who were these people? 'I need to know now. I must know that everyone's safe. I'm not going to take the boat, not now.'

The arms tightened round her.

'I need my man, my beautiful, beautiful man. You don't understand, do you? No one understands. He's the father of my child.'

Her voice was a tiny, desperate whisper. She studied her Rolex. All those days and years of belonging were shattered, gone in the space of minutes. The timing was immaterial. Fancy being able to measure devastation with the hands of a watch. She let out an agonised wail. The pearl necklace, which kept her knitted together, anchored her composure, snapped. Pearls scattered to the ground and with them went Carla's reserve. A shower of gems and tears sprinkled around the two women.

The old woman put her hands into Francesca's; her flesh

was grey, punctuated with brown spots. For a moment she looked as if she was praying, with her head bowed low. Her lined palms lifted skywards and Francesca held them to her chest. Carla sobbed stiletto tears, great streaks of sorrow. She sat rocking and hugging her friend. Francesca started to cry too. A woeful crescendo of desolation rose above the women like an angry *djinn*, a black cloud was ready to haunt them. Francesca's tears weren't for herself; they were for Carla and Mussa.

An ambulance arrived to take away the broken black-porcelain body. Dr Hussein sedated Carla. The diminutive frail woman lay like a wrinkle on the sofa in the same place that Mussa had lain.

'You know he didn't mean to do it. It was an accident . . .'

The doctor looked up from his notebook.

'What's that, Francesca?'

'He didn't mean it . . . He wouldn't have it in him to kill anyone. You believe me, don't you?'

The doctor sat beside Francesca. 'Now, tell me, what's all this talk of an accident?'

Francesca felt her lip tremble and another set of tears slide down her face. 'I don't know. I don't know anything any more.'

'You've had a very upsetting time this evening. It's always sad when someone dies. Here, take this. It will help you sleep.'

Francesca thanked him and asked him to leave; they would speak the next day. He left her sitting with a guilty secret, the unbearable consequence of not having told him about Abdul's visit. She kept telling herself that Abdul hadn't killed Mussa, although the blurred image of him pushing the old man was looped through her mind.

*     *     *

# Evacuation

For three days Frank Millichip was the only contact the Jacksons had with the outside world. Although his information about the fighting was cloudy he'd heard unsubstantiated reports about massacres taking place near Mazazini. Even more rumours were flying around the kitchens and staff quarters. But – other than act as an impotent stringer – all Millichip could do was advise the Jackson household to pack up what they could and prepare to leave. He'd already given them the nod that a warship would be in the area soon.

'Frank, I can't just shove off. What about Imperial and Eastern? They must be doing something back home. Isn't Parliament onto this yet?'

'Nothing doing right now, John, and I don't see them getting involved. They won't want to get into a bust-up with the Commies over this place. I mean, would you?'

Sima brought in tea and left it on the table. She disappeared quietly.

'Do you have any baccy, old chap? I've quite run out.' John packed his pipe with the cadged tobacco and drew on it, glugging like a fish as he lit up. 'So, that's it, Frank? Cheerio and all that . . . We just leave?'

'What else do you expect, John? A revolutionary council is setting itself up as we speak and I'm pretty damn sure they'll not need the likes of us to give them a helping hand.' Millichip poured himself a drink. 'I got news of the ship this morning. She'll be here within twenty-four hours. Let Carla know. She'll be sailing on it.'

'And what about me, old boy?'

'You'll be leaving later with the rest of us chaps. Women and children only tomorrow.'

Life in the house was agonising. Claustrophobia and heat compounded the nausea Carla continually felt. Concrete word of the boat had cultivated in her a hopeless feeling of misery. She saw it as a punishment rather than as a means of escape. 'Can't I go later with you, John?'

'What's the matter with you, woman? No, you bloody well can't. You should get this one. For God's sake, people are trying to help you. Not everyone is as fortunate as you.'

She knew that: Cook had lost his brother, and Sima had received news that her father was badly injured. There were terrible stories in the servants' quarters about Arab and Indian merchants being burned alive in their homes and of all the poorer Arabs in the countryside being exterminated. Carla felt ashamed. There was still no communication from Mussa. She found that unbearable. She wanted to scream but, perversely, rage suppressed her.

'Sima, I need your help. Will you take these letters for me? I am leaving today on the boat and I need you to deliver them for me when I'm gone . . . when it's safe, my darling.'

Carla disguised the true nature of the correspondence by addressing envelopes to the doctor's son Ramil and to Felix Gomez as well as to Mussa. There was only one letter that she wanted to get through.

38 Shrewsbury Square
WC1

Darling Moose,

I pray that this letter finds you in good health; I can't bear to think otherwise. By the time you read it I will be gone, back to the grey skies and cruel wind of England. I have no choice in the matter. I am being evacuated on a British warship. Who knows? Perhaps you even saw it far out in the harbour . . . I feel so empty at the prospect – at least without you I do. But there is nothing I can do, I am helpless. I can't quite believe we're being separated like this. You must write to me at the above address, I have to know that you are alive. I can't bear the idea that anything might happen to you. If there is a God then we will be together again. Believe me, trust me, love me,

Yours always

Lar

PS I have spoken to John. Keep the car, maybe you could sell it. That sounds so thin, I know.


## Radio News

Abdul's rage and unhappiness were tempered by the incident at Malindi Villa. He hadn't expected to find Francesca sitting outside with the other two; nor had he anticipated the old man's foolish antics. He'd not thought about what would happen after he had sprung from the undergrowth. He wanted nothing to do with the old people: his problem was Francesca.

Abdul returned to his mother's house in Mombassa. He shared a bedroom with two of his brothers and they were already asleep when he let himself in. He climbed on to his bunk clutching a small radio to his head. The blather helped him to sleep – it kept away the voices in his head. Francesca would speak with him in the morning; he'd wait for her at the flat in Shangani.

He awoke with the static hiss of the radio echoing in his ear. The programme of the dead drifted in and out of reception. He didn't turn off the transistor. Instead he propped it on a wooden box while he sat cross-legged on the bed and stretched. He recognised a name. Who was that? It was a name so familiar, but he couldn't put a face to the man. It was a new name. Abeidi . . . Abeidi . . . Abeidi . . . Mussa Abeidi. Abdul froze. It couldn't be him, surely? Panic swirled through his head.

He ran, dodging puddles, to the *dala dala* stand and caught a bus into town. Francesca wasn't in her flat. The night-watchman was leaving his shift: he told Abdul his boss hadn't returned that night. She was still with her friend. So it must be true, the old man had died. He headed back out to Malindi Villa, unsure what he was going to do on his arrival. Nothing was as it seemed. They would accuse him of murder, but he'd not killed anyone. Deep in his head he heard a crack, and the demon laughed at his fractured life. He had to escape. He had to leave Zanzibar.


# The Truth


The rain was heavy. Thick velvet sheets scoured the gardens, obscuring and smacking the flowers. The torrent seemed to last for ever, playing tricks with the hours. It had been pouring since about seven that morning. Francesca hadn't slept properly; she felt light-headed. A well of nausea weighed heavy in her throat; the strange, sickly softness was stuck below her chin. Instinct told her that the urge to vomit was a sign of change. She sat staring at the greyness, hoping the deluge might provide an answer. Mussa was in her thoughts. If only she could tamper with time and change the events of the last few months.

Someone touched her shoulder. She turned to see Carla. The old woman was breathing slowly. Her age had crept up around her. She was shrouded in antiquity.

'How are you feeling?' It seemed like the right thing for Francesca to ask.

Carla gripped her friend's shoulder and steadied herself.

'You must sit down, Carla, here. That's right, easy does it.' It was like settling an infant.

The old woman shivered, even though the room was hot.

'Would you like some tea? A drink of water, maybe?' Francesca feared that Carla might still be fighting the horrors of 1964 instead of confronting the awfulness of today. She couldn't stand the idea that her friend might lose her mind. Perhaps she could create a semblance of sanity if she spoke in platitudes. 'It's been raining like this for hours now, Lar. Would you like something to eat?'

Carla smiled weakly.

'I'm sure the sun will be out soon. This can't go on for ever, Lar. How about some toast?'

'Francesca dear, why not make me a coffee if you have to do something? My head feels groggy – I need to wake up properly.'

Ali was already in the kitchen, preparing vegetables. It was obvious from the way he looked up that he knew something had happened. Francesca asked him to make a light breakfast, then said, 'Ali, you should know that Mr Mussa died last night.'

The houseboy nodded and went to boil the kettle.

'Francesca, I've got a lot to do today. If you're willing, I'm going to need your help.'

Was this the pursuit of an agenda from four decades ago? Francesca was half afraid to ask. 'What must you do? What do you need help with today, Lar?'

The old woman sat up straight. 'A funeral, my darling. Mussa's funeral. He was a good Muslim, and he should be buried today.'

Her reply was oddly reassuring. There was nothing wrong with Carla other than grief.

# CHAPTER 10: ANOTHER ROAD

## Wake

Carla and Francesca arrived back at the villa in the early evening, exhausted by sadness. They sat outside quietly on the terrace, listening to the birds and the faint hush of the sea.

'What are you going to do now, Lar?'

Carla tapped at a cigarette. 'I'm staying here. It's what I should have done forty years ago. I'm staying right here on the island.' Her voice had recovered some of its dignity. 'This place is my home. Deep in my heart it always has been. I've spent my whole life running away and lying, Francesca. I think it's time I did the right thing. I'm staying.'

Carla's fine hair was a messy, lucent halo. Her eyes looked hollow.

'And what of you, Francesca, what will you do?'

The younger woman looked away from her friend. Her lips buckled inwards. She blinked and tears splashed down her cheek. Carla brushed them away.

'I'm going home, Lar.'

Francesca fidgeted with a chain round her neck; a small silver-coloured dolphin hung from it. It was a scrap of cheap evidence. Proof of her guilt.

'Will you ever forgive me, Carla?'

'What type of foolish question is that?'

'This awful thing, Lar. It was all my fault. If I'd not got you involved, Mussa would still be here.'

Carla embraced her. 'All your fault, Francesca? I don't think so. This heartache started years before you were born. It started when I agreed to marry John Jackson. There is one person responsible for this unhappiness. You're looking at her now.'

Ali brought tea out to them. Carla asked for the whisky bottle, soda water and ice.

'Bibi Carla, when you were gone today a man came looking for your friend.'

For a heart-stopping moment Carla thought the stranger had been looking for Mussa. As if the act of someone seeking him would create the alchemy to bring him back to life. 'My friend, Ali, or Francesca's?'

'Yes, Francesca *bibi*. He leave this.'

Ali seemed unsure to whom he should give the scrap of paper – the addressee or his boss. Carla nodded towards Francesca, then poured the drinks. It seemed like an hour before Francesca opened the note. She sat looking at it, rubbing the coarse paper between her fingers in an attempt to divine the message without reading it. Ali left them.

'What does it say, Francesca?' Carla spoke with tenderness, not a hint of anything other than concern in her voice.

Francesca unfolded the note.

dear fransesca

I no the old man Abeidi he die. Me i am sorry for all that becos Ali he tell me truth. Me I dont kill him – I try and be with you to make life good. That cant be I no. So I go to mainland. It better for me there away from you and problem. I go today. Kwaheri. Abdul

\*      \*      \*

'Here, Francesca, drink this, my darling.'

They sat beside each other, sipping whisky and smoking. The sun left the sky and the muezzin called the virtuous to their prayers. The day's heat lingered, overwhelming the senses, deadening the landscape. A vast crimson veil lifted on the horizon across the water – the red dust of the mainland had caught the last rays to turn the world bloody. Everything changed with the sunset.

Francesca felt weighted: she knew there was something else to be done. 'I should speak to him, Carla. I must. It can't be left like this.'

A female voice spoke a recorded message in Swahili, then repeated the same in English. The number dialled was no longer obtainable. Abdul had sold his phone: he had needed the money for a ticket to Dar es Salaam. Francesca would be there soon enough, bumping through the odd mix of office blocks and shanties on her way to the airport. Maybe she'd see him at the Karibu Hotel. She knew she wouldn't. He'd vanished. He'd gone for ever.

Carla pulled Francesca tenderly towards her, so that her head rested lightly on her friend's shoulder.

'I can't ask you to visit me here – I know that – but you're my daughter now. I must never lose you. You'll be safe, won't you, my darling?'

A silent tear trickled down Francesca's face as the mother waved goodbye to the daughter. Francesca felt nauseous again, a fundamental sickness that could surely mean only one thing? She walked slowly to the taxi and set off into the darkness of the road, towards the tearoom of her dreams, her flat in Zanzibar.